Running
Still

A Novel by

Steven Sheiner

Chapter 1

When Jack heard the diagnosis, he refused to believe it. The doctor's next words made it to his ears, but they didn't register. Everything from that moment on was just noise.

Cancer. Invasive. Aggressive. Terminal. Again.

He vaguely heard the doctor mumbling about advanced treatments, experimental drugs, and survival percentages, but none of it registered. This was the third time Jack sat in the same chair, in the same office, listening to the same doctor speak the same words. His shoulders sagged as he let out a deep breath. He had feared the worst, and now the nightmare became real.

"How is this possible?," Jack managed to utter.

"Sometimes it just runs in the family...," the doctor began.

"But it DOESN'T run in the family!," Jack shouted, before the doctor could finish his thought. "Not mine, and not hers!" He jerked a thumb in his wife's direction. Amy, sitting in the chair next to him, put a hand on Jack's arm in a futile attempt to calm him.

They'd been married for 16 years and for the first 15 it had been idyllic. They met in college, his fourth year, her second. Jack was a scholarship athlete, a distance runner. He was a great runner, but not elite. He had never won a race, not in high school, and not in college. There always seemed to be someone faster. He was second best in high school, and ranked fourth among Division I college runners. Some said it was just bad luck, others poor timing.

One day, during a training run, he slipped on a wet track and scraped his knee badly on the rough surface. Amy was the assistant team trainer who patched him up. There was an instant attraction, and the relationship blossomed quickly. They dated for just under two years before tying the knot, right after she graduated with a degree in Alternative and Complementary Medicine.

Jack's degree was in Sports Science, though his primary focus coming out of school was running. While Amy studied and went to class, Jack ran. He had hoped one day to figure out how to make money at it, to make a career out of running, or coaching, or both. But none of that was going to happen.

In addition to running, Jack also worked part-time with a locksmith, a teammate's uncle nice enough to give him a job. Jack liked it mainly because of the flexible hours. It allowed him the freedom to run when he wanted and work when he felt like it. He was a good worker, picked up some skills, and learned what he needed to do the job. When he wasn't at the shop, he was focused on his endurance and speed.

Shortly after the wedding, Amy got pregnant. She often joked that when the baby kicked, it was really running laps around her uterus. Emma was born just before their one-year anniversary. Two years later came Nate. With a boy and a girl, both happy and healthy, Amy declared the 'factory closed'. Emma was running practically before she could walk. Nate did everything he could to keep up with his big sister.

They were a postcard family. Healthy, attractive, fit... everything an American family could hope to be. They exercised together, ate dinner together every night, read together, and Jack and Amy were always there to tuck the kids in at night.

"Jack, are you hearing me?" the doctor asked, interrupting his thoughts.

"I hear you Dr. Holst, but I don't understand," Jack said, exasperated. "How is this possible?" Jack was on his feet now, pacing around the office. "How can three people from the same family, two of them KIDS, have cancer? All diagnosed within a year! Amy and I never smoked, we never did drugs, we don't drink, we eat healthy, we exercise, we drink nothing but water... it doesn't make sense!"

"You're not alone, Jack. I have other patients with this cancer, too," Dr. Holst submitted, but instantly regretted the words.

Jack stopped pacing, turned to face Dr. Holst and said, a little too loudly, "Is that supposed to make me feel better?! You just told me my son, my 12-year old son, is going to die from cancer! First Amy, then Emma, and now Nate. I'm going to lose my whole family to this shit, and I'm supposed to feel better because other people get cancer too?! Is that what you're saying?"

Dr. Holst was all too familiar with the emotional outbursts that often happened in these types of meetings. He took a breath and replied calmly, "We don't know that any of them are going to die, Jack. So far, the new medication seems to be working for Amy and Emma. We'll get Nate started on it as soon as all of his tests are complete."

Jack loaded another retort, but before he could fire it off, Amy stated calmly, "Jack, sit down. This isn't helping."

Jack grudgingly plopped back into his chair. He always bent to Amy's will, now more than ever. He didn't know how much longer he would have her, and upsetting her was the last thing he wanted to do. He looked at her and offered a weak smile. "Sorry," he muttered.

"I know how you must be feeling," Dr. Holst began. Jack whipped his head around and focused his intense gaze on the doctor. Realizing the poor choice of words, Dr. Holst moved on. "We've talked about this. Sometimes genetics play a role in these things, and there's nothing we can do."

"Dr. Holst," Jack said calmly as his wife gently squeezed his hand, "Amy and I have subjected ourselves to every genetic test you requested. We went to the experts YOU recommended!" Jack made air quotes with his hands around the word experts. "The tests found nothing. No tumor markers, no genetic alterations, nothing. We have no family history of ANY kind of systemic disease, certainly not life-threatening cancer. Our parents are still alive and in good health. Our grandparents lived well into their 90s. Our family is the picture of health. Or was."

Suddenly Amy was up from her seat, moving quickly to the side of Dr. Holst's desk. She doubled over and began to vomit into his garbage can. Jack was immediately at her side rubbing her back, speaking comforting words and trying to convince her (and himself) that it was going to be ok. He looked up, locked eyes with the doctor and said softly, "What is happening to my family?"

Chapter 2

"Hey, Lisa? What am I looking at here?"

Dr. Arush Patel was the head of clinical pathology at the BSC Medical Center in Chicago. His office was responsible for analyzing blood and tissue samples for Chicago and the surrounding areas. He sat on a stool with his head down and his eyes focused through the oculars of his microscope. He was fascinated by what he saw. Fascinated and horrified. The cells on the slide were oversized and irregularly shaped, and they were often clumped together abnormally.

"There's virtually no normal tissue here," he said, more to himself than anyone else. "Lisa?"

"Yes, Dr. Patel."

He picked his head up and turned to look at his lab assistant.

"Is this the same slide as yesterday?"

"No, Doctor. This is a different patient. That sample came in last night."

He paused for a moment before saying, "This is a *different* patient from yesterday?," not sure he was hearing her correctly.

"Yes, Doctor."

He shook his head. "Let me see the paperwork."

She walked over to her desk, leafed through some files, and then brought the appropriate paperwork to him. He matched the file number on the folder to the number on the vials before opening it. He scanned the paperwork inside, and then looked up.

"This patient is fourteen years old," he said. His voice was low and his words were soft, as if he could somehow keep them from being true.

Lisa moved to stand next to him, and looked into the open file.

"Yes, sir," she said, pointing at the date of birth. "Why, what is it?"

"It's the same cancer again." He scratched his head, and asked, "How many is that now?"

"I'm not sure, Dr. Patel. I'd have to check. But that's at least five this week."

"Five this week," he repeated in disbelief. "Overall... Give me your best guess, Lisa."

"Since we started seeing samples like this? Must be a hundred by now."

Dr. Patel sat back down on his stool. The open folder rested in his hand on his lap as he stared out into space. Just over a year ago, he began seeing strange cancer cells appearing in blood samples and biopsies. At first, he thought it was just an anomaly. Some rare cancer rearing its ugly head. But they kept coming. The samples slowly trickled in, but recently he began seeing more of them. More and more samples revealing the same disease. And now he would have to write a pathology report confirming that a fourteen-year-old had late-stage cancer.

"What is going on here?," he asked.

Chapter 3

The sound of the pavement under his feet was almost therapeutic. After years of running and thousands of miles, Jack could still find solace in a long run. Today, however, was different. His body was running, but his mind was racing. How could this be happening? His whole family was dying. Why? He refused to believe it just 'happens', despite what Dr. Holst said. Things like this don't just happen. They passed every genetic test they'd been subjected to. They were borderline neurotic about what they ate. No processed foods. No high fructose corn syrup. No GMOs. They ate only organic. They were vegetarian. And they only drank water. No soda or other sugary drinks.

As the scenery passed in a blur, Jack's mind continued to wander. He'd run this route hundreds of times, he could do it blindfolded. He paid no attention to the buildings he ran past, the turns he made, not even the ground under his feet. It was late at night, so he had the streets to himself. That's how he liked it. Dark, cool and quiet. Alone with his thoughts was usually a good thing. Not today. Not in a while. Not since Amy got sick. Then Emma. And now Nate. He tried to fight the emotion that was welling up inside him, but a few tears managed to find their way down his face.

He'd cried a lot over the last year, especially in the beginning. Recently, though, his feelings had changed from sadness to anger. This was new for Jack. He was raised in a happy home, the youngest of three boys. And while his older brothers picked on him now and then, it was the usual brotherly horseplay. They always had his back. No one else dared pick on him, and Jack never invited it from others. He was a kind kid, not a mean bone in his body. He'd never been in a fight his whole life. Not even with his brothers. Sure, they'd push and shove and wrestle around, but it was always half-hearted, never with any anger behind it. Jack never had any reason to be angry. Until now.

Jack pushed his lean frame a little harder as he ran towards the lake. He had reached the outskirts of town and the wind picked up a little. As he saw his rippled reflection in the edge of the water, the question he'd been avoiding came back. Why wasn't HE sick? His wife, his daughter, and now his son. Why? And why not him?

If it truly was genetics, like Dr. Holst was pushing them to believe, it must come from Amy's side of the family. That would explain why it was affecting her and the kids, but not Jack. But they thoroughly investigated her family tree and couldn't find anyone who had cancer. Her parents were still alive and well, and her grandparents lived long, full lives. No aunts, no uncles, no distant cousins. Nothing. Jack's family history was equally unremarkable. And it couldn't be a recessive gene. It takes both parents to contribute that for it to appear in their children.

"Maybe spontaneous mutation," Dr. Holst and the other specialists had postulated. The way it was explained, it's possible for a genetic sequence to experience a sudden change, or mutation, without any known cause. So no rhyme or reason. Just a natural mutation. But these are rare, and Jack found it hard to believe Amy could have experienced a spontaneous mutation after 37 years of life, and shared that genetic anomaly with both kids. It didn't add up. The doctors wanted to agree, but since they had no other ideas, they stuck with it as the most plausible explanation.

Jack started thinking about external factors, food being the likeliest of suspects. But if it was something Amy and the kids had been eating, wouldn't it affect Jack also? They all ate the same stuff. But how could it be from food, Jack wondered. He and Amy had eaten clean for years, and the kids followed suit. They'd been disciplined regarding their diet, mainly to avoid this exact situation. Amy always railed against the food industry and how they've been poisoning people for years. Nearly 60% of Americans are taking prescription drugs, largely because of their poor diets. She recited the statistics all the time. She learned all kinds of scary numbers while studying for her Alternative and Complementary Medicine degree. Amy was the main reason they ate as clean as they did. When Jack was in college, he was running so much, burning so many calories, he ate whatever he wanted. He was lean and trim, regardless of what he put in his mouth. He couldn't gain weight even if he had wanted to. But over time, Amy helped him understand how much diet matters, both in performance and long term health.

No, Jack thought. It couldn't be their diet. Short of growing their own food (which they had discussed more than once), they'd done everything right. Or so they thought. Maybe the food they'd been eating wasn't so 'safe' after all. They'd read plenty of commentary on the world of organic food. It was big business, and some believed there was NO way a farmer could grow entire crops of food without using a single drop of pesticide. The amount of crop loss to insects, animals, weeds, etc. would be staggering and would dramatically eat into the farmer's profits.

During her final semester while she worked on her thesis, Amy learned that most organic farmers DO use pesticides. But instead of chemical or synthetic pesticides, they're 'natural'. They're still designed to kill bugs and protect the crops, but the natural version isn't as effective, so farmers actually wind up using more of it. And because they're studied less, scientists know little about the potential side effects they may have.

As Jack rounded the lake to head back, he made a mental note to look deeper into what they were eating. But for the return run, he decided to focus on other things. Clear his head. On the run out, he was oblivious to everything around him. Now he noticed everything. He looked up at the stars, spotted Orion's belt. He watched the trees go by, counted them. He passed an old warehouse that, judging by all the broken windows and rusty panels, had been abandoned for years. He ran by the tall fences that surrounded the town's water treatment plant. As he approached the edge of town, he spotted the local radio station. He wondered if the folks on the other side of town got good reception. The town offered more distractions for him as he ran. He enjoyed the architecture, the simplicity of the buildings. He ran past the local stores, many of which he knew well, some he'd never visited. He used to think there would be plenty of time. Now he wasn't so sure.

Chapter 4

"Whadda we got?," Detective Mercer asked. It was early evening and the sun had just begun to set. He stood on the north bank of the Chicago river, just inside the yellow police tape. He was surrounded by fellow police officers, EMTs, and two assistants from the Cook County

Medical Examiner's office. Lights were being set up and a small crowd was beginning to form.

"We got a floater," Officer Blake said. He pointed to the gurney parked ten feet away, near the ambulance. "Two joggers found that guy floating face down about an hour ago."

"We got an ID?," Detective Mercer asked.

"His driver's license says his name is Arush Patel."

"His driver's license?"

"Yep. His wallet was still in his back pocket. All the credit cards were still in it. There was even some cash," said Officer Blake.

"So whoever did this clearly wasn't interested in money."

"What do we know about Mr. Patel?," asked Detective Mercer.

"Doctor."

"Pardon me?"

"It's Dr. Patel," Officer Blake replied. He took out a small notepad from his pocket and referred to his notes. "Apparently he was some kind of pathologist here in Chicago. Worked for the BSC Medical Center for the last eleven years. Originally from India, he came here as a college student and liked it so much, he decided to stick around. Northwestern University for undergrad, medical school at the Feinberg School of Medicine, also at Northwestern."

"Impressive," Detective Mercer said. "And how did Dr. Patel wind up face down in the Chicago River?"

"We don't know that yet, Detective. But according to his office, he had no enemies. He was a real sweetheart."

"Well clearly someone didn't think so. Did his office have anything helpful to contribute to the investigation?"

"Not really," Officer Blake replied. "According to his lab assistant, he spent the last hour of the day on the phone."

"Who was he talking to?," inquired Detective Mercer.

"She said he made several calls. The first few were to other doctors. I have their names and numbers. But his longest call was to the Centers for Disease Control and Prevention."

"The CDC? What's that all about?"

"Honestly, it was kinda confusing. She was speaking a little above my pay grade. But it had something to do with a cancer they'd been seeing a lot of."

Chapter 5

Her flight landed shortly before nine p.m. Every time she came back, Cheryl forgot about the cute little airport with only one terminal. The one with no shops, no news stand, no Cinnabon, not even a Starbucks. The one where big commercial planes can't land. She hated flying as it is, but the puddle-jumper prop plane she was forced to take on the last leg of the trip added new dimensions to her loathing. She'd thrown up on it twice in the past, but managed to keep her dinner down this time. Cheryl walked down the few steps from the plane onto the tarmac, and let out a deep breath, grateful to be on solid ground once again.

Looking around, she couldn't help but smile. She had always likened her home town to Mayberry, and it didn't take long for all the memories to come rushing back. Earlier in the day, she was fighting through the crowded terminals of JFK airport in New York. A packed flight that landed in Atlanta, another airport overflowing with travelers. A few hours later, she was in the Twilight Zone. But she loved her sister, and adored her niece, so it was all worth it. Plus, they needed her now.

She rolled her carry-on across the tarmac and into the deserted terminal. Other than one person at the ticket/baggage/lost luggage/customer service counter, Cheryl had the place to herself. She walked by the lone vending machine. It was the kind that still took change, actual coins, and required you to pull the little handle out to get your chosen item. She shook her head as she made her way through the sliding glass doors and out front.

Cheryl always expected Barney Fife or Andy Griffith to be parked at the curb when she emerged, but they never were. Her sister, however, was there, standing next to her 1988 Ford Explorer. The same car she'd been driving for at least ten years. Cheryl had lost count. Brenda was five years younger than Cheryl, but she looked ten years older.

When she first got sick, they both refused to believe it. Cheryl flew home the same day and, together, the two sisters cried. Cancer was the last thing she was expecting to hear. Brenda had smoked on and off as a teenager and early into her 20s, but she kicked the habit years ago, when she first got pregnant. She suffered a miscarriage in her first pregnancy, and though it was not smoking related, she never lit up again. Brenda was five feet three inches tall and about fifteen pounds overweight, but overall in good health. So it was a shock when she called Cheryl to break the news.

Her doctor had started her on traditional therapy right away. Chemo, radiation, the works. But when her cancer was deemed 'too aggressive' for traditional methods, her doctor recommended a new medication that had recently become available to the public. Because her cancer was unresponsive to the standard treatments, her doctor fought for Brenda and made sure the insurance company paid what they were responsible for. The new drug slowed the progression of her disease, and her doctor was happy. But her long term prognosis was still not good. 'Terminal' is what Brenda had been told, but the timetable was unclear. That was just under a year ago.

Cheryl managed a weak smile as she walked up to Brenda. She parked her rolling suitcase at the curb and hugged her little sister. Cheryl was five inches taller and enveloped Brenda like a parent does a child. She felt Brenda begin to sob and hugged her even harder.

"You doin' ok?" Cheryl asked softly.

"Not really, " Brenda replied through the sniffles. After a while, they released each other and Brenda looked up at her sister's sympathetic face. "I'm trying to be strong," Brenda said, "for Lily's sake. But I haven't figured out how to tell her."

"What does she know so far?," Cheryl asked.

"Just that she's sick, like me. She doesn't know how bad it is. I never told her. How in the world am I supposed to tell her this?"

Cheryl touched her sister's face. She had no words. After a brief silence, Brenda trudged around to the other side of the car and got in the driver's seat. Cheryl threw her bag in the back and jumped into the passenger seat. The door creaked as she closed it and for a second she was afraid it would fall off.

Brenda started the car and, as they pulled away from the curb, Cheryl asked, "Did you call the specialist like we talked about?"

"I can't afford it, you know that. Our doctor here seemed pretty sure of what's going on. He said Lily's blood test came back the same as mine." Brenda's eyes started to water again, and Cheryl wanted to change the subject. But there was no getting away from this. No matter what they talked about, it would always be in the front of their minds.

"She really needs to see the specialist, Brenda. Maybe they're wrong, maybe they..."

"They're not wrong!" Brenda exploded. "Lily has cancer and there's nothing I can do to save her!" Tears

17

streamed down her face as she wept. The airport was in a remote stretch of town and the streets were basically empty, so Cheryl wasn't worried about them hitting anything or anyone. Let her cry, she thought.

When they came to a red light, Cheryl reached over, put her hand on Brenda's arm and said "I'm so sorry, Brenda." She couldn't imagine what her sister was going through. Facing your own death is hard enough. But when it's your child, it must be devastating. Lily was all Brenda had. Her husband left shortly after she got pregnant with Lily, and hadn't been heard from since. It was no great loss. He hadn't worked in a year and a half and was not qualified to do much.

Brenda was an assistant information security officer for U.S. Ally Security, a national security company that provides everything from security systems to security guards to cyber-security. Their clients were typically large companies and corporations with hundreds or thousands of employees, with a ton of data to protect. U.S. Ally Security had monitoring stations and server warehouses all over the country. They protected financial information, product information, employee information, customer information, and so on. Research indicated that small town workers were more willing to accept lower wages, so many of their monitoring stations were placed in low population communities. It certainly wasn't glamorous work, but it was a good job. And the benefits, including and especially health care, were excellent.

Cheryl never had kids. She was a career woman, or hoped to be. When she moved to New York seven years ago, she vowed to stay single until her career was in full swing. She took an internship at the New York Journal, with a goal of being an investigative reporter. But so far, she'd spent most of her time fact checking and doing research. She had submitted a number of articles to her editor, only to have them rejected for not having 'enough teeth', whatever that meant. She knew, one day, her work would make a difference.

They pulled up to Brenda's two-bedroom house, and Cheryl thought she might wake the whole neighborhood as the rusty door of the Explorer loudly squeaked its way open. Inside, the house was quiet. Lily had already gone to bed, and the sitter was on the couch half-asleep herself. She stirred as the two came in. Brenda made quick introductions and they exchanged quick hellos. By Cheryl's estimate, Tanya, the sitter, couldn't have been more than sixteen. She wore blue jeans, white sneakers, and a dark hoodie.

"How did she do?," Brenda asked.

"Ok, I guess," Tanya said with shrug. "She was pretty tired, so she went to bed not long after you left."

"It's the new medicine. It makes you tired, especially in the beginning." Tanya nodded, not knowing what else to say.

"Did she throw up?."

"No, she was ok," Tanya said.

"Good," Brenda said, relieved.

Once paid, Tanya added, "Call me if you need me," and left quietly.

Cheryl rolled her bag into the den. The pull out couch against the wall would be her bed for the next several nights. She came out into the kitchen as Brenda was tossing back a couple of pills with some water. "I just reminded myself," she said.

"What was that?" Cheryl asked.

"The cancer drug. They just started Lily on it too. I'm supposed to take it twice a day, but sometimes I forget mine when I'm busy dealing with her."

Cheryl gave her a look.

"I know, ok. But Lily has been a handful recently. She's tired, nauseous, cranky, irritable, sad...." Brenda started to tear up again. "It's just not fair," she whimpered. "Why her?"

"Brenda, I know this is hard, but Lily really needs to see a specialist. I'll help in any way I can. We'll make it work. But these small town doctors can't handle this. Are they even up on the latest research, the newest methods? Have they ever had to deal with anything like this? This is not a scraped knee or runny nose."

"I know, Cheryl," Brenda snapped. "Don't you think I know that? But I don't have the money to pay a specialist, and neither do you, for that matter! I've already spent most of our savings on the medication, and now we both need it. The insurance company covers a lot of it, thank god, but I'm still responsible for the rest. And it's expensive."

"But the doctor..." Cheryl began before Brenda cut her off again.

"Dr. Bosh is a good doctor. He's been managing my case for almost a year and I'm still here. When he first discovered my disease, he said he consulted with a specialist up north. In New York, I think. That's how he found out about the medication we're taking. He even helped us get it covered by our insurance. I trust him. Besides, he said there are other families in town with the same condition, so he knows what he's doing."

"Wait, what? What do you mean 'other families'? What does that mean?"

"I don't know. He said he's seen a few other cases like ours. Where people are sick like us."

"Other families...with terminal cancer? In this town?" Cheryl spoke slowly, not sure she was hearing her own words correctly. She couldn't fathom how a town with a population of just over fourteen hundred could produce multiple cases of the same cancer, let alone two in the same household. "How many?!"

"I don't know!," Brenda answered, exasperated. "How am I supposed to know that, Cheryl? I have my own problems, ok? What does it even matter?"

Chapter 6

They'd moved here just under three years ago, but it still felt strange. Jack knew it would take time to adjust to small town life, he just didn't realize how long. In their first few months, things moved slowly. A snail's pace compared to where they came from. No more hectic big city life. No more crowded streets. No more smog or pollution. No more coffee shops on every corner. No more sirens at all hours. It was a different life, and it was exactly what they'd hoped for. For Jack, it also meant miles and miles of unexplored territory to run, and the fresh air of the country. The kids had a yard to play in. Amy got to focus on her book.

Amy came from a uniquely dysfunctional family. Her father was a chiropractor, and her mother a physician's assistant. She had seen both sides of healthcare, (or *sick* care, as she'd come to call it). Her mission in life was to educate people so they could better understand how the body works, what it needs, and how they can get healthy and stay that way. She hated how dependent we, as a country, had become on medication.

Not quite a year after they moved, Amy started feeling different, strange. At first she couldn't explain it. She was tired a lot. Normally she would attack the day, practically leaping out of bed like a kid on Christmas morning. Whether she got five hours of sleep or nine, she was ready and raring to go. But soon, even twelve hours wasn't enough. She had no energy to do anything.

When her diagnosis was initially made by a local doctor, Jack and Amy decided she wasn't going to get the care she needed in a small town. Jack spent days online researching experts and specialists. East coast to west coast, Jack wanted the best. Then he found Dr. William Holst. Harvard University School of Medicine, board certified in internal medicine and medical oncology, residency at Harvard, fellowship trained at Sloan Kettering in New York. Clinical expertise in advanced, late-stage, and terminal cancers. He was *the* guy. When Jack made calls to different doctors, looking for the best, the name they always came back with was Dr. Holst.

It took six weeks, but when they finally got in to see him, Amy had every test under the sun. Blood tests, biopsies, ultrasounds, mammograms, CT scans, MRIs, PET scans... the works. And every test was accompanied by the same sense of fear and dread. Would the next test confirm the last? Or would they finally discover this was just a horrible mistake.

When Dr. Holst's assistant called to schedule an appointment "to review the test results," Jack and Amy both knew. They don't ask you to come in when it's good news, Jack had thought. They say "your test results came back negative" and tell you to have a nice day. This was not one of those calls.

Dr. Holst's office was beautifully adorned. Solid oak desk that looked like it had just been polished. An entire wall of medical books and journals behind it. An oversized aquarium with all nature of fish swimming about. A large window overlooking the city. And medical degrees everywhere. It was warm and comfortable, yet terrifying. As Jack and Amy sat in chairs across from his desk, holding hands, waiting, they knew what was coming. Though they prayed they were wrong. They weren't. It was called Omnicarcinos, a new form of aggressive and often terminal cancer. The words still echo in Jack's ears.

Amy quickly rejected the idea of chemotherapy, radiation and/or surgery. She didn't know how long she had, but she knew she wasn't going to spend it throwing up every fifteen minutes and living in hospitals. Jack tried feebly to persuade her, to consider treatment, to think about the kids. But to no avail. She knew the chances of traditional therapies prolonging her life even a little bit were slim at best. Besides, cancer was big business, and she refused to feed the beast.

After a lengthy discussion of their options, with Amy refusing essentially all of them, Dr. Holst proposed one more. A new drug called EBF-14. He made no promises, but said it was very possible that it could slow down, or even stop, the progression of Amy's cancer.

Discovered in a remote area of the Amazon jungle, Dr. Holst explained, EBF-14 is a chemical isolated from an obscure berry found in only one region of Brazil. It had demonstrated tremendous potential as a tumor-killing agent. The results of the clinical trials were astonishing. There were reports of tumors shrinking, and even vanishing, in forty-eight to seventy-two hours. A huge pharmaceutical company called AstaGen held all the patents and conducted the clinical trials. Because of the astounding results, and it's potential to help cancer patients, EBF-14 received FDA approval faster than any drug ever brought to market.

Dr. Holst urged them not to get excited, but it might be their best, and only option. But it's expensive, he cautioned. At Jack's insistence, Amy started taking it later that afternoon.

A few weeks later, the bills came flooding in. All the tests, the doctor's visits, airfare, the new medication... and no insurance. Before their world came crashing down, Jack was training and Amy was writing. They never made much money, so they never had much money. Amy's parent's weren't much help. Her father had a small, one doctor Chiropractic clinic, and her mom was working for someone she called 'the cheapest man alive'. They paid their bills and put a little bit away each month for retirement. But they were in no position to help, though they desperately wanted to.

Jack's parents, on the other hand, had a great deal of money. His mother, Laura, was in-house counsel for one of the largest real-estate firms in New York. His father, Michael, was a real estate mogul throughout Manhattan. That's how they originally met. Together, they pulled in over seven figures a year.

When they learned of Amy's illness, and of the financial stress it was causing, they immediately offered assistance. Family was everything to the Turners. Laura and Michael had begged Jack and Amy not to move out of the city. They loved seeing the kids, and having them over for the occasional Sunday dinner. They even offered to support them while Jack trained and Amy wrote. But Jack had never been comfortable with the idea of a grown man being supported by his parents. One of the many reasons they decided to move from the city to a small town was the cost of living. Rent alone was eating up what little they brought in. Sometimes more. He'd borrowed money from his parents in the past, and hated it. This time, he had no choice.

His parents established an extremely well-funded account for them to use at their discretion. It didn't matter for what, they said. Amy's health was all that mattered. Whether it was to pay a doctor's bill, cover the cost of a prescription, or just take her out to dinner, the money was there. All they needed. Jack vowed he would pay his parents back, but deep down he knew he would never be able to.

Chapter 7

The seizure hit hard in the middle of the night. The ambulance arrived several minutes after Brenda dialed, but it felt like an eternity as Lily thrashed about. Cheryl could only watch in horror as Brenda tried to keep her from falling off the bed. Dr. Bosh warned that this might happen. He said the pharmaceutical company was still tinkering with the dosages of her medication. For kids it was more complicated. Age wasn't as important as body weight, and Lily had always been small for her age. A seizure was one of the potential side effects if the dosage was off. Right now, none of that was any comfort to Brenda as she rode along in the ambulance with Lily. Cheryl followed behind in the Explorer as they raced to the hospital.

Minutes later, Lily was being wheeled into the emergency room. The seizure had stopped in the ambulance, but she looked pale. Brenda had already called Dr. Bosh from the ambulance and he was on his way. Cheryl wondered what, if anything, he would be able to do and silently wished they were all in New York right now. Surely the doctors there would know what to do. The city had the best of everything... hospitals, doctors, specialists, the latest technology, the newest equipment, the best medicine. Many times in the past, Cheryl wished Brenda had taken her advice and followed her to New York. But never more so than now.

As Cheryl ran in, there was a flurry of activity surrounding Lily. Her clothes, now in a heap on the floor, had been exchanged for a hospital gown. She was connected to monitors, blood was being drawn, and an IV was being set up. She was half awake and crying, and the look on her face tore at Cheryl's heart. She looked at Brenda, who was sitting on the side of the bed holding Lily's hand, refusing to 'step aside and let them work'. Cheryl couldn't imagine how she was feeling.

Moments later Dr. Bosh arrived. He was clearly asleep when he got the call. He attempted to get dressed, but apparently gave up halfway through. He was wearing jeans with frayed hems, brown boots, a black and red flannel shirt that was half tucked, and his hair was disheveled. He was the same height as Cheryl, but stocky. His mustache was beginning to gray, but he wore it well. Add a cowboy hat, thought Cheryl, and he was the epitome of a country doctor.

Dr. Bosh immediately gave the nurse instructions to administer some medication neither of them had ever heard of. He looked at Brenda and informed her it was an anti-seizure medication to settle her down and avoid any further convulsions. He glanced at Cheryl, and Brenda introduced her as her sister, Lily's aunt. A nod and he was back to Lily. She was quiet, but still breathing, somewhat rapidly. He reviewed her vitals, looked through her chart, and mumbled a few words to the nurse.

He motioned to Brenda and they took a few steps away from Lily. Cheryl followed a step behind. "She'll be ok," he said to them both. "The convulsions have stopped and the meds we're giving her now will keep it that way. Her vitals are already normalizing. We'll run some tests, but at this point, she just needs rest." Brenda breathed a large sigh of relief. Cheryl put an arm around her and squeezed.

"We'll skip her next dose of medication," he said, more to himself than Brenda. "In the meantime, I will put in a call first thing in the morning and see what I can find out about adjusting her dosage. We'll move her to a room where she can get some rest."

Brenda nodded, relieved.

"I'll have the nurses set up a cot for you in Lily's room," Dr. Bosh said to Brenda. Turning to Cheryl he added, "It's not a very big room. Sorry."

Brenda looked at Cheryl and said, "Take the truck back to the house. Get some sleep, and when you come back in the morning, bring us a change of clothes."

"Will do." Before she left, she had to ask, "Doctor, are we sure it's the medication Lily is reacting to?"

"Pretty sure. It's a relatively new drug. It was FDA approved less than 18 months ago. A colleague up north made me aware of it just over a year ago. That was right before Brenda was diagnosed. And honestly, they still haven't nailed down the dosages for younger patients yet. When the dosage is right, it works great. When it's off, there are side effects."

"Brenda mentioned there are other families in town with this same condition...," Cheryl said, more than asked. "Are there a lot?"

Dr. Bosh paused before saying, "One is too many, if you ask me."

"But how many? That are sick like Brenda and Lily?"

Dr. Bosh took a deep breath and cast a sideways look at Brenda.

"She's always been like this," Brenda offered. "And now she works for a newspaper. Sorry."

"I'm just curious, that's all," Cheryl said. "Isn't it weird that a town this small is producing multiple cancer cases?"

Dr. Bosh looked down at his watch and sighed. He looked back up at Cheryl and suggested, "Maybe this is a conversation for another time."

"You're right, Dr. Bosh," Brenda agreed. "Thank you SO much for coming in for Lily. I really appreciate it."

Dr. Bosh smiled. "Anytime. You know that. I'll be back to check on her in the morning." With that, he returned to Lily's bed, gave the nurses a few final instructions, and strode through the automatic doors out into the night.

When he was gone, Cheryl looked at Brenda and asked, "What's the name of the medication you and Lily are taking?"

"EBF-14. They really need to come up with something better..."

Chapter 8

'In 2014, the pharmaceutical industry generated revenues of over $1 trillion worldwide for the first time in history. Earnings from prescription drugs are expected to surpass $1.3 trillion by 2018, and Big Pharma sales are greater than the gross domestic product of 15 countries, combined. This colossal industry generates higher profit margins than any other industry and, incredibly, is expected to see continued growth. AstaGen, the California-based biotech company, leads the charge with revenues of $82.4 billion in its last fiscal year. With over 120,000 employees, AstaGen is the global leader in gene-based medicine. Founded in 1987 by Dr. Albrecht Müller, the company primarily develops gene-based drugs which target diseases on a molecular level. They recently wowed the medical community with their latest innovation, EBF-14, what many doctors and scientists are calling a wonder drug for cancer patients. With a cure rate of 95% during clinical trials, EBF-14 (trade name still pending), is a potential miracle for the millions of cancer patients worldwide. And with 23.6 million expected new cases of cancer (estimated) each year by 2030, it's no surprise EBF-14 is now the most expensive drug in the world. The annual cost for this medication is just over $300,000 a year, or $25,000 a month. Some insurance companies, however, will not cover all or a significant portion of the cost, leaving many families and affected individuals to handle the costs themselves...'*

Jack threw the paper down in disgust. Yeah, no kidding, he thought to himself. He was enraged at the enormous gall of these drug companies. They create these life saving drugs, then turn around and gouge the people that need them most. Where was the humanity? Where was the compassion? It's a business, I know, Jack thought, but $25,000 a month?!

Thanks to his parents, Jack and his family had more than enough money. They could afford the medication, buy whatever they needed, and still sleep well at night. But he imagined the families out there, many of whom suffered from a very different reality. People mortgaging everything, families going broke, parents fighting with insurances companies, begging them to help. And people dying.

Sickened by the whole thing, Jack pushed away from the kitchen table. Already back from his run and showered, he washed what was left of his organic oatmeal down the drain. The kids were already at school, and Amy was upstairs in her office working. He took the stairs two at a time as he ran up, leaned in from behind, gave her a quick kiss on the cheek, and said he would see her later.

A few weeks ago, Jack decided he couldn't keep sitting around dwelling on things. It was frustrating and upsetting. All that negative energy was affecting his mood. He needed a distraction, something light to unburden his mind for a few hours. He decided to get a part-time job. His degree in Sports Science was still collecting dust in a box somewhere, so he went back to the only thing he knew how to do.

Keeler Locks and Bolts had been in business since before Jack was born. Bobby Keeler was in charge now, but Big Daddy Keeler, as everyone knew him, started and ran the place for nearly 60 years. They called him Big Daddy because of his size, but also because he was like a father to so many in town. There was a time when the people never locked their doors, and business was slow at KL&B. For years, they were more hardware store and less locksmith. But as times changed, so did people. They started locking their doors at night.

Bobby had been running the shop on his own since Big Daddy passed a few years ago. A local high school kid would come by some afternoons to help out around the shop. Bobby had spent a lifetime learning about locks. Not just from Big Daddy, but from books and videos. It was said that Bobby could open any lock, any where. The problem, for Bobby anyway, was that there was little to no demand for the newest and coolest locks. Except for a few businesses, like the bank, most of his customers only needed a standard tumbler deadbolt. He could open those in his sleep. So Bobby would order the latest high tech locks and gadgets for himself. Digital locks with touch pads, locks that communicated with smartphones, biometric fingerprint locks... whatever they came out with, Bobby ordered it. He'd study it, take it apart, learn how it worked, figure out how to defeat it, master it, and return it to the vendor as 'too advanced for the customer'.

Jack was moderately proficient at working basic locks from his time spent at the shop during college, and always fancied himself as 'handy'. He knew a few things about tools and parts, and most importantly, was willing to work for little pay. Bobby hired him on the spot.

When Jack strolled in just after nine that morning, Bobby was already elbow deep into something.

"Morning," Jack said as he walked behind the counter. Bobby's grunt in return meant 'busy, leave me alone'. It looked like a cell phone had exploded on the counter, pieces of it everywhere. Bobby was holding up the touch screen, inspecting it closely.

"You still working on that thing?" Jack chuckled as he asked.

"I'll get it eventually," Bobby retorted. "They haven't invented a lock I can't crack." Bobby had been stumped for nearly a week. Samsung's most recent innovation, the AZOE, was a door lock that resembled some of the latest smart phones. By programming in a unique password, the owner simply used the touch screen to unlock the door. There's also a small key card that can be held over a sensor that will open the lock. It even comes with a manual backup key should the technology fail and lock the user out.

"Why don't you just bypass the keypad and pick the lock?," Jack asked.

Bobby raised his head slightly and eyed Jack. "Excuse me?"

"Sorry," Jack said quickly with his palms up defensively. Bobby hated the term, 'pick the lock'. He felt it was far too crude for what he considered an art.

"Why don't you just bypass the keypad and open the lock without a key?," Jack said with a smirk.

"Can't," Bobby said, as he went back to examining the keypad. "The tumbler won't move with the tech in place. Unless there's a complete failure of the technology, not even the key will open it. With previous models, the key would override the tech. But for real security, the tech is the first line of defense."

"So why not just fry the thing? Hit it with enough juice to burn out the electronics."

Bobby looked up, gave his head a little tilt and said, "Now how am I supposed to return the thing if I do that?"

"Ah yes. Your return policy."

"Besides," Bobby went on, "that won't work either. The tech has to release the control of the tumbler on its own. There's coding in here that releases it if there's an internal failure. But frying the circuits before that happens will lock it down tight. And once this thing is mounted, there's no getting inside it."

"Sounds like you're stuck."

"I'll get it sooner or later. It's only a matter of time."

Chapter 9

They kept Lily overnight for observation, but she had no further seizures. In fact, she hardly stirred during the night. Brenda was sitting on the edge of her cot in full yawn, rubbing her eyes when Cheryl walked in. Lily was still asleep. Cheryl couldn't help but smile when she saw her resting peacefully.

"I brought clothes and coffee," Cheryl said softly. Brenda motioned for the door, and as they walked she whispered back, "Thank god. The coffee here is dreadful. It tastes like it's been filtered through a dirty sock."

Cheryl snickered, then asked "How's she doing?"

"She's ok. She's been sleeping since you left. No more seizures, not even a bad dream. Hopefully they'll send us home today. But Dr. Bosh wants to speak to the specialist up north before making a decision."

"He seems like a nice guy," Cheryl admitted. "I know I was hard on him, but now that I've met him...'

"Whoa, whoa. Hold it right there," Brenda stopped her. "Don't get any ideas. He's married and you don't live here."

"What are you talking about?," Cheryl asked innocently.

"You know what I'm talking about."

"I don't believe this. Just because I'm single doesn't mean I fall head over heels for every man I meet. And Dr. Bosh? First of all, you know I hate mustaches. Second of all, I would never date a man who wears that much flannel."

"It was just a shirt," Brenda said.

"And that's more than enough." They both giggled. Neither could remember the last time they laughed together. "What I was going to say was, now that I've met him, he seems to know what he's doing, that's all."

"Uh huh," Brenda teased.

Cheryl changed the subject. "Does he think you'll go home today?"

"Not sure yet," Dr. Bosh said as he came up behind them in the hallway. They both jumped, and wheeled around, startled. "And I only own two flannel shirts." He winked at Brenda as he walked by and into Lily's room.

Cheryl turned beet red while Brenda had a good laugh at her expense.

After a long look at Lily and her chart, Dr. Bosh rejoined them in the hall. "She's stable, her vitals look good. Seems like she's had a quiet night."

Brenda nodded in agreement.

"That's good. I have a call in to the specialist, just waiting to hear back. I forwarded him the results of her blood work. That will help us dial in the dosage of her medication. But I'm leaning towards keeping her here a day or two longer."

Brenda started to protest, but Dr. Bosh cut her off. "Once we modify her meds, I'll want to make sure she's not having any adverse affects to the changes. This is the best place for me to monitor her, and for her to be in the event of any problems."

"Are other patients having seizures on this medication?," Cheryl probed.

"A few," Dr. Bosh offered, "usually kids. Again, it's the dosage."

"How many other patients of yours are taking it?"

"Cheryl...," Brenda said, giving her sister a look of disapproval.

"What? I'm just curious."

"I'm sorry, I really can't talk about my other patients. Now if you'll excuse me...." Dr. Bosh returned to the nurse's station.

"That's the second time you've driven him away in the last twelve hours," Brenda said accusingly.

"Brenda, how are you not looking into this?!," Cheryl asked incredulously. "You and your daughter, both otherwise healthy, have been diagnosed with cancer. Both in the last year. You've been prescribed a new, seemingly experimental, medication. Lily just had a seizure from it. And then you tell me there are other families with the same disease taking the same medication, and you're not the least bit concerned?! Not even curious?"

Cheryl's voice got louder as she spoke and a few of the nurses looked over. Brenda peered into the room to make sure Lily was still asleep. She took her sister by the elbow and led her down the hall, away from Lily's room.

"I'm not like you, Cheryl. I have so much on my plate, I really don't have time for anything else. My focus is one-hundred-percent on Lily. Her health is all I care about right now. I can't worry about anything or anyone else."

"I'm *talking* about her health, Brenda. And yours. Whatever this is directly affects both of you," Cheryl stressed.

"Whatever **what** is, Cheryl? Don't a lot of people have high cholesterol? Or high blood pressure? And don't they all take medication for it? I don't know what you're looking for, but don't stir up trouble. There's no story here, if that's what you're after."

Chapter 10

The sun had just started to peek over the horizon as Jack rounded the lake. This was his favorite time of day to run. The air was cool and crisp, the sky was turning a beautiful burnt orange, and the silence was only broken by the sound of his feet on the pavement. He left the lake behind him. He ran past the old warehouse, the high fences of the water treatment plant, the radio station at the edge of town.

Today was going to be a busy day. Last night, Jack had started working on the list. He was determined to find out what, if anything, could be in the food they'd been eating. What could possibly have caused Omnicarcinos, the cancer now affecting his wife and two kids? There had to be something, and if it was the food, he was going to find out.

The list wasn't as bad as he had expected. He had broken down their food into groups and by meals. He listed all breakfast, lunch and dinner foods separately. He wrote down anything they snacked on more than a handful of times. He categorized fruits, vegetables, proteins, dairy, grains, and oils. As vegetarians, they never ate meat, but did have fish now and then. That fell under dinner/protein. He wrote down any treats or desserts they would have now and then. There weren't many, since high fructose corn syrup was high on their list of no-no's. And sugar, while not avoided entirely, was something they monitored as well. Everything in moderation, Amy would always say.

The drink list was short... water. No soda, tea, coffee, sugary drinks, or milk. On any number of occasions, Amy had informed Jack and the kids that humans were the only species on the planet that drank milk past six months of age. Not even cows. They all drank water. Humans not only keep drinking milk, but they got it from another species altogether. And who knows what's in it these days, Amy would say. Government regulators allow producers to simply list 'milk' as the lone ingredient on the label regardless of whatever hormones, antibiotics, steroids, or other chemicals or additives may be present. For a while, they turned to almond milk as a substitute, but some frightening rumors surfaced a while back, so they gave it up. They hadn't had milk of any kind for years.

Jack ran through town swapping nods and "morning"s with a few early birds that were already out and about. He turned a corner and headed home. His street was quiet, and when he ran up to the back door, all the lights downstairs were still off. He crept into the house, trying not to wake the kids. Amy was an early riser like Jack, but while he was hitting the pavement, she was hitting the keyboard. She loved to work early in the morning. She felt like her thoughts were freshest and she could get them down before the distractions of the day sidetracked her. She also had more clarity and energy in the morning. Between the cancer and the medication, it was a wonder she could manage her way up and down the stairs by the afternoon.

Amy heard Jack return. The back door squeaked as he opened it, the floorboards moaned as he moved through the kitchen, and the stairs creaked as he tried desperately to navigate them quietly.

"Could you make a little more noise?," Amy asked sarcastically.

"Probably," Jack replied with a wink. He threw his shirt in the hamper and headed for the shower.

Looking at her from the threshold between the bathroom and bedroom, he still couldn't believe she was dying. She looked as beautiful and healthy as the day they met. He stood and watched her as she scanned websites, turned pages, and made notes. Sometimes, during a long run, he would pray for more time with her, for the medication to keep the cancer at bay. He would pray for the kids to live long, healthy lives. Countless times he wished he could switch places with any one of them. But he knew better. He was a realist. The first time he heard Dr. Holst confirm their diagnosis he knew. He put on a brave face, but he knew.

"What do you have today?," Jack asked.

Amy looked up from her work and swiveled in her chair. "I have to bring the kids in for their blood work after school."

"Has it been thirty days already?"

"Yup. And we need to make sure the office sends the results to Dr. Holst this time. He was pretty peeved he didn't get it last time. He said he needs to know about any changes in their tumor markers or protein levels."

"Ok. What time is their appointment? Maybe I'll meet you there," Jack offered.

"You don't have to. It should be pretty quick. Besides, don't you need to tackle that list you worked on last night?"

"I do. Starting right after I eat something. You sure you don't want me to come?"

"It's fine. We won't get the results for a couple of days anyway."

As Jack looked over the list, he was surprised to find they ate a lot of the same food. They were just good at mixing and matching so it never felt like they were eating the same things over and over again. He felt pretty good about the fruits and vegetables. All came from local growers who were known to use no genetically modified seed and no pesticide. The fish, though they ate it rarely, was always wild, never farmed. The eggs came from a local farm with free roaming chickens that eat no genetically modified feed. Or so they said. At this point, he wasn't taking anyone's word on anything. Those would be his first stops today.

Chapter 11

"New York Journal, Health Desk, Matt Cunningham...." he answered.

"Matt, it's Cheryl."

"Hey. I thought you were out of town. You miss me already?."

"Not exactly," she retorted.

Matt Cunningham was a veteran columnist who had been writing for the Journal for over a decade. His first assignment was in Foreign Affairs, but he hated it desperately and quickly got transferred to Health. It was a much better fit. Matt was a true health nut. He was a vegan, a CrossFit devotee, and he was absolutely obsessed with pulling the curtain back on as many health issues as he could. He had asked Cheryl out on a number of occasions, but she'd always turned him down. It's not that he wasn't attractive, he was. He was tall and muscular, and had a perfect set of matching dimples when he smiled. She loved dimples. But her penchant for cheeseburgers and weekend movie marathons did not, in her mind, mesh with his veggie burgers and hot-box workout sessions.

"I need you to do something for me," she said.

"What's in it for me?," he asked, only half jokingly.

"Maybe a story. Maybe not. But I'll owe you…" Cheryl couldn't even finish her sentence before Matt jumped in.

"Drinks when you get back to the city," he said enthusiastically.

Cheryl sighed audibly through the phone. "Fine," she said.

"Whaddaya need?"

"I need you to find out whatever you can about a new drug called EBF-14."

"Ah, AstaGen's `wonder drug'," he said with some disdain.

"You know it?!" she asked, excited.

"I know *of* it," he replied. "Cancer drug. Supposed to be some magical anti-tumor drug. I heard about it when it came out, and I've read about the results the company claims. Why, what's up?"

"I don't know yet. It's probably nothing. But please let me know when you have something."

"On it," he said. "When are you coming back?," he asked, a little too eagerly.

"Bye, Matt," and she was gone.

Chapter 12

Cole Larkin was a third generation farmer. It was all he knew, all he ever wanted to do. He loved his work, had been doing it most of his forty-seven years. He made it through seventh grade before he decided school wasn't going to take him anywhere he wanted to go. He wanted to be on the farm, helping his father, all the time. Quadratic equations weren't going to help him produce hearty crops. He learned everything he needed to know from his father. And the Larkin's were proud people. Proud to provide fruits and vegetables for their hometown, proud of the food grown on their own land.

When Jack first decided to investigate the food his family had been eating, he started asking around to find out what he could about the local produce. Because they ate so many fruits and vegetables, it seemed the logical place to start. The manager of the market told Jack the bulk of their produce came from three local farms. Jack had been to two already. The Larkin Farm was his third and final stop of the day.

The 220 acres had been in the Larkin family for more than a century. They had been growing crops and farming the land nearly as long. And like the first two farms Jack visited earlier in the day, it was said the Larkin's never used pesticides, chemicals, or genetically modified seed.

Jack drove up the long gravel drive and parked. When he got out, there was no one around. The house was fifty yards to his left, with a large shed just off to the side. In front of him were crops as far as the eye could see. As he scanned the fields, Jack held a hand up to shield his eyes from the sun. One of Larkin's farm hands popped out from the shed and the bang of the metal door startled Jack. He was a strong looking teenager, someone who spent a lot of time lifting heavy stuff. Jack remembered seeing him at the market once or twice. The boy told Jack that Cole had gone to "mend the fence" on the far side of the property, but would be back soon. Jack decided he would wait in the car with the air conditioner running.

Fifteen minutes later, Jack saw a large tractor chugging along the outskirts of the fields, pumping smoke into the air and bouncing up and down like a carnival ride. It pulled up alongside the shed, and Cole Larkin jumped off. He wore a blue and white checkered shirt, a straw hat with a brim that resembled a cowboy hat but with better ventilation, and blue jeans tucked into tall boots.

"Jack Turner, we spoke on the phone," Jack said as he approached. He reached out to shake Cole's hand, but quickly noticed the blood. Cole's hand had been hastily wrapped in a handkerchief that was now about halfway soaked in red.

"You ok?"

"Damned barbed wire. Gets me at least once a month."

"You don't wear gloves?"

Cole, already aggravated by his injured hand, decided he wasn't going to have this conversation. Not with a stranger, anyway. He'd hear plenty about it from his wife, and that was enough.

"Mr. Turner, is it?"

"Jack, please."

"What can I do for you?," he asked, clearly more concerned about his hand, and less about some transplanted city-boy asking questions about his farming methods.

"Well, I'll be honest. My family is sick. My whole family. Cancer. My wife and both of my kids. All within the last year or so. And I'm just trying to figure out how it happened, what might have caused it. I'm really sorry for the intrusion, but I'm looking into everything we've been eating since we moved here. I'm just trying to rule things out."

Cole softened a bit hearing Jack's story, and apologized for being short with him. "What would you like to know?"

"Over at the market, they told me you use no pesticides on your crops and plant no genetically modified seed. Is that right?"

"Hundred percent. Never have, never will."

"If you don't mind me asking, how is that possible? How do you keep the insects away? How do you deal with the weeds? How do you keep the pests and critters out?"

Cole held up his bleeding hand. "The fence keeps the critters out," he said with a smirk. "The weeds and the bugs, that's a different story. We have a few tricks."

"Such as...?"

"Well for starters, we rotate our crops."

"What does that mean?"

"We alternate the species of crops we plant each year. It keeps the bugs from getting used to the type of plants we're growing."

"And that works?"

"Yep. Even helps with the soil. Makes it more fertile. Chemicals and pesticides can kill the soil."

"Hmmf," Jack said, surprised.

"As for the insects, it's simple. Bugs on bugs."

"What does that mean?," Jack asked, eyebrows raised, genuinely curious now.

"Certain insects are predatory, like ladybugs and wasps. They kill the pesky bugs, but leave the crops alone. Our crop yield is actually much higher than farms that use chemicals to fight pests."

Jack listened intently as Cole went on.

"Sometimes, if we're seeing more bugs than usual, we'll also plant catnip."

Jack shook his head. "Catnip?," he asked. Born and raised in a big city, Jack was clearly out of his depths.

Cole quietly sighed. He imagined this must be how a first grade teacher felt explaining simple math.

"It helps ward off the bugs too. Every farmer has their tricks, Mr. Turner." He refused to call him Jack. "But we know what works. And it ain't chemicals. They're expensive and they don't work nearly as well."

"Wow. How do you keep the weeds out?"

"After a harvest, we plant rye. In the winter it decomposes and produces a natural weed killing substance.

It protects the fields throughout the spring. It's natural and harmless."

"Amazing. And you said you never use GMO seeds...?"

"Why would I? It may grow bigger, but it's definitely not better. Plus, it's more expensive and doesn't taste as good. It's not natural."

"That's great," Jack said. "I appreciate the time. Thank you so much."

"Sure."

"One last thing, if you don't mind..."

"Ok," Cole said, as he stood there, bleeding.

"I stopped at a few other farms earlier today... they all said the same as you. No pesticides, no GMOs. Do you know if that's true?"

"Farmers around here are proud, Mr. Turner. They will never put chemicals on or in the food that family and friends are going to eat."

Jack nodded, feeling somewhat relieved.

"So look, I don't mean to be rude, but I should really take care of this hand..."

"Of course. I'm so sorry. And thanks for your time. I really appreciate the information."

Cole gave a quick nod, turned and headed up toward the house. Jack relaxed a bit. He had a few things left to look into, but after today, he was feeling pretty confident the food they were eating wasn't to blame. He began to wonder what else it could be. He already ruled out the eggs and fish. Now he could cross fruits and vegetables off the list. He started to mentally consider the other possible suspects when his phone rang. He pulled the phone from his pocket and saw his wife's face on the caller ID. He hit the button to accept the call, but before he could even say 'Hello', he heard Amy scream, "Jack, come quick! It's Nate!" Her voice was panicked as Jack sprinted to his car.

Chapter 13

Cheryl longed for the high speed internet she had back in New York. Trying to do research on a computer with dial-up internet speed was testing her patience. Brenda had a computer which sat in the corner of the den, the same room Cheryl had slept in the past few nights, but it was ancient by technology standards, and had a fairly thick layer of dust covering most surfaces. Brenda spent her workdays in front of a computer, so when she got home, it was the last thing she wanted to see.

Cheryl had wisely brought her laptop with her. And while it was new and high-tech, it was still being hindered by the internet speed in the house. There was no Verizon FiOS, like they had at the New York Journal. No Comcast XFINITY like she had at home. Both were blazing fast compared to what she was working with now. But she had no options, and was forced to make due.

Dr. Bosh had finally heard back from his colleague up north and they got Lily's dosage adjusted. He made good on his promise of keeping her a few more days. He wasn't expecting any problems, but if Lily was going to have a reaction, it would happen in the first twenty-four to forty-eight hours. The hospital was the best place to be right now.

Lily was awake and alert, and had no memory of her seizure. And most importantly, she appeared to have no lingering effects from it. No headache, no speech or vision issues, no fatigue or soreness. She slept it off, was feeling well rested, and wanted to go home. Brenda explained to her about the adjustment to her medication and how the doctors wanted to monitor her to see how she responded to the change. If all went well, they'd be home in a couple of days. Brenda refused to leave her, so Cheryl volunteered to go back to the house for more clothes and a few of Lily's favorite snacks. She imagined a little contraband would be overlooked by the nurses.

While at the house, Cheryl decided to do a little digging. Brenda may not be curious about whatever was going on, but Cheryl was. Maybe it was the reporter in her. Maybe it was the fact that she was on the outside looking in. Either way, her gut was telling her there was more to this than Dr. Bosh was letting on. It gnawed at her. She felt awful for Brenda and Lily. To live under this cloud of uncertainty, not knowing if death was right around the corner or down the road a ways. It's a terrible thing to even think about. And it was happening to her family.

But it was happening to other families too. And Cheryl wanted to know how many. Having spent years researching stories for the Journal, Cheryl was well versed in navigating the web for information and statistics. And she had worked on a number of health related stories for Matt, so this wasn't exactly new territory. But this time, it was personal.

Thanks to the glacier-like internet speed, her progress was slow. Pages would ultimately load, but not before causing Cheryl a few gray hairs in the process. It was slow, but she was making some headway. She spent the next few hours toggling between the websites of the World Health Organization, the National Institutes of Health, and the Centers for Disease Control. When she was done, she wasn't sure what to make of the information. According to the numbers, less than 0.3% of the U.S. population have been diagnosed with Omnicarcinos. Per the Rare Diseases Act of 2002, a rare disease is defined as "any disease or condition that affects fewer than 200,000 people in the United States," or about 1 in 1,500 people.

Cheryl did some quick math and discovered that Omnicarcinos fell just short of the 'rare' classification, but it wasn't far off. Fewer than a million people out of nearly 320 million were diagnosed with it, and yet in a town of less than fourteen hundred, there were multiple cases. She still didn't know exactly how many, but she was more curious than ever.

Chapter 14

The screaming could be heard across the entire floor of the hospital. Amy was crying uncontrollably, her screams interrupted only by exhausted gasps for air. Emma was on the floor in the corner with her head between her knees sobbing. Jack was numb. He stood, holding Amy in a tight embrace, her face buried in his neck. She was crying hysterically and nearly collapsed out of his grasp. Jack sat only because she needed him to. He had no words. He couldn't even produce a tear. He felt nothing but rage. He wanted to lash out at someone, anyone. And he wanted answers.

They were in a private family waiting room, the only one in the hospital, and no one dared approach. Dr. Bosh was just down the hall at the nurses' station yelling into a phone. People started gathering on the floor trying to find out what happened. Patients were peeking their heads out of their rooms, nurses were congregating around the station, and visitors moved slowly by the waiting room with far too many windows for Jack's liking.

Nate was dead, and Jack was ready to explode. Amy had brought both kids to their scheduled appointment for blood work at Dr. Bosh's office. As the big sister, Emma wanted to show Nate there was nothing to be afraid of, so she went first. They drew a single tube of her blood and she was brave for him. When it was Nate's turn, he sat up tall, wanting to show his sister he was brave too. But before the nurse could even get the needle in his arm, a massive seizure struck. Nate lurched off the table and fell forward, head first onto the floor. He began violently convulsing and the nurse screamed for Dr. Bosh, who was in the room a moment later. He immediately turned Nate onto his side to prevent choking. He instructed everyone to stand back so Nate wouldn't hurt himself further while he convulsed.

"Shouldn't we hold him down?" Amy asked, panicked.

"No!" Dr. Bosh barred her with his arm as she reached for Nate. "It could hurt him. We just have to let it run its course."

Initially, Dr. Bosh was not overly concerned. He'd seen these seizures before, particularly in kids taking EBF-14. He figured Nate was just reacting to a dosage problem, and expected the convulsions to stop within minutes. But when Nate suddenly vomited, Dr. Bosh asked how Nate got on the floor. He fell, the nurse told him. Did he hit his head, Dr. Bosh asked. Yes, the nurse told him. Dr. Bosh quickly got down on his knees at Nate's side. He lifted Nate's lids, pulled a pen-shaped light from his pocket and shined it into Nate's eyes. The situation went from bad to worse. One of Nate's pupils was fixed and dilated, and the other was sluggish responding to the light. Nate's most recent MRI had confirmed a small tumor near the base of the brain, and Dr. Bosh believed Nate was now also hemorrhaging in the brain.

"Get an ambulance here right now," he told the nurse with a sense of urgency she had not seen before. In

54

minutes, the ambulance arrived and Nate was en route to the hospital with Dr. Bosh, Amy and Emma riding along. Amy tried calling Jack but couldn't get through. In her state of panic, she couldn't be sure if she was dialing the right number or even pressing the right buttons. They pulled into the ambulance bay of the hospital and Nate was rolled into the ER with Dr. Bosh running alongside. They wheeled the gurney into a nook, pulled the curtain, and got to work. Dr. Bosh briefed the emergency room physician.

Nate had stopped convulsing. In fact, he didn't appear to be moving at all. A nurse checking his blood pressure and pulse shouted 'Code Blue!'. He had been active and breathing in the ambulance, but something had happened. Another nurse finished attaching electrical leads, and the monitor displayed a flat line. Nate wasn't breathing, and his heart was not beating. A crash cart was hurriedly rushed up to Nate's bed. They began CPR, injected epinephrine into his IV, and hit him several times with the defibrillator. Nothing. Amy was pacing frantically a few feet from the foot of the bed, repeating 'Oh my god, oh my god!' She called Jack again and again, but couldn't get through. After ten minutes of hitting redial, the call finally connected. Jack answered, but before he could say anything Amy screamed into the phone, "Jack, come quick! It's Nate!"

By the time he arrived, it was too late. Jack drove as fast as he dared, on the edge of out of control. He almost ran off the road several times, but managed to make it to the hospital. It didn't matter. The Larkin farm is on the opposite side of town, a good 20 minutes from the hospital.

They worked on Nate for over 30 minutes before calling it. He was twelve years old.

Chapter 15

Cheryl pressed the button for the elevator. She and Brenda were headed up to the third floor, excited to take Lily home. The third floor was also the top floor. Cheryl still couldn't believe that a hospital could only have three floors. New York Presbyterian Hospital has twenty-three, she thought to herself.

Cheryl had convinced Brenda to go home, take a shower, and get some rest. Cheryl drove her home, dropped her off, and took the car back to the hospital to ensure Brenda stayed there. Lily and Cheryl enjoyed some time alone together while Brenda got a chance to rest and relax. Early this morning, Dr. Bosh had dropped by to check on Lily and he assured them she would be going home today. She was showing no ill effects from the seizure and had taken well to the adjusted medication.

After a hot shower and a long overdue nap, Brenda decided while she was home, she'd get things ready for Lily's return. She tidied up, made Lily's bed (it was still disheveled from when they raced out of the house in the middle of the night), and took some pork chops out of the freezer. Brenda decided to make skillet cooked pork chops with apples and onions for dinner. Lily's favorite. She smiled when she pictured Lily's face eating it.

She got teary eyed thinking about what might have been. The seizure was just a mild one and, according to Dr. Bosh, simply a result of the medication. But what if there was more to it? What would she do if she lost Lily? She didn't know how she would handle it. Lily was all she had. It has been just the two of them for years, and that was fine with Brenda. She didn't need a man to take care of her. But she needed her precious girl. It wasn't right that someone so young had to deal with doctors, medications, seizures... with cancer. It wasn't fair. She didn't want to think about it. But the question that kept creeping in every time she started thinking this way was 'What if Cheryl is right?'.

She prepped dinner, set the table, and had everything ready for Lily's homecoming. She was excited to have her little girl back home. And for the first time since Cheryl arrived, the three of them would have a meal together.

Cheryl spent the day with Lily, playing cards, reading magazines, and watching TV. They even shared the bed and took a nap together. They both enjoyed every minute of it. Since moving to New York, she saw her niece only a few times a year. The holidays mostly. And she rarely got her one-on-one. This wasn't exactly the ideal situation, but she made the most of it.

While Lily napped, Cheryl quietly snuck out to pick up Brenda and bring her back to the hospital. They were back in less than thirty minutes. Downstairs, they waited for the elevator to arrive. When the doors finally opened, Brenda told Cheryl about her dinner surprise for Lily.

"Sounds amazing," Cheryl said. "Lily is excited to go home," Cheryl added. "When I left to come get you, she was napping, but the nurse said as soon as the discharge papers are ready, she's outta here."

"Good," Brenda said. "I've had enough with hospitals and doctors for a while."
Cheryl smiled. She was thrilled that Lily recovered so quickly and was heading home.

They rode the elevator up to the third floor, just the two of them, excited about taking Lily home and the evening ahead. When the elevator dinged and the doors opened, they moved to exit. But before they could get to the door, a man hurriedly shoved his way in, barreling between the two of them. As he pushed by them, he stuck out a leg and slammed his foot against the handrail on the back wall of the elevator as hard as he could.

"FUCK!," he shouted. He grabbed the rail with both hands and shook it violently. When he stopped, he just stood there for a moment, hands still on the rail. Then he bent over, hung his head, and started to sob.

Alarmed and frightened, the girls backed their way out of the elevator. The man never looked up. A couple of nurses at the station, having heard the commotion, leaned over the edge of the counter, watching.

The elevator doors closed, and he was gone.

"What was that?!," Brenda said, still startled by the whole thing.

Cheryl shrugged, "I don't know."

"His son just died," one of the nurses said softly.

Chapter 16

Nate's death was the first among EBF-14 patients. To date, it had done a spectacular job of halting the progression of cancer in nearly every patient. But the dosage issue with younger patients was clearly still an issue. Dr. Bosh later discovered that Nate was the youngest and smallest patient taking it. After several days of pounding the phones, and getting the runaround from a bunch of corporate stiffs, he was finally connected to the medical director at AstaGen. Dr. Nassan Habib was a fellowship trained graduate of the Imam Medical College in Saudi Arabia. According to his bio on AstaGen's website, he and his family had emigrated to the United States so he could 'further his research and make a meaningful contribution to medicine'. Dr. Bosh remembered reading one of Dr. Habib's papers a few years earlier regarding the advancement of genetic mapping and what it could mean for the future of medicine and the treatment of disease.

Dr. Bosh repeated Nate's tragic tale for what felt like the hundredth time. It upset him every time he talked about it. The autopsy had revealed that the small tumor at the base of Nate's brain, while unchanged in size, had a sizeable artery snaking around it. When Nate's seizure launched him to the ground, his head impacted with enough force to jolt the tumor and tear the artery, causing a massive intracranial hemorrhage. The location of the bleed combined with the amount of blood lost sealed his fate instantly. No one could have saved Nate.

"These things happen sometimes," Dr. Habib said with as little sympathy as humanly possible.

Dr. Bosh gripped the phone a little tighter. "Dr. Habib," he began calmly, "we're talking about a twelve-year-old boy here. This is not some eighty-year-old brittle diabetic. This is a child. The seizure that resulted in his death was caused by your medication. He'd still be alive today if it wasn't for EBF-14..."

"Excuse me," Dr. Habib interrupted. "I hate to correct you, doctor, but EBF-14 was keeping this boy alive. Were it not for 'my medication', as you like to call it, his cancer would have progressed, his tumors would have kept growing and spreading, and he would likely have already died. Wouldn't you agree?"

"Perhaps," Dr. Bosh conceded. "So let's talk about the fact that no one over there seems to be able to figure out the proper dosage for these young patients. Nate was my second EBF-14 patient to suffer a seizure this week!"

"Every patient, every case is different. You know that, doctor." The way Dr. Habib said 'doctor' had a degree of condescension that was hard to miss. He was clearly talking down to Dr. Bosh. "And these 'young patients' are of different ages, heights, weights, metabolisms, immune systems, stage of disease, and so on. There is not a 'one-size-fits-all' solution. We are still working on the dosage schedule for every scenario. As I said, these things happen. It's an unfortunate byproduct of a scientific breakthrough. But what is it you Americans say? 'You can't make an omelette without breaking a few eggs?'"

Dr. Bosh was aghast at Dr. Habib's heartless response. And he was equally enraged that a fellow doctor could have such a callous attitude toward the death of another human being, especially a child. He was at a loss for words, but it was clear he wasn't going anywhere useful talking to Dr. Habib. He thanked him for nothing, ended the call, and immediately dialed Dr. Holst's private line.

As the doctor that originally recommended EBF-14, Dr. Holst had been horrified to hear the tragic account of Nate's death. It was one of the first calls Dr. Bosh made that day. Both doctors felt somewhat responsible for what happened to Nate. Calling AstaGen to report the incident was a mutual decision. They expected a more cordial, and certainly more professional, response than what Dr. Bosh received. What exactly they were expecting, they weren't sure. But they were both disheartened and angered by the attitude displayed by AstaGen.

"Perhaps it's time to take things to the next level," Dr. Holst suggested.

"What did you have in mind?"

"We call Dr. Albrecht Müller, the founder of AstaGen. If he's not responsive or helpful, then we talk to the FDA. They may be interested to know they approved a drug with poorly investigated dosage regimens. And that a child has died as a result of their haste. If that doesn't work, there's always the media."

Chapter 17

Brenda, Cheryl and Lily shared a delightful dinner at home. Lily raved about the pork chops with apples and onions and ate them with gusto. Brenda was thrilled to have her home, to see her eating, and feeling better. She knew she wasn't 'healthy', but she was still here. And for now, that was all that mattered.

They sat around the table sharing stories. Lily of her school and friends, Brenda of her job at the security company, and Cheryl of her life in the big city. Lily's eyes widened as she imagined the sights and sounds of New York. She asked Cheryl questions, and Cheryl told her about the people, the places, the food, the shows, the history. Lily was completely entranced listening to her aunt talk about this magical place a thousand miles away. She wished that one day she could visit there. Cheryl promised her it would happen, and silently prayed it would.

Apple pie ala mode was for dessert. Already stuffed, Cheryl barely took two bites of pie. She had enjoyed the pork chops more than she expected and ate more than she'd planned. Brenda and Lily each ate half a piece of pie. By nine o'clock, Lily was wiped out and ready for more sleep. She quickly changed into her pj's, brushed her teeth, and climbed into bed. She got tucked in twice, got two hugs, two kisses, and loved every second of it.

Brenda closed the door behind them, and they resumed their positions at the kitchen table for some coffee. They talked about the incident in the elevator at the hospital, both clearly still rattled by it. They couldn't imagine what that poor man must be going through. And Brenda didn't want to. She felt terrible, but at the same time she was grateful it wasn't Lily.

"You ok," Cheryl asked.

"Yeah. Just glad she's home. I don't know what I would do without her."

Cheryl nodded.

"There's something I have to tell you," Brenda said slowly.

"Go on." Cheryl held her coffee cup in both hands and sat up a little taller in her seat.

"You were in the bathroom when Dr. Bosh came in with Lily's discharge papers. He went over the instructions, told me when he wanted to see her again, and signed us out."

Cheryl didn't know where this was going, but she was listening closely.

"We said our goodbyes and he started to leave, but I had to ask."

"Ask what?," Cheryl's curiosity completely piqued.

"About the boy that died. Did he know him? Did he know what happened? Did he know the guy in the elevator?"

"And?," Cheryl said, now on the edge of her seat.

"He was his patient, Cheryl. He had cancer too. Dr. Bosh is the one that originally discovered it. But his parents didn't think he could get the kind of care he needed here. They sought out a specialist. It was Dr. Holst. The same doctor that Dr. Bosh has been consulting with for Lily. The same doctor that recommended EBF-14. The little boy was taking it too."

Cheryl sat there, unmoving as Brenda talked. Her jaw slowly widened as she listened.

"You know what that means, right?" Brenda asked.

Cheryl took a second to regain her composure as her initial suspicions were suddenly confirmed. She nodded and said, "It means if there's one, there are others. And Dr. Bosh has been holding out on us."

Chapter 18

Word of Nate's death spread fast. There were no secrets in a small town. The waitress at the diner usually knew more than the local TV reporters. His funeral was well attended. It was a clear day and the air was cool. The family sat graveside in folding chairs under a tent that had been erected to shield them from sun or rain. Jack's parents

64

flew in that morning. His mom, Laura, got airsick on the final leg and was still queasy as she sat between her husband, Michael, and Jack. The three held hands. Amy sat to the right of Jack, next to Emma and Amy's parents, Sean and Marie Anderson. Amy and Emma were both crying. Amy was trying mightily to control her emotions for her daughter's sake, but she wasn't succeeding.

Jack was stoic. Inside, he was seething with anger. His son was dead and he wanted answers. His beautiful, sweet, innocent boy was lying in a casket five feet in front of him, dead. Why? It was easy to blame the medication. It caused the seizure that began the unimaginable chain of events that led to this moment. But, according to Dr. Bosh and the doctor that performed the autopsy, it was the tumor at the base of his brain that was the ultimate cause of death. It tore through an artery and Nate stroked out and bled to death before anything could be done. The medication was only part of the equation. Jack needed to know the rest of it. How did a twelve-year-old get cancer? How does something like that happen? And would his wife and daughter suffer the same fate? He refused to let that happen. It may not have been the food that caused this, but Jack was convinced, now more than ever, that this wasn't by chance. He would find out what caused the death of his son, and someone would pay.

As Jack stewed with anger, the minister gave a beautiful eulogy about love, family, and peace. Though he had only met Nate a few times, it was clear he was a compassionate man who truly cared about the people he served. He shared a few meaningful quotes from scripture and tried to rationalize why a young life was taken so early. Something about God's plan, but Jack wasn't hearing it.

Jack recognized a few faces in the crowd that stood opposite him. Bobby Keeler, his boss at Keeler Locks and Bolts, was there. He had a look of compassion and sympathy on his face for his employee and friend. Dr. Bosh was there as well. He hung his head with a somber look on his face. He couldn't bring himself to look Jack or Amy in the eye. Much of the town had turned out to support the Turner family in their time of need.

There were a lot of unfamiliar faces as well. Faces he'd seen in passing, but now didn't recognize. And faces that belonged to people he'd never met. One face in particular stood out. She was removed from the crowd, at least twenty yards back. She was tall, about five-seven or five-eight if he had to guess, wearing all black, including sunglasses and the scarf wrapped around her head. He couldn't help but think she looked a little like Audrey Hepburn from afar. He didn't recognize her, but she seemed out of place. Definitely not small town.

"Would anyone like to say a few words?" The minister's question snapped Jack back to the moment. They had decided that Amy would speak for the family. Jack was not in a good place and neither of them thought it was a good idea for him to stand up and speak in front of others. Amy cried her way through a beautiful summary of Nate's twelve short years. When she finished, there wasn't a dry eye among the mourners.

Except Jack's.

When the service was over, the crowd slowly dispersed. A few came over to offer their condolences, including Dr. Bosh, who looked like he'd lost a child of his own. When the last of the mourners had gone, Jack and his family stood and watched as the casket was lowered into the earth. Each of them took turns tossing a small handful of dirt on the casket. When they had all wiped their hands clean, Jack's mother suddenly wheeled on him. "We begged you to stay in New York!," she shouted. "We begged you! How could you let this happen?!" She reached up and pounded on her son's chest. Jack took a step back, both from the force of the blows and the shock of her unexpected reaction. Jack's father quickly stepped in, took his wife by the arm, mouthed "sorry" to Jack, and walked her down the slope to their waiting car.

The words echoed in his ears. How could he let this happen. Indeed.

Chapter 19

Getting on the phone with Dr. Albrecht Müller was like getting an audience with the Pope. As the founder of AstaGen he was practically royalty. And impossible to get in touch with. Dr. Holst had taken up the mantle of getting some answers and he had called AstaGen a number of times. He left messages each time, but never got a call in return. Words like 'urgent', 'pressing matter', or 'child death' made no difference. He wasn't getting through.

The FDA was equally unhelpful. He called a dozen different departments, left messages with every relevant office, and got nowhere.

Stonewalled at every turn, Dr. Holst was out of options. He and Dr. Bosh spoke regularly, and both were equally frustrated.

They had already decided on their next course of action.

A few years back, Dr. Holst read an article published in the New York Journal. It was a powerful story on the dangers of statin drugs. Commonly prescribed to lower cholesterol and reduce the risk of heart disease, it detailed the different health risks and the potential side effects associated with taking a statin. It laid out how they weaken the immune system, how they're linked to muscular and neurological problems, how they increase the risk of prostate and breast cancer, and how they are known to cause liver damage.

But it also revealed the massive amounts of money statin drugs generate for Big Pharma. In 2013, sales were in the neighborhood of $26 billion. How one-in-four Americans over the age of forty-five now takes a statin drug. It even went on to mention that the FDA had somehow been 'convinced' that 200 was no longer the appropriate threshold for what should be considered elevated cholesterol. By adjusting the number down to 190 as the new baseline, 33 million previously healthy Americans suddenly needed a statin drug.

Dr. Holst remembered thinking how bold and eye-opening the article was. He did a quick internet search to find the author. It didn't take long to find his name or a contact number.

"Matt Cunningham, please."

"He's out on assignment," said the voice on the other end. "Can I leave a message for him?"

"This is Dr. William Holst. I'm an oncologist here in New York. Could you please have him return my call at his earliest convenience?"

"Oncologist?," was the reply, sounding both surprised and concerned.

"Oh, it's not about him or his health. I may have something to share he might find interesting."

"Ah. Ok doc, you got it."

He took the number and assured Dr. Holst he would deliver the message.

Chapter 20

After the funeral, Jack, Amy and Emma returned home, joined by both sets of parents. Jack's mom had calmed down in the car ride from the cemetery, but she was clearly still upset. They all were. She apologized to Jack for attacking him. He shrugged it off. He couldn't help but wonder if she was right. Who knows what might have been had they stayed in New York. They made trips up to the city several times a year to visit different doctors and specialists. But maybe it would have been better, maybe Nate would still be here, if they never left in the first place.

Over the last few days, a number of townspeople had dropped off food to the Turner's. Salads, platters, hams, casseroles, pasta dishes, fresh vegetables, cakes and cookies. There was certainly no shortage of things to eat. The family sat around, picked at some food, and tried to make each other feel better. There were a few smiles, even a few laughs, and plenty of tears. Jack chose to sit alone in a chair by the window. He tuned out the conversation behind him and just stared blankly into the distance. His worst nightmare was now a reality and he feared for Amy and Emma.

After a few hours, Amy's parents were the first to leave. They lived nearby so they'd be back sooner than later. Their help, just their presence, would be a great comfort to Amy and Emma in the coming days and weeks. As Jack's parents prepared to leave, he thanked them for coming, for everything they did financially to help them, and apologized for what happened, even though he knew it wasn't his fault. They kissed him, kissed Amy and Emma, and said "Anything you need..." before heading out.

After the parents had gone, the house was suddenly very quiet. Amy instructed Emma to go change her clothes, and for Jack to do the same. She was determined to keep them busy and distracted. After some prodding, Jack reluctantly went upstairs to change. As he walked by the open door to Nate's room, he stopped. He turned to face the room of his only son. The bed was neatly made, toys were in a box in a corner by the closet, books lined the shelves over his bed.

Jack went in and sat down on the bed. He picked up the pillow and held it to his face. It still smelled like Nate. Jack hugged the pillow tight, and stared out the window. He wanted to cry, to mourn his son. He hadn't shed a tear since the day Nate died. He felt guilty about not crying at the funeral and, sitting on his bed, smelling on the pillow, he genuinely wanted to cry. But his anger kept the tears at bay. He sat there for a while, his mind shuffling through different questions, thoughts and ideas. But it always came back to the same one: how did this happen and who is responsible?

He wasn't sure how long he sat there before Amy's touch startled him. She stood over him with her hand on his shoulder. He looked up at her and she put her hands on his face.

"I can't lose you too, Jack," she said with a tear in her eye. "I need you here with us. Your daughter needs you. We're all hurting. But the only way we're going to get through this is together. Ok?."

Jack put the pillow down on the bed, took her hands from his face and kissed them both. Then, still sitting, he wrapped both arms around his incredible wife, and hugged her tight. "Ok," he whispered, and silently vowed to do anything he could to protect her and Emma.

Chapter 21

It wasn't hard to find him. The funeral was well publicized, so learning his name was easy. Finding his address equally so. Following him without being spotted was not. He ran early in the morning, and he ran for a long time. She quickly decided she wasn't going to try to follow him on his runs, not even by car. He did a few errands sporadically during the day, and he had a part-time job in town. She needed to find the right time to approach him. But first she needed to know more about him. And more importantly, would he go along with her plan.

He looked right at her at the funeral. Stared at her for a long time. He wasn't sure who she was or why she was there, but he was curious. And that's what she needed. He was angry and upset at the hospital, but he didn't shed a tear at the funeral. She was fairly certain this was the right guy, but she needed an opening.

Cheryl decided that his work would be the best place to approach him. The store was never very busy, so it was only a matter of time before he was alone. But the owner, whom she assumed from the sign was a Keeler, rarely ever left. He was always at the counter or at the work bench behind it tooling away. After an hour of sitting in the car, walking in and out of neighboring stores, and drinking too much coffee, she decided to take matters into her own hands.

She had never crank-called a locksmith before, but there was a first time for everything. She found the number in the phone book and chose an address that was about as far from the shop as possible near the edge of town. She feigned being locked out of her house and could Mr. Keeler come right away. It had to be Mr. Keeler. Her husband only trusted Mr. Keeler. He walked out of the store a few minutes later carrying a toolbox, got into his work truck, and drove off. She figured she had about forty minutes.

She swallowed hard, got up her nerve, and stepped out of the car. When she walked into the store, a little bell jingled over the front door. There were no customers in the store, and she didn't see anyone behind the counter. "Hello?," she said quietly.

"Can I help you?," he said, popping up from behind a row of shelves to her left.

"Oh," she said with a start. "I didn't see you over there."

"Sorry. What can I do for you?"

Jack Turner was taller in person than she expected. A lean, muscular physique, dark hair, green eyes, dimples on both cheeks, and for a second she forgot why she was there.

73

"I'd like to talk to you for a minute if you don't mind."

He slowly walked past her towards the counter, then behind it. "What about?" he asked. His tone was distant, indifferent. He picked up one of the locks Bobby had begun dissecting and started fiddling with it.

She gulped and said, "Your son."

He stopped what he was doing and looked her right at her. Any warmth that was in his face was now gone. His eyes were cold and suddenly grey. "What about my son?," he said. It came out as a question, but it sounded more like a warning, cautioning her to be careful with her next words.

"There are others. In this small town. Families, children, with the same kind of cancer he had, being treated with the same medicine, by the same doctors. My sister and niece are among them. I think there's more going on here than we know. I think the doctors aren't telling us everything. And I think people will continue to suffer and die unless we figure out what's going on."

"Tell me everything," he said.

Chapter 22

"Cheryl, this is Matt. You need to call me back as soon as you get this. It's urgent." She replayed the message and listened to it again. This wasn't the same Matt that was always hitting on her and asking her out. Something was genuinely wrong, she could hear it in his voice.

She called his cell number, but it went straight to voicemail. She called it again. No answer. She tried his direct line at the Journal, but it also went to voicemail. She called a friend in research who said she hadn't seen Matt all day. Wasn't at his desk, wasn't sure where he was.

The little hairs on the back of Cheryl's neck were on high-alert. Unless Matt was out on assignment, he was *always* at his desk. He lived for his work and devoted himself to it. He was a single guy with a cause, and he was committed to revealing the lies and corruption in the food and drug industry whenever and wherever he could. She had found him asleep at his desk more than once, and there was a rumor that he even kept his own pillow at the office for those nights when a couch was his bed.

His editor told Cheryl he was unaware of what Matt was currently working on, but admitted Matt operated with a certain amount of autonomy and didn't always check in when working on a story. Sometimes he'd be out of the office for days, he told Cheryl. Other times, he lived there.

She couldn't imagine what the urgency was about. The last time they spoke, she asked him to look into EBF-14. A simple enough request, she thought. He loved that kind of stuff, so it was right up his alley. She assumed he would use his connections, reach out to his sources, and find out whatever he could about it. That was over a week ago. Now this.

She decided he was working on a story and would call her back when he could. In the meantime, she would spend some quality time with Brenda and Lily before heading back to New York. After talking at length, she and Jack had put together a rough outline of a plan, the first part of which was happening tomorrow. She was looking forward to it. After that, it was back to New York for her. Until then, some family time.

Lily had recovered completely from her seizure and was back to her usual, silly self. The three girls ate pizza, played a game of charades (Lily won), then watched a movie and ate popcorn until Lily fell asleep on the couch. Brenda carried her to bed, they took turns kissing her on the forehead, then turned out the light and closed the door. Brenda wasn't far behind. She still struggled with her energy at times, and often got tired in the evening. She said goodnight and turned in.

Cheryl, on the other hand, was wired. She had a lot on her mind and did not expect to get much sleep. Between her meeting with Jack, their plan for the morning, the call from Matt, her trip to New York... it was going to be a long night.

She got her bags packed and ready to go for the morning. She tried to print out her boarding pass, but the sluggish internet connection in Brenda's house wasn't going to let that happen. Hopefully, whoever was manning the only counter at the airport tomorrow, could assist her with that. Cheryl brushed her teeth and climbed into bed. It was after midnight and she thought at least an effort at sleep was wise. She laid on her back and stared at the ceiling for a while. She thought about how tomorrow would go, and what they would learn. A hundred scenarios ran through her mind.

She closed her eyes and started to drift when her cell phone vibrated. She picked it up from the night stand, looked at who was calling, but didn't recognize the number. She sat up, swung her feet around to the floor and answered it.

"Hello?," she said, warily.

"Cheryl, it's Matt."

"Where have you been? I've been calling you all day? You left me this panicked message to call you back, but you don't answer. I tried your cell, the office..."

"CHERYL!," Matt shouted over her. "Stop talking and listen!" His voice was filled with panic and fear. "Have you been online today?"

"Not really. The internet connection around here is pretty bad. Why?"

"Dr. Holst is dead."

"What?!" Cheryl was on her feet, a hand over her mouth.

"They found him slumped over his desk. An overdose, supposedly. It's a lie."

"What do you mean?," she asked. "How do you know that?." She hoped none of it was true.

"He called me, Cheryl. He wanted to meet. He told me he had some information about EBF-14. Things the public needed to know. Things AstaGen is hiding. They're the ones who make it. Anyway, we were supposed to meet for lunch yesterday at the coffee place on the ground floor of our building. You know the one?"

"Yeah, I get coffee there every day when I'm coming into work."

"Ok, well he didn't show up. I waited a while, but he never showed. I called his cell, his office, even his home. Couldn't reach him, and no one knew where he was, not even his wife. He didn't see any of his patients that afternoon, and his staff had no idea where he was. They found him the next morning, dead. Pills scattered across his desk. I spoke to his wife. The only thing Holst was taking was Ambien occasionally for sleep. So we're supposed to believe he raided the pill cabinet at his office in order to commit suicide? And that he was missing for twelve hours, but decided to drive back to his office to do the deed?"

"Isn't that possible, Matt? You don't know him. Maybe he was depressed. Maybe he couldn't handle the stress of spending every day telling people they had cancer."

"Don't be naive Cheryl. The man was one of the foremost experts in his field. From what I've been able to piece together, he loved his work. He had plenty of money. He continued to see patients because he loved it. He did it because he wanted to, not because he had to. He was involved in two different ongoing medical studies, he was the featured speaker at a couple of upcoming seminars, and he had plans to travel to Switzerland with his wife next month. This isn't a guy that just suddenly decided that it was all too much for him and popped a bunch of pills. They killed him."

"Who killed him?"

"AstaGen."

"What? Why?"

"I don't know. Maybe he was asking questions they didn't want asked. Maybe he was about to tell me something they didn't want the world to know. All I know is he called me, wanted to talk, and now he's dead, on the same day we were supposed to meet. As I was walking into the cafe, he texted me a bunch of gibberish. Totally nonsensical stuff. Couldn't make heads or tails of it. That's probably when they grabbed him."

"Matt...," Cheryl started to say.

"Oh," he interrupted, "and I'm pretty sure I'm being followed."

"What?"

"I haven't been back to the office all day. I'm calling you from a prepaid cell phone because I'm pretty sure all my phones have been tapped. Hopefully they know Holst didn't tell me anything, otherwise I'm a goner too."

"Matt, this is crazy. You need to go to the police...," Cheryl began.

"And tell them what? I have no proof of anything. People in this city already think I'm a whack job for all the so-called 'conspiracy theories' I write about, no matter how much evidence I have to support it. No. I just need to lay low for a little while and hope they're not worried about me."

Matt took a deep breath.

"Cheryl, I learned some things about EBF-14. I can't tell you over the phone. I just bought this thing and I'm already paranoid that someone is listening."

"I'll be back in New York tomorrow afternoon," she said. She wrote down his new, temporary number and agreed to call him when she landed. They said their goodbyes, she told Matt to be careful, and hung up. Her head was spinning. If she thought sleep would be difficult before, it would be impossible now. And to make matters worse, somehow she had to find a way to tell Jack.

Chapter 23

Dr. Bosh's office was located on the second and third floors of a quaint building on main street less than five minutes from the hospital. His neighbor to the left was a traditional barber shop, with the classic striped pole out front. To the right was a small bookstore that sold only used books, mostly hardcovers. It was still early, so neither of them were open yet. The door from the street opened onto a narrow set of stairs that led up one flight to Dr. Bosh's office and opened on to the reception area. Cheryl had scheduled the first appointment of the day, so the waiting room, which consisted of four chairs against the wall opposite the receptionist, was empty. Since they were meeting with the doctor and not being examined, they were led into Dr. Bosh's private office.

"He'll be in a minute," the receptionist said as she deposited them in the empty office. Jack remembered the last time he was in this office. He and Amy sat in the same chairs before him now. Dr. Bosh had been reviewing the results of Amy's tests and broke the news. Jack immediately dismissed the findings as 'impossible' and insisted upon seeing a specialist. Dr. Bosh nodded. Denial was a common reaction to bad news, but, unfortunately, he'd seen similar results before and was confident in his diagnosis. However, confirmation from a specialist was a good idea, for everyone's benefit. He asked Jack if he wanted some suggestions, but Jack said no, he would handle it on his own. Ironically, he'd landed with Dr. Holst anyway. Other than periodic blood work, that was the last time Dr. Bosh saw Amy as a patient. That was also the last time Jack had set foot in this office. Everything from that point on had gone through Dr. Holst.

Jack sat in the familiar chairs, Cheryl joined him. She sat with her hands folded on her lap, twiddling her thumbs nervously. Jack sat upright, arms folded across his chest, getting more agitated by the second.

"Relax," Cheryl said. She could hear the frustration in his breathing. "Let me do the talking, ok?"

Jack exhaled and nodded, though he couldn't promise anything.

The office door opened, and Dr. Bosh came in. He took two steps towards his desk before seeing both of them, then froze. The meeting had been scheduled with Cheryl, or so he'd been told. He assumed it was to talk about Brenda or Lily. Jack was the last person he expected to see, and his mind struggled to comprehend the meaning of these two together.

Dr. Bosh gathered his composure, made it to his desk, and took a seat behind it. He folded his hands on his desk, cleared his throat and said, "I didn't realize you knew each other...."

"We've met," Cheryl said, without offering any further details.

Jack remained silent, arms folded, eyes locked on Dr. Bosh.

"What's this about?" Dr. Bosh asked.

"When we first met," Cheryl began, "my niece, Lily, just had a seizure. She and my sister Brenda are both patients of yours. Both have Omnicarcinos. Jack just lost his son, evidently to the same type of cancer. His wife and daughter are sick too. You know all this. But we know there are others. Something is going on here, Dr. Bosh... something you're not telling us. I asked you about this a couple of times before, and you said it was a conversation for another time. Well, now's the time."

Jack sat quietly still, his anger slowly building. A small tear had formed in the corner of his eye at the mention of Nate's death, but he didn't speak. Jack was waiting to see how Dr. Bosh responded. But he was fully prepared to leap across the desk and throttle him if that's what it took to get some answers.

"I agree," Dr. Bosh said plainly.

Jack and Cheryl looked at each other, stunned. Jack uncrossed his arms and sat up in his chair. Cheryl blinked twice trying to register the words. She wasn't sure she heard him correctly.

"Pardon?," she said. They hadn't expected this. In fact, every time Cheryl and Jack role-played what Dr. Bosh might say, it was never 'I agree'. It was always something argumentative or dismissive. Why wouldn't it be? He had been resistant to discuss the matter previously, and never volunteered anything. But now he seemed ready to talk.

"You're right, it's time," he said. "Nate's death was a terrible thing. I'm so sorry, Jack. I wish I could have done more to prevent it. He was a sweet boy and didn't deserve any of it. None of them do."

Dr. Bosh spoke with genuine remorse and a transparency neither of them were used to from a doctor. He had always been guarded with his words. Now they came freely.

"I thought the new medication was enough. I listened to the specialists, followed their recommendations, and believed I was doing right by my patients. I was naive. I never asked the important questions, and I should have."

He paused to rub his temples and then continued.

"As a doctor, we're taught to treat disease. Cancer is the toughest of them all. So when I learned about this new miracle drug I got excited. We all did. Finally, a way to not only treat our patients, but to save them! And it was working! Patients with Omnicarcinos, an advanced terminal cancer, that should have already died are still alive. None of them would be here without EBF-14. The medication worked. It slowed, or even stopped, the progression of the cancer in every single patient."

"Except Nate." Jack finally broke his silence. Tears were slowly running down his face as he listened to Dr. Bosh's confession. It was the first time he cried since Nate's death. He'd been holding on to his anger for so long now, but Dr. Bosh's frank comments softened him, and grief had taken its place.

"Except Nate," Dr. Bosh repeated. "But even Nate," he countered. "Nate's cancer had halted its march through his body. There had been no increase in tumor count or size over his last several scans. And his tumor markers were the same or lower over his last few blood tests. It was the seizure. We were told seizures might happen, particularly in the younger patients. I've seen a few, as you both know." He looked between the two of them as he spoke. "But they usually recover well and, once we get the dosage adjusted, it typically doesn't happen again."

Dr. Bosh turned to Jack. "Nate's situation was an extraordinary one. The location of the tumor, the malformed blood vessel, the seizure, the fall to the floor... it caused a horrific cascade of events that no one could have seen coming, or prevented. Dr. Holst and I spoke at great length about his condition and his death. It affected both of us greatly. We decided to inform AstaGen of our concerns about EBF-14. We reached out to the medical director. We tried contacting the founder. We made a number of calls the FDA. No one wanted to hear it.

Dr. Holst consulted with a lot of doctors around the country. He has probably prescribed or recommended EBF-14 more than anyone. So he felt slighted, and rightly so, when no one took or returned his calls. It made us both start to think maybe there was more going on than we initially believed. We agreed that the public needed to be warned about EBF-14, particularly families with kids on it. So we decided to reach out to the media. Dr. Holst said he knew of someone that would be willing to listen."

"Matt Cunningham," Cheryl said.

"Yes," Dr. Bosh said, looking somewhat surprised. "And now Dr. Holst is dead, and I'm in fear for my life."

Chapter 24

Sleep was hard to come by. In his ten years of writing exposes and shedding light on important health issues, Matt was never concerned for his own safety. He'd never received a threatening call, an angry letter, or a single piece of hate mail. Sure, he'd gotten letters from people disagreeing with his take on a particular issue, but never anything worrisome. Maybe it was because people quietly considered him a 'conspiracy theorist', and didn't take his work seriously. Right now, he was thinking maybe it was better that way.

Matt never really thought much about the term 'seedy motel'... until now. His original plan had him hiding out at a hotel in the city. But he quickly discovered that no reputable hotel chain allowed it's guests to check in without showing any ID and paying in cash. As he rode north, headed upstate, he found a motel that allowed both of those things.

By the time he left the city last night, Matt was convinced he was being followed. Walking down the steps from his apartment, he saw him again. The same guy from the day before. Matt didn't believe in coincidences. And New York City was simply too big and had too many people to just randomly run into the same stranger two days in a row.

He had found a small electronics store in the city that sold pre-paid cell phones for cash. He bought two, quickly pocketed them and, as he came out of the store, he saw him. He was standing about thirty feet away, looking in Matt's direction, and appeared to be talking on a cell phone. Matt had been on high alert since Dr. Holst's sudden death, so he took notice. Not because there was anything suspicious about the guy. He was white with dark hair, about five-feet-ten, and weighed about a hundred and eighty pounds. The only thing even remotely interesting about him was an angular scar below his right eye. Aside from that, he could have been anyone.

But Matt found it odd nonetheless. Who stands around in New York, he thought. Even when you're on the phone, you're on the move. Places to go, people to see. But not this guy, he was waiting for something... or someone. People walked by him in both directions, but he just stood there with his phone. Something just wasn't right about the guy.

Matt saw him and he saw Matt. As soon as their eyes met, the guy turned and walked away. Matt walked to his car, got in, and began to drive off. But in his rearview mirror he saw the guy turn around, walk back in his direction and go into the same store Matt had just come out of. At first he wasn't sure if he was being paranoid. But seeing him again the next day outside his apartment convinced him it wasn't just paranoia.

Later that day, he packed a gym bag and threw it in the trunk. He drove to his CrossFit gym. He didn't want to deviate from his routine in case anyone was watching. But that day, he didn't work out. He spent the hour looking down at the street from an upstairs window. He wanted to see if his friend showed up. He didn't.

Normally Matt would head back to the office after a trip to the gym. It wasn't unusual for him to spend sixteen hours a day or more at his desk, so returning to the office after a workout and some dinner was pretty typical. He debated it for a few minutes before driving back to the

Journal. He parked in the employee parking lot and went in. But instead of heading up to his desk, he called for an Uber from one of his prepaid cell phones. He instructed the driver to pick him up in the back of the building near the loading dock under the overhang. The car arrived a few minutes later, and Matt quickly got in. As they drove upstate, he kept looking behind them, but never saw anyone that appeared to be following them.

Sitting in his motel room in the early morning hours, he was feeling pretty pleased with himself. He hadn't slept much, and he spent a lot of money on the Uber, but none of that bothered him. He'd outsmarted whoever had been following him and was now safely tucked away where no one could find him.

One of the two prepaid cell phones sitting on the nightstand rang. He glanced over to where they sat and any feelings of safety and security vanished. He'd only given that number to one person, Cheryl. And she wasn't due back in New York until this afternoon. Before he even picked up the phone, he knew it wasn't her.

"Hello?," he said nervously.

"How's the room, Matt?" It was a man's voice, a deep unfamiliar voice.

"Excuse me?," Matt gulped.

"The room. You know, room 27, Motel Six, just off I-81. Seems like a pretty dodgy place, Matt."

"Who is this?"

"You know who this is. Don't you, Matt?"

"How did you find me?"

"Really, Matt? Giving Uber a fake name is not enough, my boy. The prepaid credit card was a nice effort, but easily traced back to you. Uber doesn't accept cash, so I guess you had no choice. And tracking the driver's GPS really wasn't all that difficult. So here we are."

Matt had no words. His mouth was dry, his heart was pounding, and he couldn't have pieced together a reply even if he knew what to say. He bought the prepaid credit card with cash from the same store where he got the phones. Clearly the guy that was following him got all the information he needed after Matt had driven off.

"Listen up, bright boy," the voice went on. "You're done with this whole EBF-14 thing, got it? Dr. Holst killed himself. The end. He was overworked, stressed out and couldn't take it anymore. No more digging. No more questions. No more calls to that pretty little coworker of yours. Am I making myself clear?"

"Yes." Matt managed to choke out.

"Good. Because I'm sure you know what happens next if I see even a single mention of EBF-14 in your paper, right?"

"Yes."

"Now, call someone to come pick you up from that shithole, drive back to the city, and go back to work. I'm sure there's some asparagus somewhere that needs your attention."

And with that, he was gone.

Chapter 25

"We have questions...," Cheryl said.

"I thought you might," Dr. Bosh admitted.

"How do you know Dr. Holst didn't kill himself like they said?"

"Not a chance. He's not the type. And he certainly wouldn't choose to overdose on a bunch of pills at his desk. No, that was a message. And it was received loud and clear."

"What kind of message?," Jack asked.

"A warning. The kind of message that says 'we can get you whenever and wherever we want'. If they're willing to kill him, they're willing to kill just about anyone."

The significance of those words weighed heavily on Cheryl and Jack.

"So you're convinced it was AstaGen?" Cheryl asked the question, but she already knew the answer.

"Without a doubt," Dr. Bosh said.

"And you think they know about you?," Jack asked.

"Of course. I had a very unproductive conversation with their medical director not long ago. I imagine they started bugging our phones as soon as we began making calls. Dr. Holst and I talked frequently, especially in recent weeks. By now, they have printed transcripts of our conversations."

"What about this office? How do we know it's not bugged too?," Jack asked, looking around.

"Unlikely," Dr. Bosh said. "There's no one in this town they would be concerned about me meeting with or talking to in person. I doubt they know either of you even exist."

"Are you in danger?," Cheryl asked, concerned.

"Maybe. I think the murder of Dr. Holst was meant to dispose of the bigger threat, and motivate me to drop it. I'm a small town doc with a handful of patients. He was a major player with connections across the country."

"How many patients? Patients of yours with Omnicarcinos? The same as Jack's family and mine?" Cheryl finally got around to the question she'd been dying to ask.

"Nineteen,," he confessed with a sigh.

"Nineteen?!," Cheryl repeated loudly. Jack and Cheryl had speculated on the number a few times and were expecting six, maybe eight at the most. "Nineteen?!," she said again. "Nineteen. Out of fourteen hundred."

Jack leaned forward in his chair, put his elbows on his knees, his head in his hands, and began shaking it side to side in disbelief.

"Five of those are from your families," Dr. Bosh reminded them carefully. "But we should also assume there are people out there that either don't yet know they're sick, haven't come in for an examination, or have no insurance and are in no position to pay. And that's just here. Dr. Holst said there were others."

"Unbelievable," Cheryl said, still struggling to wrap her mind around the number.

"How many did Dr. Holst know about?," Jack asked.

"I don't have a specific number. Between his personal patients and the cases he consulted on... probably quite a few."

"What was he planning on telling Matt?" Cheryl asked. "They were going to meet. Matt told me. What was he going to say?"

"He was going to tell him what we'd learned about EBF-14. About the dosage issues. The seizures. About what happened to Nate. We wanted to warn parents."
He paused, and looked at both of them.

"What?," Jack said.

"EBF-14 doesn't work on every cancer. It only works for patients with Omnicarcinos."

"I don't understand," Cheryl said. "Cancer is cancer, isn't it? A tumor is a tumor?"

"Well there are different types of tumors. But the cancerous ones, the malignant ones, like the ones we're talking about are largely the same. So it didn't make sense to us either that EBF-14 was ineffective on other patients," Dr. Bosh admitted. "It works incredibly well on the right type of cancer, but when Dr. Holst began administering it to his other cancer patients, it didn't work. We were baffled."

"What does that mean?," Cheryl asked.

"It means the drug targets a specific type of cancer. And AstaGen knows it."

"Holy shit," Jack said.

"How is that possible? How does a drug know what type of cancer a patient has?," Cheryl said.

"Dr. Holst had a theory."

"Which was....?," Jack asked.

"He wouldn't tell me until he was sure he was right. He knew we were treading in dangerous waters with our questions. But we never expected this. Maybe we should have."

Jack turned to Cheryl. "We need his files," he said quickly.

"What do you mean?," she asked.

"We need to know what he knows. We need to find out what his theory about all this was. And we need to know how many patients are out there. If we can access his files, maybe we can figure out what's going on."

"That's not going to be easy," Dr. Bosh chimed in. "His office is a crime scene. Sealed off from everyone, staff included. I'm sure both the police and FBI are in and out of there regularly. You can't just knock on the door and look at his files."

"I have an idea," Jack said.

Chapter 26

Her flight landed shortly after four o'clock. As much as she loved her sister and her niece, she was thrilled to be back in New York. She moved there ten years ago to begin her journalistic career, but things were going slower than she'd like. She'd learned a lot about how a story develops, how the research is done, how to get confirmation of facts, and how the writing takes shapes. She'd also made a lot of professional connections and several close friends.

She walked through the airport's sliding doors out into the cool, crisp New York air. There was no feeling like it. She was a New Yorker now, and she loved it. She waited twenty minutes on line before she hopped in a cab and headed straight to the Journal.

She swiped her badge at security, rode the elevator up, threw her bags under her desk and went looking for Matt. He was at his desk where he always was, and she made a beeline straight for him. She poked him on the shoulder, and kept walking, straight into the conference room. He slowly got up and followed her.

"Well?!," she said, excitedly.

"Well what?," he replied, with much less enthusiasm.

"What do you mean 'well what'? What did you find out about EBF-14? Tell me everything."

Matt vividly remembered the phone conversation from the other day. The one that included threats to him and to Cheryl. He had every intention of dropping the subject like a hot rock. "Oh, that. It's a dead end. There's no story there."

"You're joking, right?"

"Nope. The trail ran dry. I've moved on. Plenty of other stuff to write about."

"Matt, c'mon. Be serious. This thing is huge, and getting bigger by the minute. Kids are having seizures on this medication because they can't figure out the proper dosages. A child has died. Dr. Holst has been murdered. And I just found out EBF-14 doesn't work on every type of cancer. In fact, it only works on one, very specific, form of cancer. Somehow it targets the tumors a cancer called Omnicarcinos. And a lot of people have it. More than should. And we think Dr. Holst knew why. That might be why they killed him. We're going after his files."

Matt looked at her for a long moment. He cared about her and knew with every word she spoke she was in danger. But he didn't dare encourage her. He knew what was at stake.

"Cheryl, Dr. Holst killed himself. I questioned a few of the investigators. They're convinced there was no foul play. He just cracked. That's what they're saying. They already swept his hard drive, both at his home and office. They didn't find anything other than his patient data. As for EBF-14, AstaGen said it was specifically designed to combat Omnicarcinos. It's aggressive, terminal, and affecting more kids than any other form of cancer. So it makes sense that's where it would work best." He watched for her reaction, and it was pretty clear she wasn't buying it. But for her sake, he needed to convince her.

"Matt, what the hell? Since when do you believe anything 'they're saying'. Can't you see what this looks like? They're covering it all up, and you're telling me you're buying this crap?"

"I can't write a story that isn't there, Cheryl. I've moved on. I suggest you do the same."

With that, he walked out of the conference room and back to his desk. She practically fell back against the edge of the conference table in disbelief, the air effectively let out of her balloon. Matt was supposed to be her biggest ally in this fight. She was counting on him. What just happened? He was so persuasive on the phone. He was the one that convinced her Dr. Holst was murdered by AstaGen and EBF-14 was at the root of the matter. What changed? He had completely flip-flopped. Did he actually believe what he was saying? Cheryl had a hard time accepting that.

But maybe he was right. Maybe it was all just coincidence. Dr. Bosh didn't seem to think so. He said Dr. Holst didn't either, but now we may never know, she thought to herself. She and Jack were thoroughly convinced this was a conspiracy of epic proportions. But maybe Matt was right. Maybe Brenda was too. Maybe Cheryl was looking for a story that just wasn't there. Now more confused than ever, she wasn't sure what to believe. She needed to talk to Jack before they moved forward with his plan.

Chapter 27

It was after midnight and Jack couldn't sleep. The meeting with Dr. Bosh left his mind reeling. The numbers were terrifying. How could nineteen people living in a small town be affected by the same form of cancer? At least, nineteen! Probably more. How did AstaGen develop a drug that targets the exact type of tumors associated with Omnicarcinos? How did they do it so quickly? And why is it ineffective for other cancers? He was looking for answers, but now had more questions than ever.

Cheryl had returned to New York, but her conversation with Matt did not go as planned. She and Jack were both anxious to hear what Matt had uncovered, but he wasn't talking. She called Jack right after they spoke and told him what happened. They both had time to think about it and there was only one logical conclusion... someone got to him. And they both knew who. If AstaGen knew Dr. Holst was talking to the media, then they knew exactly who he was talking to. Getting to Matt must have been easy. A threatening phone call perhaps. Maybe they even confronted him somewhere. But after what happened to Dr. Holst, it was easy to understand Matt's sudden change of heart.

Jack started thinking about his plan for getting Dr. Holst's files. Several things needed to go his way if it was going to work. He hated involving others, but if he was serious about getting in, he knew he needed help.

Earlier in the day, he told Amy about his planned trip to New York. He gave her as little detail as possible. The less she knew, the better. He told her he was going to a trade show in the city as the designated representative of Keeler Locks & Bolts. He hated lying to her, but protecting her was more important. She and Emma would both be safer with Jack out of town. He had no intention of raising any suspicion, but he wasn't taking any chances. The last thing he wanted to do was land on AstaGen's radar. He knew what that meant. And if something were to happen to him, he wanted to be far away from his girls.

Since sleep wasn't happening, he decided to go for a run. He slipped out from under the covers, so as not to wake Amy, and grabbed a pair of running shorts off the dresser. He crept down the creaky stairs, tip-toed across the noisy kitchen floor, laced up his running shoes and went out the back door. He was immediately reminded that the hinges still needed oil. Hopefully the squeaking didn't wake anyone.

He left the house behind, ran down his street and headed toward town. Over and over he reviewed what they had discussed with Dr. Bosh. The number of patients, the way EBF-14 worked, the death of Dr. Holst, his theory... and he remembered the fear in Dr. Bosh's eyes. They all knew they were playing with fire. And right now, Dr. Bosh was closest to it. It was a dangerous game, but if they were going to find the truth, it had to be done.

Jack wrestled with the numbers. Nineteen. He still couldn't believe it. But what's more, he still didn't know why. AstaGen had a drug that worked on only this particular form of cancer. But where was the cancer coming from? And how did so many people have it? He needed to know and he hoped there were answers in Dr. Holst's office. Getting in was just the first step.

Jack rounded a corner and proceeded to run past nine consecutive fast food joints blanketing both sides of the street. He shook his head as he ran by. He couldn't believe people still ate that crap. He and Amy had sworn off junk food years ago. And as much as he'd like to lay blame there, he knew it wasn't that. They never ate it, and still Amy and Emma were sick. It was something else. And not knowing what gnawed at him.

He spent the better part of his run through town mentally reviewing his to-do list for his trip to New York. Everything he could do was done, but there were a lot of 'what ifs' looming.

Before he knew it, he had left the town behind him and was approaching the lake. He ran the long loop around and started heading back. He ran past the old abandoned warehouse he'd see a hundred times. It looked different at this hour. Spooky, Jack thought. He looked up at the sky. He still couldn't believe how clear the air was and how visible the stars were here. He never got a view like this in the city.

As he ran along the tall fence behind the water plant, his focus elsewhere, he was nearly run over by a large tanker truck coming through an open gate. In the dim illumination, the driver never saw him. If it weren't for the squeaky brakes, Jack would surely have been run over. The sound jolted him back to reality and he stopped dead in his tracks, his heart pounding out of his chest, less than six feet from the side of the truck. It was a large tanker truck like the ones that that deliver fuel or milk. Jack could make out the word Sagante' printed on the side. Sagante'. Sounds like some kind of Spanish wine, Jack thought. He'd never seen any trucks coming or going on previous runs. But then again, he'd never run by at this hour before.

Jack watched the tanker pull out and drive off. The gate slid closed automatically. After having nearly been killed, he needed a minute to settle himself. He took a few deep breaths, stretched a few muscles, then started back home, in the opposite direction of the truck.

Chapter 28

Every day at two in the afternoon, Matt ran the stairs in the building. You could set your watch by it. He was serious about his health and fitness, and spending sixteen-plus hours a day behind a desk wasn't exactly conducive to either of those things. He ran up all twenty-one flights of stairs, and back down, as many times as he could. He started on sixteen, where he worked, ran up to the top floor, and started back down. He would do this for an entire hour. His co-workers thought he was crazy. But then again, most of his co-workers were overweight and out of shape.

If anyone was looking for Matt between the hours of two and three in the afternoon, they knew where to find him. And it wasn't at his desk. Everyone knew his routine. Including Cheryl.

Just before two, like clockwork, Matt got up from his desk and headed to the bathroom for a quick change of clothes. He threw his bag under his desk and headed for the stairwell. He pushed the door open, hoping to stretch for a few minutes, but instead Cheryl was waiting in ambush.

She pushed him with both hands, and he stumbled backwards, more from the surprise than the shove itself. "What the hell are you doing?," she asked sharply.

Back against the wall, Matt replied, "Running the stairs, like I do every day."

"Don't play dumb, Matt. Who got to you?"

"What are you talking about?"

"Matt, I'm not stupid. You call me and tell me you've got information about EBF-14, information that's so important you can't tell me over the phone. And less than twenty-four hours later, you've completely changed your tune. So it's a dead end now? Have you dropped the story entirely? What did they say? Did they threaten you?"

Matt looked around nervously and whispered, "I can't talk about it, Cheryl. And for your sake, you shouldn't either."

Cheryl held both arms out, feigned looking around, and said, "There's no one here, Matt. It's just us. Tell me."

"I can't," he said, his voice barely above a whisper. "Not here."

"Not here? We're alone in a stairwell, Matt. No one is listening. My cell phone is in my purse locked in my desk. I'm sure yours is somewhere in your desk too, right?"

He nodded. It was obvious they gave him a good scare.

"What did they say?"

"They threatened me, Cheryl," he said softly. "They said if I wrote anything about EBF-14 or AstaGen, I'd end up like Holst."

Cheryl wasn't really surprised. She expected this. It was the only thing that would explain Matt's flip-flop.

"They threatened you too, Cheryl."

Now she was surprised. She swallowed hard and said, "What do you mean?"

"They said I should stop talking to my 'pretty little coworker'. They said it just like that."

"I'm flattered. Look, we need to talk about this. I need to know what you found out about EBF-14 and AstaGen."

"Not here, Cheryl. It needs to be someplace quiet. Someplace private."

"More private than an empty stairwell?"

"I don't feel comfortable talking about it here, ok? Tonight. Meet me at Sushi Mara down the street. Nine o'clock."

"That place is gross, Matt. Didn't you almost die from food poisoning last time you ate there?"

"Exactly. That's why it'll be empty. Privacy won't be an issue."

"Ah, gotcha. Smart. Ok, see you at nine. I'll grab a booth in the back."

A metal door banged open loudly above them, the sound startling both of them. As Matt peered up and around the stairs, he caught a brief glimpse of someone leaving the stairwell through the door. They hadn't heard anyone come in, so whoever it was had been there a while. Matt and Cheryl looked at each other, both thinking the same thing. Someone had been listening after all.

Chapter 29

Dr. Holst's office was on the seventh and eighth floors of a ten-story medical building in midtown Manhattan, just a few blocks from the Empire State Building. He had multiple suites covering both floors. The seventh floor was primarily used for patient visits when he had office hours. The eighth floor housed his lab, conference rooms, and his own private office, which was located in the northeast corner of the building, overlooking the east river with a view of Long Island.

On the flight up, Jack studied the building plans. He'd been to Dr. Holst's office before, on a number of occasions, with Amy and Emma. But he paid very little attention to the details. He had other things on his mind at the time. Now, however, he knew every entrance and exit, he knew where the stairs were, he knew how to access the roof, and where the fire escapes were located. He even knew what kind of alarm Dr. Holst had. Bobby had been kind enough to offer his expertise in defeating the alarm, which was fairly basic according to Bobby. "The same cheap crap found in every home across America," he'd said. Jack had all the tools to defeat just about any lock he might encounter. But the alarm worried him. If he screwed that up, all hell would break loose and he'd have to make it out of the building from the eighth floor without being spotted and before the cops showed up.

The building itself had little to no security. It was an older building with a bunch of medical offices, most of which contained nothing of value other than some pills or equipment that was too heavy to move anyway. Each doctor was responsible for securing his or her own office.

The building owner was kind enough to provide an overweight, middle-aged security guard who spent more time dozing than actually patrolling the building. From a small hill top across the guest parking lot, Jack watched him for several hours and the guard rarely moved. When he did, it was usually to the bathroom, where he spent an average of twenty minutes a trip. When he wasn't in the bathroom, or roaming the halls, he sat in a folding chair near the elevators with his head down and eyes closed.

Around one in the morning, Lazy Larry awoke with a start after nearly falling out of his folding chair. Through his binoculars, Jack could see the name tag with Larry etched into it. The 'lazy' was rather obvious. After catching himself from falling on the floor, Lazy Larry stood up, stretched and headed for the bathroom. Jack was on the move too. He hurried to the front door of the building which, as expected, was locked. He worked quickly and opened the simple one key tumbler in a flash. Bobby would be so proud, Jack thought.

He re-locked the door behind him, and hurried across the lobby. He found the door leading to the stairway in the far corner where he knew it would be. He couldn't risk being caught, or even seen, in an elevator, because of the possibility of a camera. As he bounded up the stairs two at a time, he was grateful for his years of running and his current level of fitness. He wore track pants, running shoes and a hoodie, so maneuvering the stairs was a piece of cake. In no time, he had reached level seven and was barely breathing hard.

Jack slowly opened the door out onto the floor and peered around it. He saw no one. The possibility of someone working late concerned him, but the place seemed deserted. He eased out of the stairwell and made his way to the northeast corner where Dr. Holst's office was.

From a distance, he could see the yellow police tape cordoning off the hallway just before the office doors. As Jack got closer, he saw something that he never noticed before. Something that worried him a lot more than police tape. "Oh, shit," he muttered quietly to himself.

Dr. Holst may not have taken his inside security seriously, but he was very serious about keeping people from coming in the front door. Mounted on the door was the Samsung AZOE. Jack recognized it immediately. He couldn't believe he never noticed it before. But who pays attention to the kind of lock that's on the outside of an unlocked door?

The AZOE was the same high-tech digital locking system that Bobby had wrestled with a few months earlier. Bobby never cracked it. And Jack certainly had no idea how to beat it. But he needed to get into Holst's office. All of their plans hinged on what was in those files.

Jack briefly considered kicking down the doors and dealing with the alarm on the other side, but quickly dismissed the idea. The office doors appeared to be extremely solid. Jack knew the only thing that would come from kicking them would be an injury. If he couldn't beat the lock, he wasn't getting in.

He didn't know if he would have another crack at this. It was now or never. He dreaded what he had to do next. He pulled out his cell phone, dialed and waited.

"Who the hell is this?" Bobby had clearly been dead asleep, and Jack expected such a greeting.

"Bobby, it's Jack. I'm at the door. We have a problem."

Bobby sat up and turned on a light on in an effort to shake the cobwebs. "What is it? A multi-point security door?"

"No. It's the Samsung AZOE."

"Ah, shit."

"That's what I said. Did you ever beat this thing? Can you tell me how to bypass it?"

"No. I had to return it before I missed the refund deadline."

"You and your damned return policies."

"Hey, I don't make the rules. I just play by them."

"What am I gonna do? If I can't beat this thing, the whole plan goes to shit."

There was a long pause. Jack could hear Bobby breathing, thinking.

"You know, after I sent it back, I kept thinking about it. No lock or device had ever stumped me before. It pissed me off. I kept going over and over it in my head. I developed a theory, but I never got a chance to test it. Do you have a nine-volt battery?"

"No. Why would I have a nine-volt battery? Besides, didn't you tell me frying the circuits locks it down tight?"

"Yes. But you're not gonna fry the circuits. Remember, the tech has to release the control of the tumbler on its own. If you zap it with too much voltage, the system clamps down and the tumbler won't budge. But if there's an internal failure of the tech itself, it will release control of the locking mechanism and you should be able to open it without a key."

"That's great, Bobby. How am I supposed to cause an internal failure? Keep in mind I'm in an office building in the middle of the night, with poor lighting, and a fat security guard who could be here any second."

"Did you come up the stairs?"

"Yeah, why?"

"Did you see any illuminated Exit signs?"

"Yeah. On every floor. So?"

"So, every one of those signs has a back-up battery in it. Those signs are required by law to be lit at all times, even and especially during a power failure. The back-up battery is usually a nine-volt. Go look. If that doesn't work, there should be a smoke detector somewhere around there."

"I'm not going to start messing with a smoke detector! That'll set off alarms for sure!"

"Then you better go find an Exit sign pronto."

Jack sighed. He wasn't expecting it to be easy, but he wasn't expecting this either. "Ok, hang on." He walked quietly back to the stairwell and, sure enough, just inside the doorway, hung a red, illuminated Exit sign. "Found one."

"Good. It should be fairly easy to open."

"It would be if I could reach it," Jack said, irritated.

"Would a chair help?"

"Actually, yes."

"Then go get one, dumbass! Do I have to think of everything?!" Bobby was wide awake now and in true form. "Find a different office, open the lock, and grab a chair."

"Yeah, ok," Jack said, feeling rather foolish. He found a conference room on the opposite end of the hall. As it turned out, the door wasn't even locked. It was just a room with a long table, a bunch of chairs, a few phones, and a large monitor on the far wall. Nothing worth stealing, so they didn't even bother locking it.

Jack carried the chair down the hall, placed it under the Exit sign, and stepped up. He popped off the back cover and smiled. A shiny new nine-volt battery. "Bingo," he said into the phone.

"Good. Take the two wires that connect the battery to the panel also. You're gonna need them."

Jack removed the battery, snipped the two wires at their base, and headed back to the Samsung AZOE.

"Ok," began Bobby. "Here's the theory: while frying the circuits shuts the whole unit down, sending a small current into the processor *should* cause a factory reset, restoring the system to its default status. That will either be unarmed altogether, or with an unlock code of 0000, which it usually is. You'll need to remove the outer housing, then attach the wires from the nine-volt to the processor."

"Anything else?" Jack asked.

"Pray," Bobby added.

"Great. Standby."

He did exactly as Bobby instructed. When the final wire was in place, Jack heard a small click, a soft beep, and the digital display on the front screen flashed briefly. He typed 0000 into the keypad and heard the tumbler disengage. He tried the knob on the office door and it turned freely.

"I'm in."

Chapter 30

Nine o'clock came and went, and Cheryl feared the worst. Matt wouldn't just blow her off. Something was up. She couldn't reach him on any number and no one at the office knew where he was. The last time this happened, he turned up a few hours later and everything was fine. This was different, and she knew it.

She sat at the table until almost ten, hoping he would show up, offer some lame apology, and then tell her what he knew. But the hour came and went, and Matt never appeared. After two hot teas and some highly questionable sushi, Cheryl paid the check and left. She wasn't sure what to do or where to go, but she needed to talk to Jack. He seemed to have a way of talking her down when panic started to set in. But he had his own issues to contend with at the moment, so it would have to wait.

She walked the two blocks back the Journal, rode the elevator up to the sixteenth floor and went straight to Matt's desk. It looked as it always did. Organized chaos. Matt always claimed to have a system to the disarray spread across his desk. But to Cheryl it was just a mess. His computer and light were still on, but there was no sign of his bag or cell phone. It looked as though he'd gone out to meet Cheryl, with every intention of coming back to the office after their clandestine meeting. She started thinking about the stranger in the stairwell. If that person was watching Matt and monitoring his activity, then he knew about their plans to meet tonight. And he, and whoever he worked for, weren't going to let that happen.

She didn't see who it was, and Matt said he only caught a glimpse of him on his way out. But he was pretty confident it was a man. At that moment, Cheryl remembered something. Six months ago the Journal had installed security cameras in the stairwell every few floors. This after an employee was caught smoking pot and then proceeded to fall down several stairs, breaking her ankle in the process. Not surprisingly, the insurance company insisted that surveillance cameras be installed in the stairwell. Cheryl just wasn't sure where the closest camera was. She walked quickly to the stairs, opened the door, and peered in. Sure enough, there was a security camera on the far wall, pointed in the direction of the exit door on the seventeenth floor just above them. There was a camera every other floor.

She quickly made her way to the security office on the ground floor. No one appeared to be inside. She tried the handle, but it was locked. She knocked on the door, but no one answered. She stood in front of the door, hands on hips, turning in either direction looking for someone official. It was after ten, so she imagined most of the security staff had gone home for the night. Someone had to still be here, she thought.

A moment later, a security guard rounded the corner with a newspaper folded under one arm. She had a pretty good idea where he was coming from.

"Hi!," she said sweetly, screwing a smile onto her face.

"Do you need some help?," he replied.

"I sure do. Do you mind?" She gestured to the security office, the smile glued to her face.

He unlocked the door and held it open for her. Once inside, with the door closed behind them, she said, "I need a favor. A coworker of mine and I were having a private conversation in the stairwell earlier today, but we're pretty sure someone was eavesdropping from the floor just above us. What we discussed could be embarrassing for my friend if anyone else found out. You know how office gossip can spread. Anyway, I was hoping you could tell me who was up there so we know if it's anything we need to worry about."

He sighed. "I'm really not supposed to do that."

"Robert, is it?," she asked, reading his name tag. "Couldn't you bend the rules just this one time? For me? I'm just trying to look out for a friend. Please?" A few bats of her eyes later and Robert was parked in front of a bank of monitors clicking away on his mouse.

"Around what time was this?," he asked.

"Just after two this afternoon."

"What floor?"

"Sixteen."

A few more clicks and a video appeared on the center screen in front of him. It showed an empty stairwell. Cheryl stood right behind him, watching the screen closely. He began scrolling until the time stamp on the video read shortly before two o'clock.

"There!," she said, a little too loud for Robert's liking. "Sorry," she added. She watched herself on video quietly sneak into the stairwell. She had waited for Matt to leave his desk en route to the bathroom to change his clothes before she headed to the stairs. She lay in wait for only a minute or two before the video shows Matt come in, Cheryl's ambush, and her shoving him. The recording was video only, no sound, so there was no record of their conversation. She was silently relieved at that.

Less than two minutes into the video, a figure appeared on the landing above them. It was now obvious it was a man. He entered the picture from above, so she could only assume he had come down the stairs. Why and from where, she wasn't sure. But if he was truly watching Matt's movements, he must have expected to see him running the stairs. Matt should have reached the top floor and been on his way back down by that point. The figure's back is to the camera, but it's very clear from his posture and body language that he's listening intently to the conversation just below. Sixty more seconds, the conversation wraps up, and the stranger turns to leave. Cheryl gets her first look at his face. It's no one she recognizes from the Journal, no one, in fact, she's ever seen before. He looks to be of average height and weight, dark hair, with an ugly scar under his right eye.

"Can you make a copy of that for me?"

Chapter 31

Jack figured he had about thirty seconds before the beeping turned into blaring sirens and speeding police cars. As soon as he opened the door, the alarm started its countdown. Jack had silently been praying that maybe someone forgot to set it. No such luck. Whoever closed up the office after the police left stuck to routine and set the alarm. Jack popped off the plastic cover and, following Bobby's instructions, snipped the appropriate wires. The beeping stopped and the alarm display read 'standby'. Jack started breathing again.

He was standing in the office of Dr. Holst's secretary. Across the small room was a plain black desk with a phone, calendar blotter, and a two-tier paper tray. Next to the desk hugging the far wall was a three-drawer filing cabinet. A single potted plant, two chairs, and a painting of horses gallivanting across a meadow rounded out the decorations.

On his right was a door clearly designated as a bathroom. The door to his left flaunted a gold placard that read 'Dr. William Holst'. There was a deadbolt on the door above the handle, but neither were locked. The police had been in and out so many times by now that there was no sense locking the door. Jack slowly opened it, unsure of what he would find.

He reached in and flicked on the light. Before stepping across the threshold, Jack peered inside. There was a large mahogany desk wrapped in leather trim fifteen feet away, directly across from the door, with a large window behind it. The blinds were closed, but Jack has seen the beautiful water view on previous daytime visits.

To his right was an entire wall covered with books. Wall to wall, floor to ceiling. Nothing but books, mostly medical in nature. Jack silently wondered if Dr. Holst had read them all. To his left was a coat rack, a closet, and what appeared to be a small bar. Jack had always wondered about that, but Dr. Holst had never offered him a drink. Sitting atop the bar was a crystal decanter containing what was mostly likely very expensive scotch, a crystal ice bucket, and four crystal tumblers.

Jack entered, closed the door behind him, and walked over to the desk. There was no chalk outline. No taped silhouette of where Dr. Holst was found dead. In fact, the desk was practically bare. A monitor and keyboard were the only things that adorned the sleek leather surface. The pills, papers, and anything else the police found were collected as evidence and removed. There was a small dent in the carpet where the computer tower used to sit. Also confiscated. But Jack knew something the police did not.

In the weeks leading up to his murder, Dr. Holst and Dr. Bosh spoke often. They began to confide in one another. They discussed their more complicated cases, they commiserated about EBF-14 and AstaGen, and got to know each other on a personal level. They talked about their families, their medical school experiences, even old girlfriends. And, of course, they talked about work. Over the course of time, Dr. Bosh discovered that Dr. Holst was a control freak. He refused to delegate work that his associates or even interns could easily have handled. He reviewed every chart from every patient, regardless of who the examining physician was. He regularly micromanaged his schedule, despite having a full-time, and well paid assistant that was hired specifically to handle such things. He wanted everything done a certain way and believed the only way to make that happen was to do it himself.

He also never trusted computers. He constantly felt as though he was one virus or power outage away from losing all of his work. As such, he invested in a four-terabyte external hard drive. It was a sleek, black, low profile device that he could carry with him or store at the office. He told Dr. Bosh this in passing one day over the phone. It happened in the midst of a nasty thunderstorm. The sky was nearly black, lit up only by the frequent flashes of lightning. The booming thunder shook the building. Dr. Holst voiced his concern from the darkness after the power went out and his computer promptly cut off. He told Dr. Bosh about the hard drive and where he kept it. He thought it prudent to protect his work and his patient data. Dr. Bosh was kind enough to share that information with Jack and Cheryl.

Jack walked around the desk and sat down in the leather rolling chair. As he scooted himself up to the desk, he prayed the drive was where it was supposed to be. Dr. Holst brought it with him everywhere. He took it home with him when he left the office, and brought it back when he returned. Dr. Bosh told him there would be a small leather sleeve attached to the underside of the desk between the upper middle drawer and the frame. Jack reached under the desk and found the sleeve. It was empty.

Panic began to set in. Jack pushed the chair back and got on his hands and knees. He looked up at the empty sleeve and cursed. He looked all around on the floor, without actually expecting to find anything. He got up, sat back down in the chair and searched the desk. He pulled out every drawer, looked under loose papers, medical journals, and books. He found nothing. He got up and went to the closet. It was empty save for one cardigan hanging alone in the corner. The shelves had been cleared out, and the only box he'd found contained a few reams of blank office letterhead.

He closed the closet door and walked over to the wall of books. He started checking each and every book, careful to return them where he found them. Despite what he'd seen in the movies, there was no secret panel or doorway, no hollow book or shelf. Just books. And no sign of the drive. Where could it be, he asked himself. He stood in the middle of the office, looking around. He stared at the desk where they found Dr. Holst dead. Suddenly he realized his mistake. Dr. Holst didn't commit suicide. He wasn't at his desk when he died. He was murdered. And he was placed here after the fact. Which means his drive was with him at the time he was killed. On the day of his death, his car was found in the physician's lot downstairs. So the portable drive was either in his bag, which could be anywhere by now, or in the car. Jack was praying for the car.

Chapter 32

The package arrived with the morning deliveries. It was plain brown about the size of a shoe box and was addressed to John Stirling, Owner, CrossFit Gym. John was sitting at his desk in his upstairs office looking at membership numbers when one of his employees dropped the package on his desk.

"Thanks," he said, without looking up.

He spent a few more minutes looking over quarterly membership figures before turning his attention to the box. He gave the package a quick once over, but he found nothing to indicate who it was from. The return address on the label had no name, only a post office box address. He grabbed a letter opener and cut through the tape on the top of the box. He opened the lid and inside was a handwritten letter and another, smaller package. He unfolded the letter.

"Hey John, I don't have a lot of time, so I'm gonna make this quick. My life is in danger, so I have to disappear for a while. I need you to keep this for me. Protect it. But do NOT open it. Keep it somewhere safe. If you get a text from me that says '911', take it straight to the FBI. Their New York office is a dozen blocks south of you on Broadway in lower Manhattan. I'm sure you can find it. Ask for special

agent Donna Lewis. Don't give it to anyone but her. Sorry for all the cloak and dagger, but the less you know the better. You're the only one I can trust right now, John, so I'm counting on you. Remember, '911' go straight to the feds. It means I'm out of luck and out of time. Hopefully, one day, I can explain all this to you in person. Thanks.

Your friend,

Matt Cunningham

John scratched his head. FBI? What the hell, he thought. He couldn't imagine what kind of trouble Matt could be in or who would be threatening his life. He'd known Matt a long time. He'd been a CrossFit regular since John opened his gym in NoHo in the mid-2000's. He was one of the original members of the gym, and he and John had become fast friends. They often worked out together, and even hung out outside the gym. John regularly teased Matt about his job, referring to his 'boring columns', demanding to know 'who reads that crap?'. But never once did he believe Matt's work to be dangerous.

For a moment, he thought the whole thing was a joke, and was very tempted to open the second package. But he reread the letter and became more convinced Matt was being serious. He picked up the package and held it to his ear. He shook it a few times. It wasn't very heavy, and nothing was rattling around inside. He decided to lock it away before his curiosity got the better of him.

He stood, walked over to the wall across from his desk, and took down a framed picture autographed by

Channing Tatum. John had the pleasure of training Channing, who often relied on CrossFit to get in shape for a movie. Behind the picture, recessed slightly into the concrete, was a wall safe. Still bewildered, John punched in the code, turned the knob and tucked Matt's mysterious package away for safekeeping.

Chapter 33

Jack made it out of Dr. Holst's office and down to the parking garage undetected. He had closed and locked the doors behind him, left everything as he'd found it, and maneuvered through the police tape, leaving it undisturbed. The only thing he couldn't undo was his reset of the Samsung AZOE on the outer door. But he put it back together, and there was really no way for anyone to discover it had been tampered with and the code changed.

He hustled down the stairs all the way to the parking garage, never once seeing Lazy Larry. It was after two in the morning now, so Jack didn't expect to encounter anyone in the garage either. But he opened the door slowly and quietly nonetheless. As he was descending the stairs, it occurred to him he had no idea what kind of car Dr. Holst drove, or if it would even still be there. He was hoping since it likely wasn't part of the crime investigation, the police didn't feel the need to impound it. He was also hoping Dr. Holst's wife or other family member hadn't driven away with it. And most of all, he was hoping every doctor had their own parking space with their name on it. Then again, at this hour, how many cars would still be parked in the physician's garage?

Jack held the door halfway open so he could peer around inside. The garage was practically deserted. Jack's luck held out. There was but a single car parked on the physician's level. A silver Jaguar XJ sitting just off the elevator about twenty feet to Jack's right. Jack looked up and around, and found what he was looking for. As he feared, there was a security camera. And it was pointing in the direction of the silver Jaguar. There was no avoiding it. If he went to the car, the camera would see him. Considering the hour and the all but empty garage, Jack doubted if anyone was monitoring it. But it would be recorded. And if he set off the car alarm, as he expected he would, someone would hear and see it.

He had no choice. For all he knew, the car would be gone in the morning. He got the tools he would need out of his bag, pulled his hood over his head, and walked quickly to the car. He had them ready. With his majestic pick gun and tension wrench in hand, he approached the car, and started working the door lock. He fiddled with it for two or three seconds before he heard a click and the lock popped open. He swapped tools and pulled the door open. The alarm siren started wailing, and Jack jumped in, bent down, and reached under the steering column. He grabbed the bundle of wires that led to the alarm and clipped them. The alarm went dead. Jack had opened the lock and disabled the alarm in less than six seconds. At that moment he was extremely grateful for everything Bobby had taught him.

The garage was silent, but he had to move fast. If anyone heard the alarm or was monitoring the camera, they'd be along shortly. He sat up, opened the center console between the two front seats, and looked around. Nothing. He leaned over and opened the glove box. Nope. He checked the door pockets on both the driver's and passenger's door. Still nothing. He reached under the driver's seat and came up empty. He leaned over, reached under the passenger's seat, and felt something. He shifted it around under the seat and found it had a handle. He pulled it out and placed it on his lap. It was a gray, plastic case with 'Craftsman' embossed on the cover. He flipped the plastic tab and opened it. Inside was a set of eight stainless steel Craftsman wrenches in various sizes. They looked as though they'd never been used.

Jack stared at the wrenches. He never met Dr. Holst, but didn't imagine him to be mechanically inclined. Not with cars anyway. These wrenches had clearly never seen the light of day. And who keeps tools under the front seat, Jack asked himself. Don't most people keep them in the trunk? Something didn't add up.

He looked at the wrenches. He felt the weight of the box on his lap. Then he noticed the tab. There was a small plastic tab in the inside corner of the box that allowed you to lift out the tray of wrenches. Initially, Jack expected to find more wrenches underneath. But when he lifted the tab, there it was. A shiny black device about the size of his hand with a USB port on the bottom edge. Bingo. He'd found Dr. Holst's external drive.

Chapter 34

Morning arrived and Cheryl wasn't sure what to do next. She just wrapped up her weekly call with Brenda, and everything was going well with her and Lily. No change in either's status. She was relieved at that. She updated Brenda on their progress, what was happening with Matt, and Jack's adventure at Dr. Holst's office. Jack had called around four in the morning to let Cheryl know he was ok and that he found what they were looking for. They had heeded Matt's earlier advice and now both Jack and Cheryl were using prepaid cell phones. Brenda had one too. They swapped them out for new ones weekly. They also spoke in code, offering as little detail as possible, just in case anyone was still managing to listen in.

Cheryl also shared with Brenda her concern for Matt. After what happened to Dr. Holst, and the threat Matt received, his disappearance was more than a little worrisome. Brenda tried to put Cheryl at ease, but it wasn't working. The hairs on Cheryl's neck were standing at attention again, and that never meant anything good. They agreed to talk again in a few days, or sooner if anything changed.

After hanging up, Cheryl quickly showered and dressed. She picked up the flash drive containing the surveillance video from the stairwell. With a little more flirting, she had convinced the security guard to make a copy and save it on the drive for her. She had no idea what she was going to do with it, but it was their first real proof that someone else was involved in whatever's going on. She debated with herself whether she should hide it in her apartment or keep it with her. Hiding it won out and she decided to stash it at the bottom of a cereal box in the pantry. She wasn't sure why, but figured it was the last place anyone would look for anything of value.

With that done, she grab her things and headed out to the office. Her apartment was ten blocks away, an easy walk especially when the weather was nice. She thought of nothing but Matt the whole way. She feared for his safety, and also felt extremely guilty. It was her call, her request that got him started asking questions about EBF-14. And she had used his feelings for her to get him to do it. If something happened to him, it was her fault.

She beat herself up for the rest of the walk until she arrived at the coffee shop on the ground floor of the New York Journal building. It was here that Matt and Dr. Holst were originally scheduled to meet. Now Dr. Holst was dead, Matt was missing, and Cheryl feared the worst. She stood in line for ten minutes, and as she waited, she constantly checked her phone for emails or text messages from Matt. None arrived.

With egg sandwich and coffee in hand, Cheryl headed outside looking for a table, but there weren't any available. She had hoped to enjoy the cool morning air and do some serious people watching, but the morning crowd forced her to abandon that idea quickly. Having resigned herself to eating yet another meal at her desk, she turned towards the revolving doors that led into the building. But before she could take two steps in that direction, she was roughly grabbed at both elbows by two large men in dark suits.

"Hey!," she said.

They quickly steered her away from the building and practically carried her to a van parked at the curb just a few steps away. Before she could make another sound, the door slid closed behind her.

This is it, Cheryl thought. This is how I die. In the back of a dark van. She felt the grip on both elbows release, and a light clicked on. She blinked a few times to adjust to the brightness and looked around. Her two escorts were still on either side of her. Across from and facing her was a fifty-something year old woman in a dark pant suit. Her shoulder length hair was mostly gray, and was complemented nicely by her rimless glasses.

"Good morning, Cheryl," she said.

"And you are?"

"Special Agent Donna Lewis, FBI."

Chapter 35

"Who is it?"

The video playing on the screen clearly showed someone searching the office of Dr. Holst. He was looking for something.

"The same guy from down south. The runner."

"How did he get in?"

"We're not sure. That lock was supposed to..."

"Did he find it?"

"Not in the office. He didn't seem to know where it was. He was just randomly searching the place hoping to get lucky. After ten minutes or so, he gave up and left."

"Where did he go from there?"

"He took the stairs down to the parking garage. The physician's lot."

"And?"

"He broke into the doctor's car. We think he found it."

"Find him. Now."

Chapter 36

For the first time since he was in high school, Jack slept past noon. Last night was a success, but it was also tense. For hours after, his heart pounded and his adrenaline rushed. He finally managed to fall asleep as the sun began to come up. Having found what he was after, he awoke feeling excited and accomplished.

126

He stretched, stood and went to the window. With the sun at its apex, he had an incredible view of central park. People were already having lunch in the park, walking their dogs, and playing with their kids. He thought about Amy and Emma. They had been to New York a number of times for visits to Dr. Holst and other specialists. Emma loved this view. They stayed here every time they came up to the city. Jack's parents were excellent hosts. With six spare bedrooms, a full-time cook, housekeeper, and valet, it was easy.

Jack called Amy to check in. He told her a bunch of lies about the phony conference he was supposedly attending. He hated doing it, but he knew how important it was to maintain the illusion. She and Lily were both doing fine, no problems and, more importantly, no unexpected visits from anyone. Now that he had officially begun meddling, he was constantly concerned for their safety. As soon as AstaGen became aware of his identity and his actions, the girls would be in danger. He didn't know what he would do if something happened to either of them. He still ached every day for Nate. And much of what Jack did now was for him.

He and Amy talked for ten minutes catching up on her work, his parents, the conference, etc. Yes, he would be home in a few days, he assured her. Yes, he was eating right. No, he didn't eat a hot dog. Yes, he was getting his exercise in. That part was true, but he couldn't resist a Sabrett's hot dog when he first got to the city. Everything in moderation, Amy always said. He secretly used her words against her. They finished the call, exchanged I love you's and hung up.

Desperate to see what was on Dr. Holst's portable drive, Jack was eager to get to a computer. According to Dr. Bosh, Dr. Holst had backed up virtually all of his patient data, his research, everything. Jack turned the drive over in his hands. Four terabytes. That was four thousand gigabytes! Dr. Holst had more than enough room to back up whatever he wanted.

Having slept in his clothes, Jack thought it best if he showered, shaved, and changed into something a little less wrinkled. His parents didn't know the real reason he was in town, and he wasn't about to fill them in. They may know he was out late, but they don't know doing what. And he certainly wasn't going to tell them. The staff didn't need to relay to them his disheveled state either.

Clean and neat, he headed out to the kitchen. It was a massive expanse that was larger than most of the apartments in New York. He sat at the island, easily twenty feet in length. It had two sinks, an oven, a stovetop, multiple heating and cooling drawers, the works. The chef had prepared enough food for an army, even though he was the only one there. His parents had long since left for their respective offices, so he had the place to himself. Except, of course, for the multitude of staff.

He had his choice of breakfast and lunch items. He was embarrassed that so much food had been prepared on his behalf. And that so much of it would probably go to waste. He ate some of everything, mostly out of guilt, and by the time he was done, he thought he might vomit. He excused himself and made his way to his father's office.

The room was dark. His father had a penchant for always keeping the blinds closed and the sun out, so his office was more like a cave. Jack fumbled his way to the desk and managed to find the light. His father also had a thing for wood. Rich, dark wood. From the wood paneled walls to the oak wood flooring, to the walnut desk and the maple bookshelves, it was a gluttony of wood.

He pulled out his father's solid wood, leather bound chair and took a seat. He rummaged through the drawers until he found the cable he needed. He plugged Dr. Holst's drive into the computer and waited. His excitement overcame his food-induced nausea. He sat on the edge of the chair, drumming his fingers on the desk in anticipation. A few mouse clicks later and the computer was directed to open the external drive.

Suddenly a pop-up window appeared on the screen. On the top bar it read: **BlowfishEncryption-v0.1.1**, and in the center of the window there was an empty bar with a blinking cursor. The instructions stated: **Please Enter Your Distinct Password to Access this Drive**.

"Shit," Jack said. "He really was a control freak."

Chapter 37

The ride in the van was awkward, but brief. They arrived at the office of the FBI in a matter of minutes, and Cheryl was whisked out of the van, into an elevator and up to one of the top floors. She now found herself alone in a room with a plain table and three chairs. She sat in a chair on one side, the two chairs on the opposite side of the table were vacant. As she sat there, she began to wonder if this was an interrogation room. But those were only for criminals, she thought to herself. Or suspects, right? The FBI couldn't possibly consider her one of those two things, could they? She started to get nervous.

She stood and began pacing around the otherwise empty room. She couldn't help herself, so she tried the door. It was locked from the outside. Cheryl's panic-meter began to rise. Am I under arrest, she asked herself. Why am I locked in here? Her knees wobbly, she decided to sit back down.

After being snatched up and tossed into the back of a van, Cheryl's breakfast and coffee never made it to her stomach. If they had, she might be throwing them up right now. She started feeling lightheaded and queasy. Her nerves weren't helping either. She hung her head between her knees and tried to control her breathing. Between the two-way glass and the surveillance camera in the corner of the ceiling, she knew she was being watched, but she didn't care.

Just as her deep breathing was beginning to calm her, the door swung opened and she popped up, startled. The two arm-grabbers came in first, followed by Agent Lewis. She placed a folder on the table and took a seat across from Cheryl. Her two cronies stood behind her in opposite corners of the room, facing her.

"Please, Cheryl, have a seat."

Cheryl lowered herself back into her chair, her eyes nervously surveying all three of her apparent captors.

"Quite a morning so far, huh?," she said. "I imagine you have questions."

"Can I have some coffee?" Cheryl asked, trying to appear anything other than the way she was actually feeling.

Agent Lewis laughed. That was not the question she was expecting. She turned and gave a subtle nod to the goon closest to the door and he left the room.

"Why am I locked in this room?" Cheryl asked. "Am I under arrest for something?"

"Have you done something we should arrest you for, Cheryl?"

"Not that I know of..." She had spent the last few minutes thinking about that and couldn't come up anything juicy enough to warrant her arrest. And certainly nothing that would concern the FBI.

"No, Cheryl, you're not under arrest."

She let out a silent breath of relief.

"You're here because of this."

Agent Lewis opened the folder if front of her and slid a sheet of paper across the table. Cheryl picked it up and looked at it. She recognized the handwriting immediately.

Agent Lewis, my name is Matt Cunningham. We've never met, but perhaps you recognize my name. I write an investigative column on health and wellness for the New York Journal. I'm writing you this letter because I need your help. A few months ago, a colleague of mine, Cheryl, brought to my attention some things about a new cancer drug known as EBF-14. As you may or may not be aware, the drug was developed and is being produced and sold by AstaGen. At my colleague's request, I did some digging, reached out to some of my contacts, and learned some interesting things, about both EBF-14 and AstaGen.

Last week, I had a meeting scheduled with Dr. William Holst, one of the foremost cancer experts here in New York, and one of the largest prescribers of EBF-14. As I'm sure you're aware, he was found dead in his office, apparently from suicide. This happened on the same day we were scheduled to meet.

It is my contention, however, that Dr. Holst was murdered and his crime scene staged. He was killed because he had been talking to me, had arranged to meet with me, and someone was listening. He intended to confirm as fact certain things I had uncovered about EBF-14. With their wonder drug, AstaGen has been targeting a specific form of cancer. A type of cancer that didn't exist just a few short years ago, called Omnicarcinos. I don't know how that's possible. How did a new form of cancer just spring up suddenly? And how is it that AstaGen already has a drug that treats it? How did they get FDA approval so quickly? And how did the clinical trials produce a 95% cure rate? Not 95% effective rate, but **cure** rate!

These are all questions I had hoped Dr. Holst would be able to answer. He's dead, and now they're after me. I don't think my snooping was well received. I've been followed, my phones have been tapped, and my life has been threatened. I'm currently on the run and in fear for my life. All courtesy of the fine folks at AstaGen.

So here's the plan: A friend of mine is holding something for me that contains substantial evidence to support my claims. If something happens to me, it will be hand delivered to you. In the meantime, Cheryl and her friend, Jack, should now have in their possession a portable hard drive that once belonged to Dr. Holst. Don't ask how they got it. It will contain his patient files, his research, his findings about EBF-14, his theories about AstaGen, and hopefully the answer to those questions I mentioned above. There should be plenty there to motivate you to investigate AstaGen.

You may be wondering why I'm coming to you with all of this. I'll tell you. Two years ago, you were the lead investigator in the case against Dresden Pharmaceuticals. You investigated them for six months. And you were the one that discovered they were lacing their pills with oxycodone and other addictive properties. I wrote a lengthy column about it. Maybe you saw the piece?

Anyway, you went after a multi-billion dollar pharmaceutical company who was doing something illegal and unethical, and you nailed them. You weren't intimidated, bribed or forced off the case. You let the world know what they were up to, and you made them pay. I'm hoping you'll put forth a similar effort in this case.

I can't tell you where I am or what I'm doing, I still have some digging to do. But I need you to do a few things for me. First of all, protect my friends. Both Cheryl and Jack are here in New York, and I have good reason to believe AstaGen is aware of their presence. And if they know about the drive, Cheryl and Jack are both in grave danger. Second of all, check out the EBF-14 clinical trials. Maybe you can use your resources to figure out how they got it approved so fast, and how in the world they managed a ninety-five percent cure rate.

That's all for now. If a package shows up addressed from me, it probably means I'm dead. Use it to nail those bastards at AstaGen. And find Cheryl! She'll lead you to Jack and the drive.

Sincerely,

Matt Cunningham

Cheryl put the letter down and looked up at Agent Lewis, who was sitting with her arms crossed.

"Your friend Matt has been a busy little bee, hasn't he? So to answer your question, Cheryl, the reason you're locked in this room is for your protection. Plus, it seems like we have some things to discuss."

Cheryl swallowed hard. She had no idea she was even in danger, or that AstaGen might have people looking for her right now. She looked around and realized she was now in the protective custody of the FBI.

"Now," Agent Lewis went on, "who is this Jack character and where is he?"

Chapter 38

Jack spent the better part of the afternoon sitting at his father's desk searching Google for ways to hack into Dr. Holst's encrypted drive. It took him far longer than it should have, but eventually he realized he had no idea what he was doing. He didn't even understand most of what he read as he searched. He wasn't a computer hacker. He could open doors without using a key, but this was a whole different kind of lock. And this time he was pretty sure he was going to need the key.

Jack discovered rather quickly what he was up against. *Blowfish is a keyed, symmetric cryptographic block cipher*, he read. It's like it was written in Latin, Jack thought. He had no idea what any of that meant, but he knew it was trouble. He kept reading. *Blowfish security had been extensively tested and proven time and again*, and, according to one article he found, *full Blowfish encryption has never been broken*. Jack read it again. *Blowfish encryption has never been broken.*

Dr. Holst had employed one of the best encryption tools known to man. But why? What was he so serious about protecting? And who was he trying to protect it from? Jack considered Dr. Holst's level of involvement in what seemed to be an ever-growing conspiracy. How many patients was he aware of, Jack wondered. What did he know about EBF-14 and AstaGen that could have gotten him killed? And for how long had he known? All of those answers were in the drive resting in the palm of Jack's hand. But he had no way of getting to them.

Moving forward, Jack concluded he had two options. One, he could go find one of the world's best hackers and somehow convince him or her to help him break into the drive. An almost laughable notion, he thought. Or two, he could somehow find Dr. Holst's password and open the drive himself. Neither scenario seemed very likely. He wouldn't even know where to start looking, for either of those things.

Jack stood up and stretched. He'd been sitting for too long and things had gotten tight. He walked around the room in a circle, hands behind his head, trying to come up with an idea. It was unlikely that Dr. Bosh would have the password, Jack thought, but that was the easiest place to start. He'd be sure to call him today.

He considered the possibility Mrs. Holst would have it. But he doubted it, since she hadn't even bothered to retrieve her dead husband's car. He didn't know what their relationship was like, but Jack found that strange. He had no way of contacting her anyway. Their home number was private, unlisted. But he remembered Cheryl saying something about her friend Matt speaking with Mrs. Holst. Maybe he still had the number. He'd follow up on that too.

Right now, though, he had no way to reach Cheryl either. Today was the day they were scheduled to replace their prepaid cell phones. Every week, on the same day, they would each purchase a new phone, then login to a shared folder on a cloud based server, and update their contact info. They could log in at anytime from anywhere to get each other's numbers.

Jack's phone was dead. It was out of minutes and out of power. In all the running around yesterday, he never charged it. But that was their primary form of communication. They didn't dare use a landline or their personal cell phone, both were too risky. A new phone was the first thing on Jack's to-do list. After that, it was back to solving the riddle of Dr. Holst's encrypted drive.

Jack mulled over a number of different options, none of them terribly realistic. Finding someone to hack the drive seemed like a long shot. He didn't know anyone from that world and probably didn't want to. And he couldn't imagine what something like that would even cost.

But he knew one thing he had to do. He was trying to think of anything else he *could* do instead. But if there was any chance of finding the password, he would have to look for it. Anywhere it could possibly be. No matter how hard he tried, there was no avoiding it. He would have to break into Dr. Holst's office again.

Chapter 39

Lander's Market had been a fixture in town for nearly one hundred years. It was founded shortly after locals began farming the land in order to make the fruit of their labors available to the townspeople. It started as a very small farmer's market, but over the years blossomed into a full-blown grocery store. The largest section of the store was still the fresh, local grown produce, but they had become more mainstream, offering frozen foods and canned goods, as well as prepackaged and processed food.

Once a week, Amy would bring Emma to Lander's to get groceries for the house. She stuck to mostly the local grown food, but anything else she bought was organic, without artificial colors, and was not genetically modified. Emma loved going to the store. It was mother-daughter time, and they often played games as they walked up and down the aisles. Today's game was 'I Spy'.

"I spy something that starts with the letter B," Amy said.

Emma walked slowly down the aisle, looking up and down the shelves before shouting "Bread!"

"You got it," Amy said with a smile.

Lander's had their own bakery where everything was made from scratch. The smell of fresh bread permeated through the entire store and hit you as soon as you walked through the front doors. Amy took a loaf of their usual off the shelf and placed it in the cart. Emma spotted something she thought would stump her mom.

"I spy something that starts with the letter 'P'," she said, excited.

"Hmm, something that starts with the letter P," Amy repeated. She looked around slowly, trying to prolong the excitement for Emma. "Is it peanut butter?," she guessed.

"Nope!" Emma giggled.

"Pretzels?"

"Nope! Only one more guess!"

"I know. Popcorn!"

"Aggh! You got it!" They both laughed.

Amy never hurried when she took Emma grocery shopping. Emma loved it so much and Amy didn't want to rush it. She normally liked to shop in the middle of the day, while everyone was at work, so the store was quiet anyway. When they got to the last aisle, Amy noticed the cart wasn't very full. With Jack out of town, she was shopping for just two, and Emma had never been a big eater.

Jack's trip had been extended by a few days. He said there had been some kind of power issue at the convention center, delaying a number of the presentations and pushing everything back. On the bright side, he was spending some quality time with his parents and was enjoying the distractions of the city. It took his mind off Nate and everything else that had been going on. Or so he said.

Emma drove, and she steered the cart to an open cashier, then helped her mom unload the groceries onto the belt. Amy paid and they headed out to the car. Much like the store, the parking lot was nearly empty. They were still giggling from their game as they approached the car. Amy looked down and reached into her purse for the keys.

"Mommy!," Emma screamed.

Amy turned quickly towards the sound of her daughter's panicked scream. A man she'd never seen before was holding Emma. He had a clump of her hair in one hand, and a knife pressed to her throat with the other. She had a look of absolute terror on her face.

"Please...," Amy began. But before she could finish her sentence, another man grabbed her by the throat and slammed her against the car. Her toes barely touched the ground as his grip tightened and he pushed her harder against the car. Her eyes began to water and redden from the pressure on her throat, and she struggled to take a breath.

"Listen to me very carefully, Amy" he said, staring into her eyes. He knew her name. "I want you to deliver a message to your husband. Can you do that for me?"

Amy tried to speak, but couldn't make a sound. She nodded slightly, barely able to move her head. Her eyes turned to Emma and the knife at her throat. Tears streamed down her face. There was a small drop of blood where the knife tip pressed against Emma's throat. Amy struggled, but could not break the strong grip around her throat.

"Tell him to stop. Stop right now before things get ugly. Let him know what happened here today, and tell him to stop. You make sure Jack gets the message." He tilted his head and brought his face close to Amy's. "Do you understand me?"
She efforted another small nod.

"Do not make us come back here, or today will seem like a picnic. Got it?"

Another forced nod.

"Good." And with that he released her. She fell hard to the ground. Emma was also free and raced to her mother. Amy grabbed her and held her tight. They sat on the ground against the car, Emma in a tight embrace, both breathing hard and crying hysterically. Amy hadn't seen her assailants leave or where they went, and she didn't care. They were gone, Emma was ok, and that's all that mattered.

Chapter 40

Cheryl logged into the shared folder with amazing speed and ease. The FBI's Wi-Fi was much faster than anything she'd used before. Certainly faster than the prehistoric Wi-Fi back at Brenda's house. Agent Lewis was kind enough to allow Cheryl the use of a laptop computer in an effort to locate Jack. She tried reaching him on his last burner phone, but it was out of service.

Looking at the spreadsheet they'd been using to keep track and update their numbers, Jack had not renewed his yet. Then again, neither had Cheryl. She'd been keeping company with the FBI all day and a trip to the store for a new phone was not high on their priority list. Brenda's new number was here. She updated it as scheduled and on time. Agent Lewis was watching over Cheryl's shoulder with great interest.

"Nothing yet," Cheryl said. She sat back in her chair, and started to fear for Jack's safety. Matt's letter had freaked her out. She never seriously considered what they were doing to be dangerous. She knew they might make some people unhappy, but never did she think their lives would be at risk. What did they think we were going to find, she asked herself. While she was safe and sound in protective custody at FBI headquarters, Jack was out there somewhere. He could be anywhere, she thought. He could be in the hands of AstaGen, or worse. She didn't want to think about it.

"What was the next step in the plan?" Agent Lewis asked.

"Jack was to go through the contents of Dr. Holst's drive and then call me. Depending on what he found, we would plan our next move."

"How did he come to be in possession of the drive?"

Cheryl feared this question would be asked. She had thought about what she might say, but now that it was upon her, she couldn't come up with anything good. So she went with "I thought Matt said not to ask."

"I'm asking anyway."

"I'd rather not say."

"I'll let it go for now, Cheryl. We have bigger issues." Agent Lewis said. "But we will come around to it again."

Cheryl nodded, and hoped to have a better answer when the subject came up again.

"I should have heard from him by now." Cheryl's concern for Jack's safety was on the rise. "He hasn't called and he hasn't updated his number in the spreadsheet. Something happened."

Agent Lewis put a hand on Cheryl's shoulder. "We don't know that yet, Cheryl. From what you've told me, Jack is a smart guy. He could be holed up somewhere, laying low. Or he could be on the run. Either way, he could be perfectly fine, and just hasn't had a chance to buy a new phone or use it."

"Maybe," Cheryl admitted. She reached around with her hand to feel the hairs on the back of her neck. They weren't standing at attention yet, so that was a relief. "There's something else we should consider."

"What's that?" Agent Lewis asked.

"Maybe he doesn't have a new phone yet, but maybe he does and just hasn't updated the spreadsheet yet. But he might still be trying to reach me. My phone is dead, and

I haven't updated the spreadsheet with a new number either. If he's been trying to call, he doesn't know where I am, how to reach me, or if I'm alive or dead."

"Good point," Agent Lewis conceded. "Do this." She pointed at the computer screen over Cheryl's shoulder. "Insert a text box where you would normally update your phone number and fill him in on what's been going on. And give him this number." She placed her card on the table next to the computer and pointed at the number. "That's my direct line. It get's forwarded to my cell phone no matter where I am."

"Ok," Cheryl said. She moved the mouse, put the cursor in the box where she would normally update her phone number, and began typing:

Jack, hopefully you'll read this sooner than later. I'm ok. I'm with the FBI. They picked me up after they received a letter from Matt sharing his/our theories about EBF-14, AstaGen, and the murder of Dr. Holst. He claims to have evidence. He's being followed, he's been threatened, and he believes you and I are both in immediate danger. Somehow AstaGen knows about us. I don't know how, but they do. The FBI wants you to come in. They know about Dr. Holst's drive and the agent in charge seems willing to help, but she needs to know what's on it. Call me at this number: 212-555-1084. That's Agent Lewis's direct number. Hope to hear from you soon!

"Good," Agent Lewis said.

Cheryl turned slightly in the chair to look in Agent Lewis's direction. "Now what?"

"Now we wait."

Cheryl sighed. "I hate waiting."

"Let's make good use of the time then. Why don't you tell me everything. Start from the beginning, and don't leave anything out."

Chapter 41

A quick Google search revealed a small electronics store that also sold prepaid cell phones just a few miles from his parents' penthouse apartment. Jack made a mental note of the address and location and shut down his father's computer, without ever logging into the shared drive. He returned the office to its previous cave-like status and walked back to his room to collect his things. He put on his watch, pocketed his wallet, and picked up his personal cell phone. The screen displayed a notification of one missed call and one voicemail. It was from Amy. He hadn't told her anything about the burner phones, or the need for them, so she was still calling his personal cell phone. He opened the voicemail screen and pressed play.

He held the phone to his ear and as he listened, his jaw went slack. His knees got weak and he started to tremble. He nearly fell, landing on the edge of the bed, still listening, but not believing what he was hearing. Amy described, in detail, their encounter with the two men in the parking lot of Lander's Market, and the message they asked her to deliver to him. When the recording ended, he listened to it again. He could hear the terror in Amy's voice. She was obviously still shaken when she left the message.

Stop, they had said. Even if Amy didn't know, Jack knew exactly what they meant. He could not recall a time when he felt guiltier. It was his actions that brought this on his wife and daughter. He put their lives in danger and he wasn't even there to protect them. He pictured the scene. His wife pinned against the car, a man with his hand wrapped around her throat. His daughter in the clutches of a stranger, a knife pressed against her neck. Jack felt helpless and weak. His heart pounded as he imagined it.

One thing was abundantly clear. AstaGen was on to him. How they knew about him, he had no idea. Maybe the break-in at Dr. Holst's office? He couldn't be sure. What if they knew about the drive? Suddenly the prospect of going back there to search for the password was terrifying. The prospect of simply stepping outside was now terrifying! How many people were looking for him right now, Jack wondered. AstaGen has unlimited resources, so if they genuinely believed he was a threat, they would stop at nothing. Look what they did to Dr. Holst.

His thoughts quickly turned to Cheryl. Where was she? Was she safe? Were they looking for her? Had they already found her? The questions came fast and furious, and Jack began to feel queasy.

He needed to call Amy. Their home phone was almost certainly tapped by now, so it didn't matter what phone he used on his end. The phones in his parents' penthouse might already be tapped too. And they definitely must have cracked his personal cell phone. They would hear the conversation either way. He would just have to be very careful with his words.

He picked up the cordless landline in his room and dialed. She answered on the second ring.

"Amy, it's me. Oh my god, are you ok?! How's Emma?!"

At the sound of Jack's voice, Amy started crying again. "She's terrified. I'm terrified. You can't imagine what it was like."

"I'm so sorry, Amy. I'm so sorry I wasn't there. Did you call the police?"

"They just left. But it won't do any good. I couldn't tell them much about the two men. I was so scared, Jack. I just didn't want them to hurt Emma."

"I know. It's ok. No one could be expected to give a description after something like that."

"Who were those men, Jack? What did they want? And what did they mean 'stop'?"

"I don't know who they were." That was mostly true, Jack thought, efforting to justify his lie.

"Jack, they knew your name. They knew my name. They had a knife at your daughter's throat. Don't play games with me. Tell me what's going on. Who were those men and why are they telling you to stop? Stop what?"

"Now is not the time, Amy."

She started to protest, but he cut her off.

"Listen," he said firmly. "I want you to lock the doors. Pack a bag, and in the morning go straight to the airport, and get on the first flight to New York. I'll be waiting for you at the airport when you get here."

"Why can't you just come home?"

"You'll be safer here."

"Safer from what?"

"I'll explain more when you're here, I promise. Now go. Just do what I'm telling you, ok?"

They hung up and Jack immediately called Bobby. He knew what Jack had been up to and the danger it might present. When he answered, Jack skipped the pleasantries, gave Bobby a quick rundown and asked him to hurry over to the house and make sure the girls got to the airport in the morning safely. Bobby was incredible with locks, but he was equally gifted with guns. Born and raised in the south, he was well trained and always carrying. Jack knew they'd be safe with him. Bobby assured him he'd head right over and see the girls off in the morning. Jack thanked him and they hung up.

Still sitting on the edge of the bed, Jack leaned forward and hung his head. Everything just got a lot more complicated.

Chapter 42

Cameras were pointed at her, a digital recorder was running on the table, and an FBI stenographer was sitting at the end of the table, ready to take notes. Cheryl never particularly enjoyed the limelight. That's why she chose to be a newspaper reporter, not television. She liked to be involved, to make a difference, but still remain behind the scenes. All the attention focused on her now made her uncomfortable.

"Relax," Agent Lewis had said. "Just speak naturally, like it's just you and me."

After Matt's letter, Agent Lewis was taking the AstaGen matter more seriously. She had developed a healthy distrust of large pharmaceutical companies, particularly the ones with deep pockets and a penchant for cutting corners. In her experience, healthcare wasn't their primary concern, but rather profits. Keeping the executives rich and the shareholders happy was the name of the game.

With the cameras rolling and all eyes on her, Cheryl started from the beginning. She told them what she could remember about when Brenda was first diagnosed. Her lifestyle, diet, family history, etc. It was a mystery then, and remains one now. A few months later, Lily got sick and the mystery grew. At first, it was easy to believe it was 'just genetics', like the doctors said. After all, mother and daughter both with the same disease. But then they learned there were others. Jack's family, for starters. His wife and two kids, all affected.

"Not Jack?," Agent Lewis asked.

"Nope. Not a single tumor marker in any of his blood work. He's an athlete, so I suggested maybe his immune system was just superior to his family's. But Jack dismissed that notion quickly. He's convinced it's something else."

"Like what?"

"That's the problem. We have no idea where it came from or how it's affecting so many people. That's what we hope to find out from Dr. Holst's drive. But Jack is certain it's coming from somewhere, and it's not genetics."

"What do you think?"

Cheryl shifted slightly in her chair. She'd never said the words out loud, but she'd been suspicious from the get go. She thought about her sister and her niece. Once perfectly healthy, now living with the cloud of 'terminal cancer' over their heads.

"I think someone or something is causing this," she confessed. "And I think there's a lot of money at stake. And I think we've been asking the right questions and the wrong people noticed. And that's why I'm sitting here now."

"Ok, go on."

Cheryl talked about Dr. Bosh. Agent Lewis was genuinely surprised to learn that at least nineteen people in a town with a population of just fourteen hundred had been diagnosed with Omnicarcinos. Nineteen that they knew about. The same cancer which, according to Matt, didn't exist just a few short years ago.

Then she went on to EBF-14, AstaGen's new wonder drug. After it's incredible performance in clinical trials, it was touted as a miracle of modern medicine. When Cheryl mentioned the annual cost of EBF-14 to be in the neighborhood of $300,000, Agent Lewis choked as she was drinking her coffee.

Cheryl brought up Dr. Bosh's connection to Dr. Holst. Holst was the specialist Bosh consulted for these cancer cases. He told Bosh about EBF-14, and it was his recommendation that got Brenda and Lily started on it. He even helped push it through with the insurance company.

"Why would he do that?" Agent Lewis asked.

"I thought about that," Cheryl said. "I can't really be sure. Brenda insists he cared about his patients and was just trying to help."

"But you don't believe that?"

"At this point, I don't know what to believe."

"Ok, let's keep going."

Cheryl then gave a first-hand account of the seizure Lily suffered. The fear in Brenda's eyes. The horror of seeing her niece thrash around uncontrollably with no way to stop it. She also shared what she knew about the seizure that ended Nate's life. Jack had told her about it and she cried as he did.

She went on to talk about the dosage problems AstaGen had been having with EBF-14, particularly for younger, smaller patients. They attributed the seizures to that, and said it was "par for the course" and "no big deal." They figured a few casualties along the way as they got things ironed out was to be expected. Dr. Bosh confessed that he'd seen it happen in other patients.

As she started piecing things together, Cheryl continued, she got curious. She asked her friend at the Journal, Matt, to look into EBF-14 and see what he could find out. He had said that somehow AstaGen was targeting this specific form of cancer with EBF-14 and that it didn't work on other types of cancer. He discovered Dr. Holst, made contact, and scheduled an interview. Dr. Holst was killed the same day they were to meet. And as he said in the letter, he believed the suicide was staged.

There was a hard rap on the door that startled Cheryl. She wasn't sure how long she'd been sitting there, but she'd lost all track of time during the interview. The door opened and a head peeked through. It was no one Cheryl recognized. "Agent Lewis, can I see you for a minute?"

Agent Lewis excused herself and left the room. When she returned a few minutes later, she was holding a small brown box. She stood just inside the closed door and looked directly at Cheryl. The look on her face made the hairs on the back of Cheryl's neck stand up.

"What?" Cheryl asked tentatively.

"Your friend Matt is dead."

Chapter 43

He needed a phone, now. Jack paced back and forth
worried about Cheryl, wondering if she was alive or dead.
He was still shaking after talking to Amy and hearing about
what happened to her and Emma. They were safe, for now,
and he was relieved they were on their way to him. His
parents' building was well protected with state of the art
security. They would be safe here. He wasn't excited about
coming clean with Amy, but he had no choice.

Right now, he needed to talk to Cheryl, to make sure
she was ok. And he needed to figure out a way to open Dr.
Holst's drive. Both of those things meant going outside,
leaving the safety of the penthouse. Surely, this is the first
place they would look for him. By now they must know he
hadn't checked into a hotel. And if they were monitoring his
home phone, they knew Amy and Emma would be on a
plane to New York first thing in the morning. Would they try
to intercept them at the airport? Or would they give Jack a
chance to 'stop', to heed their warning, before taking
further action?

He knew they'd be watching him. They might even
have people waiting outside for him right now. If he went to
buy a new phone, they'd know. If he got anywhere near Dr.
Holst's office again, they'd know. To be safe, he had to
assume they were watching at all times. That would force
him to plan his movements carefully. He had an idea, but in
order to put it into action, he needed a phone.

Jack put his track pants and hoodie back on. He found a pair of sunglasses in the kitchen. He even went so far as to darken his complexion with some of his mother's makeup. I didn't think I'd be doing this when I woke up today, he thought to himself.

It was getting late in the day and the sun would be going down soon. The electronics store was open until 10 pm, so he could afford to wait. But his patience wouldn't allow it. He stashed Dr. Holst's drive in one of the many closets in the massive apartment and headed out. On the elevator ride down, he came up with a new idea and needed to make a few changes.

When the elevator doors opened, Jack went straight to the men's room just off the lobby. He washed the makeup off his face, took off the hoodie and wrapped it around his waist, and tied his running shoes up tight. He plugged his ear buds into his phone and started up his playlist on low volume. He opened the doors onto the street, spent several minutes stretching on the sidewalk, and looked at anyone and everyone who might be watching him. The street was lined with parked cars and people passing by in both directions on both sides of the street. It was impossible to tell who, if anyone was watching him. But it would also be very easy to lose them in this crowd, especially in the fading sunlight.

Jack started off with a light jog. He stayed on the same street for a mile or two, watching to see if anyone was following him. As he picked up the pace, he started turning down side streets, running through alleys and looking behind him at every turn. As he ran down the smaller streets and alleys, he thought he heard a strange buzzing sound, but whenever he got near people or cars, the sound faded. He ran in the direction opposite the electronics store for about three miles, before making a u-turn. He darted and dashed through different side streets, picking up the pace even more as he went. Every now and then his imagination would get the better of him, but he never saw anyone behind him. There was no way anyone could be following him, he thought.

As he got closer to the electronics store, about a mile away now, he continued to make sudden turns, running down side streets, and behind buildings. As he was cutting through an empty alley, he heard the buzzing sound again. This time he was sure of it. He slowed to a jog, then stopped running altogether. He bent down, put his hands on his knees, and pretended to be winded. He remained motionless, just breathing. He still heard a soft buzzing which now sounded like it was coming from directly overhead. He kneeled down and acted like he was re-tying his shoes, then stood and did some light stretching. He laced his fingers together, pressed his palms to the sky in a stretch and looked up. There, hovering about thirty feet above him was a small, remotely controlled drone quietly buzzing away.

Shit, he thought, quickly looking away. No wonder he hadn't seen anyone following him. As soon as he had looked up, the drone moved over the roof of the nearest building out of his line of sight. So they saw him, and he saw them. A slight panic set in when he realized he wouldn't be able to enter the electronics store unseen. He looked up again. The drone was still out of sight. Maybe, he thought, he could use this to his advantage. He had an idea, he just needed to find the right spot.

He started running again, slowly at first as he assessed his options. The street was still crowded, plenty of people around. He made a small loop around the side streets and ran past the electronics store. It was in a strip plaza surrounded by other retailers. On either side of the electronics store was a dry cleaner, which appeared closed, and a cigar lounge, which was open, but not very busy. Neither of those would work. On the far end of the plaza was a pizza place, and as he ran by he spotted two entrances, one in the front and one on the side. Inside was bustling with customers. There was also a back door, an employee's only entrance, which was also used for trash disposal and deliveries. This could work, Jack thought.

He ran past the plaza and kept going to avoid tipping his hand. After he put some distance between himself and the plaza, he looped back. He was two blocks away when he turned down another small, empty alley. He was running slowly now and easily heard the soft hum of the drone above him. He looked up slightly and as he did, the drone once again drifted over the adjacent building. Jack took off in a sprint. He rounded a corner, made a beeline for the back of the pizza place and ducked inside. He hugged the inside of the wall, listening for the buzzing of the drone. Nothing.

"This is for employees only, pal," someone said.

"Oh, my bad," Jack replied innocently. "Where can I get a slice?"

"Up front. Just go through here." He pointed towards the front of the restaurant through some curtains that separated the kitchen from the diners up front. "Next time use the front door, huh?"

"You got it," Jack said. "Thanks."

Jack walked through the curtains to the front of the pizza place. It was filled to near capacity. Perfect, Jack thought. He untied the hoodie from his waist, put it back on, and pulled the hood over his head. He waited for a group of college kids to leave and he followed closely behind them. They walked down the front of the plaza talking and laughing, Jack clinging tightly to the group. As they passed in front of the electronics store, he quickly dipped inside.

He took a moment to look back outside. There were too many people milling about for anyone to have seen him. And it was too noisy for him to tell if the drone had spotted him, but he doubted it.

"Can I help you with something?"

Jack turned to see the clerk behind the counter eyeing him suspiciously. This particular electronics store had been robbed once before, so a stranger with a hood pulled over his head wasn't a particularly comforting sight.

"Yeah," Jack said, removing his hood. "Sorry."

With one last glance over his shoulder, he walked towards the counter. There were several other customers in the store, being helped by other staff members. No one seemed to be looking at him. As he approached the counter, the person behind it was wearing a name tag. It said 'Walt Simmons, Manager'. His left hand was resting on the glass display case, his right hand was holding something out of sight below it. Jack could only assume it was a gun.

With his hands in plain sight, Jack said, "I need to buy three prepaid cell phones. I'll be paying cash." He didn't know if or when he'd be able to get another one, so he decided it would be a good idea to get extras.

"No problem," Walt said. He bent down and removed three phones still packed in boxes from the bottom shelf of the display case and placed them on the glass top counter.

"Would it be possible to just have the phones and leave the boxes here? I'm travelling light tonight."

"Sure thing," Walt said. He opened the boxes, unpacked the phones, and laid them out next to each other. "These are good for thirty days each. You know how they work?"

Jack assured him he did.

"Oh, and do you have... there, let me have one of those. That one right there." Jack pointed to an item hanging on the wall behind Walt. "I don't need the box," Jack said.

"No problem," Walt said.

Jack took out a wad of cash, paid Walt, and stuffed his purchases into different pockets.

"Do you want a receipt?"

"No, thanks," Jack said. "Oh, by the way, my wife and I are going through an ugly divorce and I'm pretty sure she has a private investigator following me. If anyone comes in here asking about me, or what I bought, do you think maybe you could not tell them anything?" Jack slid a twenty across the counter.

Walt looked at the twenty dollar bill and grinned. "Keep it. I've been divorced three times myself. I got you covered, buddy," and winked.

"Thanks, man. I appreciate it." Jack gave him a thumbs up and turned for the door. He peered through the window, but didn't see anything unusual or suspicious. He pulled up his hood, eased out the door and blended into the crowd. He walked with a large group for a few blocks, constantly listening for the buzz of the drone, but kept his hood up and eyes down. When they passed a narrow alley, Jack turned into it, staying close to the wall in the shadows. He remained there for several minutes without hearing any buzzing from overhead.

He removed his hoodie, tied it back around his waist, put his ear buds in and started running. He headed in the general direction of the apartment, still weaving in and out of side streets. If they spotted him between here and there, he didn't care. He got what he came for.

Chapter 44

"What do you mean, you lost him?!"

From behind his desk, the two other men in the room could feel the heat of his anger.

"He spotted the drone," said the first man. "We're not sure how yet, but he managed to evade it for a little while. We picked him up a few minutes later. He was running still." The second man remained silent.

"And where was he during those few minutes that you lost him?!" He slammed his hands on the desk.

"We're not sure. Running, we think. We just lost him in the crowds."

"Did he stop somewhere? Talk to anyone? Buy anything?"

"We don't know. We don't think so."

"And you're basing that on what?"

There was a long, awkward pause. The man behind the desk turned to the second man, who had still not said a word. "I want to know what he knows. Find him."

"Consider it done," the second man said. He rubbed the scar under his right eye and walked out the door.

"Remember, I need him alive."

Chapter 45

"What do you mean Matt's dead?!" Cheryl screeched. "How? What happened?"

"Sit down, Cheryl." Agent Lewis took her by the arm and tried to guide her into a chair, but Cheryl yanked her arm away.

"I don't want to sit down! Tell me what happened to Matt!"

"We don't know, exactly. We don't have much in the way of details."

"Well I do! I'll tell you exactly what happened! Those bastards over at AstaGen killed him. That's what happened!" Cheryl knocked over a chair in anger and started crying.

"Cheryl, please sit down. This isn't helping." Agent Lewis put her hand gently on Cheryl's back. "If you can calm down and have a seat, I'll tell you what we know."

Cheryl pulled herself together enough to sit down. Another agent handed her a small pack of tissues, which she immediately put to use. She wiped her eyes, blew her nose, and took a few deep breaths.

She couldn't believe Matt was dead. He was a flirt at the office, and had asked her out countless times. Cheryl always said no to keep things professional, but the temptation was there. He was a smart, fit, good looking guy and had become a good friend at work. He was someone she could bounce ideas off, ask questions about any project or research she was doing, and, in general, turn to if she needed help. She admired his ideals and his devotion to his work. And he wasn't bad to look at either.

With her elbows on her knees, she hung her head as guilt washed over her. She thought about the conversation that put him onto EBF-14 and AstaGen. He had asked her out again, and she rejected his offer again. She agreed to drinks, but only after he did something for her. She realized he was always doing things for her, and she never returned the favor. All he wanted was a date, to spend some time with her, and she couldn't even give him that. And now it was too late. He died doing yet another something for her.

She looked up at Agent Lewis with tears in her eyes and said, "What happened?"

"Matt knew he was being followed," Agent Lewis began. "You know that. He feared for his life. Apparently he took certain precautions to protect what he knew. In his letter, he referred to a package he entrusted with a friend. He gave that friend specific instructions that if he received a 911 text from Matt, he was to hand deliver the package to me right away. A 911 text meant that Matt's life was in immediate danger and he believed he was about to die. That package just arrived." Her tone was somber and apologetic, which only added to Cheryl's guilt.

"This is all my fault," Cheryl admitted. "I asked him to see what he could find out about EBF-14. I caused this."

Agent Lewis took a seat beside her, put a hand on her knee and said, "This is no one's fault but the people that killed Matt. If it's AstaGen, we'll find out."

Cheryl sat bolt upright and wheeled around to face Agent Lewis. "*IF* it's AstaGen?!," Cheryl protested.

"We don't know anything yet, Cheryl. Right now I'm working on a lot of he-said/she-said. You guys have given me a lot to go on, but no real facts. I know that's not what you want to hear, but we have work to do if we're going to prove that AstaGen is up to no good. And we're going to need proof if we plan to nail them."

Cheryl shook her head. Agent Lewis was right, that was not what she wanted to hear.

"Cheryl, listen to me. As of this moment, all we have are theories and conjecture. Is there any proof that AstaGen has somehow figured out how to target this one particular form of cancer? How about that EBF-14 is directly linked to seizures? Any proof, other than what some small town doc told you?"

At that, Cheryl glared at Agent Lewis. She thought about the night of Lily's seizure, about what happened to Nate. She remembered Dr. Bosh telling her the seizures were being caused by EBF-14's dosage problems, but admittedly never got into the specifics of it.

"Don't look at me like that. I know what you've seen and heard, but that's not proof, Cheryl. That's what the courts refer to as circumstantial evidence or, in layman's terms, a coincidence. Nineteen people in a small town is an alarming number, yes, but that's all it is right now. It's certainly not a big enough sample size to determine anything. Is there any proof that Dr. Holst was killed by AstaGen? Or that he was killed at all? How do we know, for sure, that he didn't actually commit suicide? You see what I'm getting at here, Cheryl?"

Cheryl nodded and let out a deep breath.

"Look, you definitely have my attention. I'm not blowing this thing off. But you have to understand you're asking a lot of me right now. AstaGen is a multi-billion dollar corporation with deep pockets and what I'm sure is a very serious legal team. I'm going to need something concrete in order to open an investigation. Are we on the same page here?"

Cheryl nodded again. "What was in the package Matt sent to you?," she asked, hoping for some good news.

"A cell phone."

"A cell phone? That's it? Is it his or someone else's?"

"No idea. I will put our analysts on it right now. We should know something soon enough."

Chapter 46

Jack made it back to the apartment building without incident. The drone had reacquired him several blocks after he left the electronics store, but he didn't care. His plan had worked. He'd hid himself from the drone long enough to get into the store, get what he needed, and get back out on the street. He was in the store only a few minutes and was back on the street mingling with the crowd. He ran back to the apartment building in the same serpentine style without ever once looking up. The whole operation took well over an hour and was exhausting, both physically and mentally, but it was worth it. His purchases were crucial to keep the plan in motion, to stay in touch with Cheryl, and to avoid AstaGen's listening ears.

When he got back to the building, Jack removed his ear buds, and punched in the six-digit code to open the front doors. He nodded to the two armed night security guards at the desk as he crossed the foyer towards the elevator. He placed his thumb on the button to call the elevator. A small horizontal red beam appeared and scanned his thumbprint up and down. After a short pause, the button turned green, emitted a small ding, and the elevator doors opened. Once inside, he inserted his access key card into the slot just above the buttons and pressed P for the penthouse. The doors silently closed and the elevator rose smoothly to the top floor. When it reached its destination, the elevator stopped and the doors opened onto a small vestibule that led to the double doors of his parents' apartment. He took a key out of his pocket, unlocked the door and went inside. The apartment's internal security system was already disarmed, meaning his parents, at least one of them, was home.

Normally Jack was annoyed by the multitude of steps necessary to get into the building and his parents' apartment. But with Amy and Emma on the way, he welcomed it. He knew they'd be safe here. He would just have to convince them to stay here and not leave the apartment. That would be easier said than done, but once

Amy heard the truth about what had been happening, Jack thought she would agree to stay put to keep Emma safe.

He walked quickly to his room, stashed his items, and jumped in the shower. The apartment was so large, he managed to do all this without ever running into another person. Not his parents, not even the staff. He dried off, put on shorts and a tee shirt and went to find out who was home. He found his father sitting in his office pouring over paperwork with the assistance of a single desk lamp. The cave was only slightly illuminated.

"Hey Dad," Jack said.

"Jack," he replied, without looking up. Michael Turner was a New York real estate baron who spent eighteen hours a day, six to seven days a week, working. He started out many years ago flipping small residential properties. Studio apartments, small homes. He could sniff out a deal better than anyone, and had a knack for convincing owners that their property was worth far less than their asking price. He reinvested his profits in more properties, eventually owning and keeping several as rentals. With both his income and bank account steadily growing, he eventually moved into larger properties, including commercial real estate. Once again, he started with smaller deals, avoiding any big mistakes that would cost him a chunk of money. He became an expert at leveraging other people's money so he could make bigger and bigger deals. Now, he wouldn't touch a deal if he wasn't going to net seven figures.

Jack's father loved his family in the non-traditional sense. He showed it by working all the time, making sure there was more than enough money so the family would never want for anything. Warmth, however, was not his thing. He preferred handshakes over hugs and emails over phone calls. Jack was used to this.

"Can you talk?," Jack asked hopefully.

"Can it wait?," his father replied.

"Sure, no problem. I have some calls to make anyway." Jack retreated back to his room and sat on the edge of the bed. His father was one of the main reasons Jack became a runner in high school. It got him out of the house every day, sometimes twice a day, and kept him out for the better part of the day. Not that his father was ever home. He was always working the next deal. Nor did he ever come to any of Jack's races. Too busy. Jack's teammates were his surrogate family and most of his best memories from his youth came from being part of the team.

"How's Emma?" Jack's thoughts were interrupted by his father standing in the doorway.

"She's good," Jack said, surprised. "She'll be here tomorrow, with Amy."

"Is there something I should know?"

"Nope. They were just jealous of my time in New York, so they decided to join me."

"Have you found a new specialist for them?"

"I'm working on it. I hope to find something while they're here." In more ways than one, Jack thought.

"Let me know if you need any help. And I'd like us all to have dinner together tomorrow night. It would make your mother happy."

"Sure, Dad. I'll see what I can do."

Chapter 47

The bed that Cheryl had been sleeping on fell somewhere between an army cot and a wooden plank. The FBI's protective custody offered little in the way of comfort, but she was indeed being protected. They offered her accommodations off premises, but that would mean entering the witness protection program, and she was not ready for that. She could be relocated anywhere in the world, but she needed to finish what she and Jack started.

Unable to sleep, she stared into the darkness of the small office that doubled as her room for the night. When she was finally alone, she cried for a long time over Matt. She had hoped to cry herself to sleep, but that didn't happen. It didn't matter what Agent Lewis or anyone else said, she knew his death was her fault. She got Matt into this and he was dead because of it. And now Jack was missing. He had never missed a scheduled call, and, as of a few hours ago, he still hadn't updated his contact number in the spreadsheet. There was also no answer on his home phone.

Her mind reeled and, despite her exhaustion, sleep evaded her. Was Jack alive? Did he still have Dr. Holst's

168

drive, or had it fallen into AstaGen's hands? Why did Matt send a cellphone to Agent Lewis? What was on it? The questions kept coming, but she had no answers. She closed her eyes and tried to quiet her mind.

As she slowly began to relax, the door to her room opened and light came streaming in. Cheryl shielded her eyes as she tried to adjust to the sudden brightness. Agent Lewis was standing in the doorway. "Cheryl, it's Jack! Get up!"

Cheryl leapt out of bed and raced after Agent Lewis. She followed her down the hall into a conference room with a large table, chairs all around, and a speakerphone in the middle. Cheryl looked around. She and Agent Lewis were the only ones in the room.

"What is it?," she said to Agent Lewis.

"Cheryl? Is that you?," came Jack's voice from the speakerphone.

The sound of his voice made her heart leap. She put her hands on the table and leaned in towards the speakerphone. "Jack! Thank God! Are you ok? Where are you?!"

"I'm fine, though I'd rather not say where I am right now. I'm sure you understand. I was worried about you! I saw your note on the spreadsheet and called as soon as I could. Sorry it wasn't sooner, I've been kinda busy. You ok?"

"Yeah. I've been holed up here for a couple of days. Safe as could be."

"What's going on? How did the FBI get involved, and what do they want with you?" Jack wasn't sure if it was a good thing or a bad thing, but he figured sooner or later the FBI would be involved. He had expected later.

"Jack, this is Special Agent Lewis. We really need to talk to you, in person. I can explain everything. How soon can you be here?"

"Not so fast, Agent Lewis. There are still a few things that need to be resolved before I show up there. I'd like to speak to Cheryl privately, if you don't mind."

"I don't know what you're up to, Jack, but that's not a good idea. By now you must know people are after you. If you want to nail AstaGen, we need you. Don't go putting yourself at risk. Why don't you let the FBI take over? Come in. And bring Dr. Holst's drive with you."

"Thank you for your concern. I'd like to speak with Cheryl, please."

Agent Lewis looked at Cheryl, and then walked out of the conference room, closing the door behind her.

"She's gone," Cheryl said. "It's just us."

"Is it?," Jack asked. "You sure no one is listening in?"

"No. But what choice do we have?"

"I suppose," Jack conceded. "Tell me what's been happening."

Cheryl told him about being snatched up by the FBI, the letter from Matt, her long Q&A session with Agent Lewis, and about Matt's death.

"Oh, Cheryl, I'm so sorry," Jack offered. "This is unbelievable."

"Yeah," she agreed. She told him about the cell phone Matt had delivered to Agent Lewis.

"What's on it?," Jack asked, excited.

"We don't know yet. The FBI is working on it."

"Are you sure we should trust them, Cheryl? What do you know about this Agent Lewis?"

"I've thought a lot about that since I got here. Here's what I've decided... Matt picked Agent Lewis consciously. He sent her the letter and then the cell phone. If he trusted her, I think we should too."

"Ok," Jack agreed, somewhat reluctantly.

"What's been going on with you? What have you been up to?"

Jack told her everything that happened over the last couple of days. Cheryl gasped when she heard about the attack on Amy and Emma. "Oh my God," she said aloud. "Are they ok?"

"Yeah. They were both pretty shaken up. Amy has some bruises on her throat, and Emma has a small cut on her neck. But overall, they're not hurt."

"Thank God," Cheryl said. She was concerned to hear they were coming to New York later today. "Is this really the safest place for them, Jack?"

"I can't leave them unprotected back home. I need them here, and to know they're safe." He gave her a quick rundown of the security features at the Turner's apartment building, and Cheryl agreed that would be the safest place for them.

He told her about the drone that had been tracking him, how he managed to evade it, and about the phones. Once they were caught up, Jack got down to business. "Cheryl, listen. Dr. Holst's drive is encrypted with some of the most state of the art software money can buy. I have no idea how to get into this thing without a password. I called Dr. Bosh, he doesn't know it. Couldn't even offer up a clue. Same with Mrs. Holst. She didn't even know he had a backup drive. I think it might be back in his office somewhere."

"You can't go back there, Jack. They'll be looking for you. They're probably watching the place right now. Maybe they have been all along."

"I don't see what choice I have, but I'm open to suggestions."

There was a long pause before Cheryl said, "Maybe the FBI can break into it. They must have teams of nerds who do this kind of stuff for a living, right?"

"Maybe," Jack said. "But if we put this into the hands of the FBI, Cheryl, we may never see it again. If it disappears or gets accidentally erased, everything we've done, all the risks we've taken, Matt's death... it will all be for nothing. No, I need to hang on to it, at least for a while. You ok with that?"

"Yeah, I am," Cheryl said.

"Listen, I gotta run. I need get a few hours of sleep before I pick up my girls at the airport. You should really try to get some rest, too."

"I'm trying, believe me."

"Tell Agent Lewis I appreciate her offer, and that I said thanks, but no thanks."

"Be careful, Jack. Please. And call me before you go anywhere near Dr. Holst's office. Maybe the FBI can offer surveillance, or even backup...?"

"I don't know if I could trust them, Cheryl. Agent Lewis may be ok, but there's no telling who might be in AstaGen's pocket. The fewer people we trust, the safer we'll be."

"Ok. Take care."

"Thanks. I'll talk to you soon."

Chapter 48

Getting to the airport in New York was always an adventure, and Jack was not excited about the drive later this morning. He was, however, excited about having Amy and Emma where he could keep an eye on them. Fortunately, his parents had a car service on retainer and with one simple call, there would be a town car waiting for him downstairs in a matter of minutes.

Jack had a few hours of restless sleep before giving up and going for a run. He heard the familiar hum above him, but he refused to look up. He ran a ten mile loop and was nearly back to the apartment building when the car hit him. It came out of the alley without the appearance of even trying to slow down. Jack saw it coming at the last second and he managed to speed up and lunge forward to avoid a direct hit. But his back leg was struck, and it spun him around and he fell hard to the ground. The car screeched to a halt next to him. The driver got out and came around the car to where Jack was lying. He grabbed Jack by the shirt and began dragging him towards the car.

"Hey!," someone shouted, but from where, Jack couldn't be sure. He was dizzy and disoriented, and his vision was a little fuzzy. At the sound of the voice, the driver released his grip on Jack. He leaned in close to his face and said, "This isn't over, Jack. We have some things we need to discuss. See you soon." And with that, he hurried around the car, got in and sped off.

Jack, still laying on the pavement, heard footsteps coming quickly from behind his head. "Are you ok, Mr. Turner?" Strong hands were suddenly under his shoulders, lifting him up. Jack took a moment to steady himself on his feet. His left leg was killing him, and when he tried to put weight on it, the pain shot like lightning all the way up to his hip.

"Tommy, how many times have I asked you to call me Jack?," he said, leaning against him. "Thanks for coming along when you did."

"It's no problem," Tommy replied.

Tommy Mitchell was one of the daytime doorman/security guards for the his parents' building. He was six-foot-five, weighed 260 pounds, and was carved from granite and stone. He would have intimidated just about anyone. As a former Navy Seal who had seen more than his share of action, Tommy relished the thought of doing nothing and getting paid for it. That's how he viewed his work in the building. All the residents were extremely wealthy, so they prided themselves on being protected by former Marines, Navy Seals, Army Rangers, and the like. As such, the position paid well, and Tommy loved his work.

Jack had known him for years. They regularly exchanged pleasantries, and would often talk sports when they saw each other. They became friends over time and often shared a beer or two at a local bar during football season. Tommy was a diehard New York Jets fan, and Jack never missed an opportunity to rib him about it. "Well, at least you're not a Browns fan," Jack would say. Tommy was the kind of guy that took it in stride, it was all in good fun. But he was also the kind of guy you didn't want to cross. Jack made sure to always stay on his good side. Twice, when an argument hadn't been going his way, Tommy opened his coat just enough for Jack to see one of the guns he carried. He did so with a big grin on his face, as if to say, "I win." Jack put his hands up in surrender, and they both laughed.

"Who was that guy?," Tommy asked.

"I don't think I've seen him before. But I was pretty woozy there for a minute. I didn't recognize the voice, but it looked like he had a pretty nasty scar under his eye."

"From the accident just now?"

"No, I don't think so." Jack knew this wasn't an accident, but Tommy didn't need to know the details. "Looked like it had been there for a while."

"Should I call an ambulance, Mr. Turner? Or the police?"

"It's Jack. And no. Help me get upstairs and then I can better assess the damage."

"You got it, Mr. Turner," he said with a smirk. He refused to call him Jack, mainly because Jack wanted him to. It was just another part of their little game.

"Hey, did you know the Jets are the only team in NFL history to lose during a bye week?" Jack teased.

"Maybe we should see how you manage on your own the rest of the way," Tommy said, starting to let go.

"No no!" Jack said, as he clung to Tommy's large frame. "Sorry," he said with a chuckle.

When they got back to the building, Tommy helped Jack navigate the gauntlet of security measures en route back up to the penthouse apartment.

When the elevator door opened, Jack said, "Thanks, Tommy. I got it from here."

"You sure?," Tommy asked. "That leg doesn't look so good. Can you even put weight on it?"

Jack took his arm from around Tommy and tried to stand. Using the wall for support, he managed to hobble over to the front door. Leaning his shoulder against the wall, he managed to extricate the key from his pocket and let himself in.

"Thanks again, Tommy. I really appreciate it."

"My pleasure, Mr. Turner," he said. Tommy backed into the elevator, pushed a button, and the doors closed between them.

Jack tried to keep the mood light with Tommy, but the truth was, he was in agony. His leg was throbbing in pain, and getting worse by the minute. He didn't even want to think about the guy who just tried to run him over.

For all ten miles of his run, Jack heard the intermittent buzzing of the drone. He did not acknowledge its presence, but he knew it was there. He never really considered that someone else might be watching or following him. What did he mean *'We have some things we need to discuss'*, Jack wondered. If they knew about the drive, and that he had it, they'd want it. They had no way of knowing it was encrypted, or that Jack hadn't seen its contents. They don't know what's on it, but they don't know Jack doesn't either, he thought. If they think he's seen information that could be harmful to AstaGen or EBF-14, his life was over. He needed to get into the drive now more than ever.

Chapter 49

"He's making a mistake."

"You have to understand his position. Our position. Dr. Holst was murdered..." Cheryl held up her hand as Agent Lewis started to interrupt. "You don't have to believe that right now, but we know it's true. Matt is dead. Jack's wife and daughter were attacked and threatened. And now Jack has been run over by a car."

Jack called shortly after the 'accident' to let Cheryl, and anyone who cared at the FBI, know that he was ok, but that the heat was slowly being turned up.

"If this is what we think it is," Cheryl continued, "there's no telling who's involved or who we can trust. The fewer people we have to deal with, the better."

"Cheryl, listen to me. If you're right about all of this, Jack doesn't stand a chance out there by himself. If AstaGen is really behind this, they have unlimited resources and will do whatever it takes to end things in their favor. I hope you're starting to see that. Jack got lucky this morning. But they'll be back. And now he's bringing his family into it. They're sitting ducks in that apartment, I don't care how good he says the security is. How long do you expect his luck to hold out?!" The volume of Agent Lewis's voice was slowly increasing as she spoke, and when she finished, she pounded a hand on the table to drive her point home.

"Then why don't you do something about it?!," Cheryl shouted back. "Get off your asses and do something! Start looking into what we've been telling you. Have someone out there protecting Jack. Stop lecturing us and start helping!"

Agent Lewis replied calmly, "We already talked about this, Cheryl. I can't open an investigation into one of the largest drug companies in the world without any evidence. All I have right now is a suspicion of felonious activities without any proof."

"Goddammit, why did you snatch me up and bring me here if you didn't have any intention of helping us!?"

"I've been helping you since the moment you got here, Cheryl. In fact, I'm helping you right now. I'm protecting you from whoever's out there trying to kill you. I'm telling you that Jack needs to get in here, with the drive, as soon as possible. And I'm telling you we need to find something concrete on AstaGen so we can nail the bastards. Maybe it's on that drive, maybe not. But if Jack gets killed or that drive is lost, this whole thing is over before it ever really started.

Cheryl put her elbows on the table and hands on her head. She let out a frustrated sigh before saying, "This is ridiculous. You know something is going on here. After all that's happened, there must be something you can do. What more do you need?"

"Cheryl, just as you've asked me to understand your position, you have to understand mine. I answer to people. I can't just use the FBI's resources whenever I want. I need something to go on. Something more than assumptions and guesswork."

Agent Lewis's cellphone vibrated loudly in its case. She removed it from the holster on her belt and looked at the screen.

"It's a text from Jack," she said. Cheryl jumped out of her seat and ran over to look at the screen. She no longer had a phone, so Jack was instructed to call or text Agent Lewis directly if anything happened.

It read: **I was a little woozy, so I forgot to mention this earlier. The lunatic who tried to run me down this morning had a pretty nasty scar under his right eye. That mean anything to you?**

"Oh shit!," said Cheryl.

"What?," Agent Lewis asked. "You know who it is?"

Cheryl turned and began pacing the room. "It's him."

"Him who?"

"The last time I saw Matt, we were talking in the stairwell at the Journal. We thought we were alone. But it turned out someone was listening. Someone just above us on the stairs. He had been following Matt, monitoring his movements. It was a guy with a scar under his right eye."

"How do you know that?"

"I have it on video."

Chapter 50

If AstaGen doesn't kill me, Amy will, Jack thought. He stood, leaning against the wall, and looked at himself in the full-length mirror. He spent the last twenty minutes soaking in an ice bath and was now trying to assess the damage.

Rosie, the Turner's private chef, was in charge of keeping the kitchen stocked and food prepared. She was working on her weekly grocery list when she saw Jack stumble in. She helped him get to the edge of the tub, brought him some of his mother's painkillers, and shuttled back and forth from the kitchen until there was enough ice in the tub for Jack to submerge his lower half. The last ice bath he had was in college, and he was quickly reminded of how much he hated them.

Looking in the mirror, Jack convinced himself that he had avoided serious injury. No broken bones, no torn ligaments. Just a massive bruise on his left thigh where the car hit and some cuts and scrapes from where he hit the ground. His head was clear despite the painkillers, so he seemed to have avoided a concussion as well. But he was having a lot of trouble putting weight on his leg without grimacing in pain, and he was walking with a severe limp. He couldn't even imagine trying to run on it.

He dressed slowly and carefully into loose fitting clothes. He still had a little time before he had to pick up Amy and Emma from the airport. He flirted with the idea of taking a nap, but he wasn't sure he'd be able to move once he woke up. He thought it best to keep moving, as painful as it was. He limped slowly around the bed to the window that overlooked the park, and stared off into the distance.

The image of the car coming out of nowhere flashed in his mind. Hitting the ground hard. Being dragged across the pavement. His assailant right in his face, threatening to return. And the scar. Jack wondered what might have happened if his attacker got him to the car before Tommy showed up. His leg throbbed and the pain reminded him just how serious this was and what they were risking. The guy with the scar under his eye would most certainly be back, and probably soon. Maybe next time, there would be more of them.

Jack needed to know what was on Dr. Holst's drive. But going out alone, now hobbled, didn't seem like a great idea. So a trip to Dr. Holst's office to have a scavenger hunt for the password was out of the question. No one he'd spoken to had any idea about the password, and Jack had no clue where to look for it. That left just one option.

He took out one of his burner phones and dialed the number for the car service. He arranged for a town car to take him to the airport, and they assured him they would be downstairs at the curb in fifteen minutes. Whoever had been monitoring his calls knew Amy and Emma were arriving today, but they didn't know when. Or maybe they did. But Jack didn't feel like cluing them in, so he used a burner phone.

He collected his things, then slowly limped his way to the front door. Ignoring Rosie's objections, he left the apartment and closed the door as she continued to protest. The elevator ride down was smooth, and when the doors opened onto the foyer, Tommy was standing there, arms folded, waiting for him. He'd seen Jack coming down in the elevator on the surveillance monitor and was at the door before Jack could step out.

"Really?," Tommy said. "I figured you'd be in bed for a week."

"I wish. I need to pick up the girls from the airport."

"Good luck explaining this one," Tommy said, gesturing to Jack's leg.

"Yeah, I know. There's going to be a lot of explaining happening today. I'm not excited about it."

Tommy laughed. He did not envy Jack right now.

"Hey Tommy, you carrying today?"

"Always," Tommy said. "Why?"

"Take a ride with me, would you?"

"Where? To the airport?"

"Yeah. I could use the company. Plus I need to talk to you about something." Jack failed to mention he also liked the idea of having an armed escort with him.

Tommy looked over his shoulder towards the security desk. "Hey Mike, think you can handle things by yourself for a little while? Mr. Turner needs some help."

"Yeah, I think I can manage." Mike was a former Army Ranger who had been working security in the building for more than ten years. He was part of Bravo Company, which played a role in Operation Desert Storm, as well as Operation Gothic Serpent, the infamous "Black Hawk Down" incident in Somalia. He went into corporate security after he got out, then the private sector, before he ultimately settled down here. Jack was pretty sure Mike could 'handle things' by himself just fine. He was ten years older than Tommy, but still incredibly fit and equally menacing when necessary.

Tommy turned back to Jack and said, "Let's go."

"Let me lean on you a little, ok?," Jack said. "Just until we get to the car."

Tommy practically carried Jack across the foyer. "A little, huh?," Tommy teased. "We should really get you some crutches," Tommy said, only half joking.

The foot on Jack's injured leg never touched the ground as he hopped on his good leg and clung to Tommy's substantial frame. "Maybe we can get through today without any Jets jokes," Tommy said hopefully.

"I can't promise anything," Jack said with a smirk.

Tommy helped load Jack into the back of the waiting Town Car, walked around to the other side and got in. Jack was still settling himself, trying to find a comfortable position when Tommy sat down and closed the door. As the car pulled away from the curb, Tommy asked, "What's going on, Mr. Turner?."

Jack painfully shifted himself in his seat so he could look at Tommy. "You're really not going to call me Jack, are you?"

"Not as long as I'm an employee at the Tower, I'm not."

"The Tower?," Jack asked.

"Yeah, that's what we, me and the other security guards, call it. You know, like the Ivory Tower?"

"I get it," Jack said. "Do the residents know you call it that?"

"A couple. Sometimes we accidentally let it slip. But it's cool. No one seems to mind. So what did you want to talk to me about?"

Jack took a breath. Tommy was the first person outside of a very tight circle that was about to learn what Jack knew. "I'm going to tell you a story, Tommy. Before I begin, know that I'm counting on your complete discretion. But for now, I just need you to listen. If you have any questions along the way, just ask, ok?"

"Fair enough," Tommy said.

Jack spelled it all out for him. He told him about the cancer, his family, Cheryl's, the others. He told him about EBF-14 and AstaGen, and what they knew about both. He told him about Nate's death, and the seizures other kids were suffering. He told him about the murder of Dr. Holst and Matt Cunningham, the attack on Amy and Emma. He told him about the drone that had been following him and, most recently, nearly getting run over by a car. Jack talked for the entire ride to the airport, trying not to leave out any details. He needed Tommy to understand the importance of what he was about to ask.

"Jesus Christ," Tommy said. The look on his face told Jack he was still trying to absorb it all. "No wonder you asked if I was carrying today."

185

Jack nodded with a grim look on his face.

"But how is this possible?," Tommy asked.

"It's not only possible, it's happening. Now we just have to prove it."

"How are you going to do that?," Tommy asked incredulously.

"That's where you come in. I hope."

"How can I help?" Tommy asked, sitting up. Jack was counting on Tommy's military-bred need to serve, and he didn't disappoint.

Jack told him about the drive he had retrieved from Dr. Holst's car, and what he believed he would find on it. He told him about the advanced level of encryption and the missing password. Tommy nodded as Jack spoke.

"You and the other security guards have all served in elite military units. I may be grasping at straws here, but I'm hoping one of you, in all your combined years of military experience, knows someone that would be considered a computer expert. Someone who has expertise in breaking into electronic devices. Someone who can help me get into that drive."

"A hacker," Tommy summarized nicely.

"Exactly."

They were pulling up to the curb at JFK when Tommy said with a grin, "I might know someone like that."

Chapter 51

"Tell me about the video," Agent Lewis said. "How did you get it?"

Cheryl was excited, mainly because something finally got Agent Lewis excited. "I flirted with the security guard in my office building and convinced him to give me a copy of the surveillance video from the stairwell. He copied it onto a flash drive for me. It's the same guy that ran Jack down. It has to be. He's probably also the one that killed Dr. Holst. Maybe Matt too."

"Cheryl, calm down. Let's not get ahead of ourselves. We don't know who this guy is, or if it's even the same guy on the video."

"You really can't see what's happening here, can you?"

"I go by the book, Cheryl. It isn't always popular, but I believe in doing things correctly, not quickly, and getting things right the first time. I didn't get where I am by playing things fast and loose. I can't build a case on hunches and gut feelings. Let's see the video. Where is it?"

Cheryl thought about what Jack had said about who to trust. And at first she was reluctant to tell Agent Lewis where the video was. But then she thought about Matt. He would have wanted her to trust Agent Lewis. Like she'd told Jack, if Matt trusted her, they should too.

"It's on a flash drive hidden in my apartment."

Agent Lewis sighed. "Dammit."

"I wasn't sure if it was safe to keep it with me," Cheryl went on. "I can go get it and be back here in under an hour. Besides, I could really use some clothes and a few other personal things," she said, letting her excitement come through.

"I was really hoping the video was on your phone, or with you here somewhere." She looked Cheryl in the eyes. "You can't go to your apartment, Cheryl. There's no question it's being watched, and the fact that you haven't been back there in a few days has no doubt raised suspicion as to your whereabouts. It's too dangerous. If they see you, they'll grab you. They'll want to know where you've been, who you've been talking to... whatever they can. I can't let you do it."

"Well someone has to," Cheryl said, deflated. "We need that thumb drive so you can identify this guy. Maybe he has a record and your computers can tell you who he is. Maybe Jack can confirm it's the same guy that tried to run him over. Maybe Jack's wife can tell you if it's the same guy that grabbed her and held a knife to her daughter's throat. Maybe this guy can confirm everything we've been telling you from the start," Cheryl said, sounding indignant.

"That's a lot of 'maybes', Cheryl. I don't even leave my desk for 'maybe'. But you're right, we need that thumb drive." Agent Lewis pulled out a chair at the conference table and sat down. Cheryl did the same.

"So send one of your agents over. I'll tell him, or her, exactly where the flash drive is and they can bring it back here."

"I can't do that, Cheryl."

"WHY?!," Cheryl shouted in frustration. She slammed both palms against the table and stood up. "Is this how every government agency operates?! No wonder we never get anything done in this country!"

Agent Lewis slowly stood and looked at Cheryl. Very calmly, she said, "Cheryl, right now, whoever is looking for you has no idea where you are. You've completely dropped off the grid. They don't know where you are, who you're with, or what you know. That's a win for us. The moment I send an agent to your apartment, they're going to know exactly where you are and who you're with. You think they're after Jack now? Wait until they think the FBI is involved. They'll put everyone they have on finding him."

"Oh," Cheryl said.

"Not only that, but I can't endanger one of my agents for an investigation that doesn't exist yet. We're still operating on speculation, theory, and now 'maybes'."

A gentle rap on the glass door of the conference room startled them. There was a guy standing just outside the door with a cellphone in his hand. He wasn't dressed like a typical agent. No dark suit, no well manicured hairdo. He looked more like he just came back from the beach. He had unruly blond hair, two or three days of facial hair, and was wearing a Green Day t-shirt, cargo shorts, and flip flops.

"Who is that?," Cheryl asked softly.

"One of our tech guys, Lonnie. He's been working on Matt's phone."

Agent Lewis waved him in. He opened the door half way, leaned in, and said, "Sorry to interrupt. I just finished going through Mr. Cunningham's cell phone. You're going to want to see this."

Chapter 52

"What happened to you?!," Amy asked as she wrapped her arms around Jack and leaned in for a kiss.

Escorted by Tommy, Jack had hobbled up to the gate where arriving passengers stream into the main terminal, trying his best not to look like he was in agony. He failed miserably. When the girls came through, Amy immediately gave him an odd look when she saw him limping. Emma, on the other hand, charged him at full speed. She practically knocked him down, but with a little help from Tommy, he managed to keep his balance, and hugged Emma tight.

"Hi Dad!," she said excitedly.

"Hi Pumpkin! Welcome to New York! I'm so glad you're here!"

"Me too! Mom and I were talking on the plane about all the stuff we want to do while we're here. I made a list. Wanna see it?!"

Jack and Tommy exchanged furtive glances, both knowing they wouldn't be doing any of the things on that list.

"Oh yeah?!," Jack said, feigning excitement. "I've got some stuff for us to do, too!"

"Like what?!," Emma said, genuinely excited.

"Uh uh, not now. It's a surprise," Jack said with a wink.

"Ok!" Emma said. She loved surprises.

Jack turned back to Amy and saw something behind her he wasn't expecting. Bobby Keeler leisurely strolling through the arrivals gate.

"I didn't want to spoil the reunion," he said with smile.

"What the hell are you doing here?," Jack asked, surprised.

"I needed a vacation. Besides, I figured you could use all the help you can get."

Jack glanced over at Amy and she returned his gaze with a look that said 'you have a lot of explaining to do'. But she let it go for now, not really sure who knew what.

"So?," Amy asked with a slight sideways bend to look at his legs.

"It's nothing," Jack said. "Hurt myself on a run this morning. No broken bones. Just a bruise."

"Hurt yourself on a run, huh?." Amy knew there was more to the story, but again she didn't feel like pushing for details right now, especially in front of Emma.

Jack nodded, not knowing what else to say.

"Hi Tommy," Amy said. "How are you?"

"I'm great, Mrs. Turner. Thanks for asking."

"Please, call me Amy."

"Don't bother," Jack said.

"What brings you here, Tommy? Did my husband drag you to the airport just to keep him company?." Amy looked at Jack again, the story getting richer with each passing moment.

"Pretty much. Plus, I didn't want him to fall down and not be able to get up. He's pretty old, you know."

Amy and Emma both laughed. Tommy joked, but his head had been on a swivel looking for any kind of trouble coming their way. Neither he nor Jack expected any in such a crowded place, but anything was possible.

"Ha ha, very funny," Jack said. "Can we go?"

As they walked to the car, Bobby stole a quick moment to whisper in Jack's ear. "The only way I could keep an eye on them was to come with them."

"Thanks Bobby," Jack whispered back with a nod.

The car was waiting for them right where they left it. The driver helped Amy and Emma with their bags, while Bobby held onto his backpack. Tommy sat in the front seat, while Bobby and the Turners sat in the back, with Emma on Jack's lap. The ride back was largely spent listening to Emma regale them with tales of their travel day. She loved to travel. She made a game of it, and Amy would play along. How many traffic lights would they hit on the way to the airport? How long it would take to get through security? How many people would get on the plane before them? How many times would the Captain turn on the seat belt sign? She and Amy would guess, and whoever came closest would win.

The highlight of the day happened at Cinnabon. Amy let Emma get a small cinnamon roll with the white frosting. Everything in moderation, Amy always said, and this was a special treat for a fun day. Emma spent a good ten minutes describing how it looked, smelled and tasted, and by the time she was done, everyone in the car wanted one.

As they salivated with the thought of a hot cinnamon roll, the car pulled up to the front of the Tower. The driver came around to open the door, while Mike was at the front door of the building, waiting for them. Jack painfully extricated himself from the car after Bobby, Amy and Emma had gotten out. Tommy was standing by the car door, close to the Turners, instinctively protecting them. They made their way to the front door of the building, entered without incident, and Mike closed and locked the door behind them. Jack quietly breathed a sigh of relief.

"Thanks for coming along for the ride and keeping me company, Tommy," Jack said.

"Not a problem at all, Mr. Turner."

"It's Jack," he said again, hopelessly. "And don't forget to look into that thing we spoke about earlier today."

"I'm on it," Tommy said as he rejoined Mike behind the security desk.

"Thanks, Tommy," Amy said. "Hey Mike."

"How are you, Mrs. Turner?," Mike replied.

"Tired. But happy to be here." She pressed her thumb to the elevator call button. The red light appeared, scanned her thumbprint, turned green, and dinged. "We'll see you guys later."

"Have a good afternoon," Tommy said.

"Bye!," Emma said with a wave.

The four of them got in the elevator, and Jack produced his access key card. Emma took it from him, inserted it into the slot and pressed the button for the penthouse. When the elevator stopped, they went inside and locked the door behind them. Emma sprinted to her room, rolling her pink suitcase behind her. Amy shouted after her. "Emma, unpack your bag, and then read your book for a little while. Daddy and I are going to talk for a bit, and then we can figure out what we're going to eat for dinner, ok?"

"Ok!," she shouted back.

Amy rolled her bag into their room, Jack limping behind her, Bobby bringing up the rear. She looked at Bobby, then back to Jack. "It's ok, he knows," Jack said.

She closed the door, then immediately wheeled around on Jack and began firing off questions.

"What the hell is going on, Jack? Why are we here? Why did Bobby need to come? What in the world happened to your leg? And what is Tommy looking into for you?"

"Sit down. It's a long story."

194

Chapter 53

Matt's face appeared on the screen. He seemed to be recording in a closet, or some other nondescript room. Clearly he didn't want to offer any clues as to where he was when he shot the video. Cheryl sat next to Agent Lewis in what the FBI called a 'viewing room'. It was not much more than a conference room with blacked out windows and more comfortable chairs. At the far end of the table, the same stenographer from Cheryl's interview was standing by, fingers hovering over her keyboard, ready to take notes. Lonnie, the tech guy, was also in the room to run the video.

"Hi Agent Lewis. My name is Matt Cunningham," the video began. Cheryl's eyes filled with tears when she saw his face. "Hopefully you received my letter. If you're watching this video, you know what it means. Cheryl, I'm sorry I couldn't be there to help you see this through. Or to take you out for that drink," he said with a wink. The tears that had pooled in her eyes now ran down her face.

"I am a reporter for the New York Journal," he continued. "Not long ago, I began looking into the pharmaceutical company AstaGen, and more specifically their cancer drug, EBF-14. This drug moved through clinical trials faster than any drug in history and was unanimously approved by the FDA in less than eighteen months. EBF-14 demonstrated a cure rate of 95% during clinical trials, which is unheard of. That statistic alone piqued my curiosity. But then I learned that it's only effective on one

195

specific type of cancer, Omnicarcinos, a cancer that didn't even exist a few years ago. Where did it come from? And how did AstaGen produce such an effective drug so quickly after its discovery?"

Cheryl looked at Agent Lewis for any kind of reaction, but she just watched and listened. Much of what she was hearing, Cheryl had told her already, but it was nice for her to hear someone else saying it for a change.

"I reached out to a prominent oncologist in the New York area, hoping to get the answers to those questions. Dr. William Holst was one of the foremost cancer experts in the country, and, as it turns out, one of the largest prescribers of EBF-14."

Cheryl glanced at Agent Lewis. Still nothing.

"I spoke to Dr. Holst a number of times. He was very personable over the phone and seemed eager to help with my research for the article. We had arranged to get together, and he said he was willing to share some things he learned about both EBF-14 and AstaGen. Unfortunately, he was found dead at his desk the same day we were scheduled to meet. His death was declared a suicide, but that's a lie. I can't prove that yet, but I would encourage you to speak to the medical examiner that received his body. There should have been a report, and any unusual findings would have triggered an investigation. There hasn't been one."

Agent Lewis turned to the stenographer who was tapping away and said, "Find out who that is."

"Dr. Holst loved his work," Matt went on. "He lived for it, in fact. At the time of his death, he was the lead doctor in two different ongoing medical studies, he was scheduled to speak at two upcoming oncology seminars, and he and his wife had travel plans to Switzerland the following month. This was not a man who had been entertaining suicidal thoughts. This was a man who was caught speaking to a reporter and was silenced."

"Since the time I began asking questions about EBF-14 and AstaGen, my phones have been tapped, I've been followed, threatened, and attacked. And now, if you're watching this, probably killed. Several times, including when I first realized I was in danger, I saw the same guy following me. He was on the street outside the electronics store where I purchased my first burner phones, and he was outside my apartment the day before. He's about six feet tall, brown hair, well built, with an ugly scar under his right eye."

Cheryl gasped. "It's the same guy! It has to be." Lonnie paused the video upon Cheryl's interruption.

Agent Lewis gave a slow, thoughtful nod. It was hard to deny the possibility. How many guys with a scar under their right eye are running around New York?

"We need to see the surveillance video from the stairwell," she said to Cheryl. "Let's finish this, then we'll circle back to that and figure out how to get it here." She gestured to Lonnie and the video resumed.

"But prior to my untimely death," Matt went on, "I found a researcher at AstaGen who was willing to talk to me, off the record. His name is Jonathan Aker. Hopefully he's still alive."

Cheryl sat up tall in her chair. "Holy shit," she said.

Matt went on. "Jonathan has a bachelor's degree in biochemistry, a master's degree in molecular biology, and a doctorate in molecular genetics. He was the lead genetic engineer on the team that developed EBF-14."

Cheryl was now staring at Agent Lewis.

"Pause the video," Agent Lewis said, pointing at Lonnie, and Matt's face froze on the screen again. She picked up the phone in front of her and pushed a button. When someone finally answered, she said, "Agent Lane, I need you to find someone for me. His name is Jonathan Aker. He's an employee at AstaGen Pharmaceuticals. Find him right now and bring him in," and, without waiting for a reply, hung up. She nodded at Lonnie and the video resumed.

"His wife, Andrea, is pregnant," Matt continued, "but has been having complications. I won't bore you with the details, but Jonathan has been forced to miss a lot of work in order to take care of his wife and tend to his two-year-old son, Riley. This sort of absenteeism is frowned upon at AstaGen and Jonathan has been feeling the heat from his bosses. They revoked all of his paid time off, and told him they would start docking his pay for every further absence, regardless of cause. They have bumped him from projects he was the lead engineer on, removed his name from pending scientific journal publications, and even threatened to fire him. Needless to say, he's not feeling the love, and decided to talk."

There was a short pause for effect as Matt let those words sink in. He had found a whistle-blower at AstaGen. Someone who was ready to confirm what Cheryl and Jack has suspected all along. Cheryl's pulse raced, and Agent Lewis was definitely paying attention now.

"I met with Jonathan on two separate occasions. I had notes of those meetings, but they were stolen. My apartment and my car were both ransacked before I went on the run, and my computers, tablets, and notebooks were all taken. But Jonathan told me something interesting that you need to know. EBF-14 was genetically engineered to work only on people with a blood type of B. The reason the clinical trials were so successful was because all of the participants had the same blood type! Find Jonathan. He could be the key to everything."

"Son of a bitch!" Cheryl said. She leaned across Agent Lewis, grabbed for the phone in front of her, and began dialing. When it started ringing, she put the call on speaker and replaced the handset.

Agent Lewis looked at Lonnie, who paused the video again.

After three rings they heard, "Hello?." Brenda's voice was quiet, uneasy.

"Brenda, it's Cheryl. What blood type are you?"

"What number is this? Where are you calling from?"

"Not now. Your blood type..."

"B-negative, why?"

"What about Lily?"

"The same. Why, what's going on?"

"I'll call you back..."

Chapter 54

Jack told Amy everything, and he filled in the gaps for Bobby. Amy became angry as he spoke, and was furious when he was done. How could he put his family in danger like this, she asked. How could he not tell her what he was doing. How could he lie to her. Jack apologized repeatedly, and tried to make her understand why he did all those things. He was doing it *for* his family, he said, and for the other families that were slowly dying from Omnicarcinos. There were a lot more of them out there. When she heard the potential numbers and learned that AstaGen was deliberately targeting their disease with EBF-14, her anger with Jack lessened slightly, and her curiosity grew.

For over an hour, Jack talked. He answered all of their questions, endured Amy's punches on the arm every time he said something that renewed her anger, and told them what he was planning next. When she finally calmed down, they left the bedroom, collected Lily, and headed for the kitchen.

Jack's parents had come home from the respective offices just as Jack was finishing up his confession to Amy. They all ate dinner together in the dining room, and Jack's parents were thrilled to have them all under one roof again. Emma sat between Jack's parents, and Laura and Michael laughed at her jokes and listened intently as she told them about school, her friends, her favorite books, and anything else she wanted to talk about. There was no talk of cancer, medication, treatments, drones, evil corporations, the FBI or men with scars under their eyes. They all smiled and laughed and enjoyed the company and the food.

Rosie had made an incredible dinner of blackened grouper with buttered carrots, a beautiful Portobello mushroom stir-fry, roasted brussel sprouts with balsamic vinegar and honey, garlic roasted broccoli with parmesan cheese, four cheese mac and cheese (Emma's favorite), garlic bread, and a mixed field greens salad. Dessert was warm apple cobbler, vanilla ice cream, chocolate chip cookies, and a platter of fresh fruit and berries. They ate as a family for the first time in a long time, and Bobby was a gracious guest.

After dinner, Emma showered and went to bed. It was a long travel day that started early, and she was exhausted. The adults weren't far behind. The Turner's set Bobby up in one of several spare rooms, and he was asleep not long after Emma. Amy showered, got into bed, and read for a while. She was too tired to continue the conversation, but she made sure Jack knew 'this isn't over'. She went to sleep shortly before midnight.

Jack couldn't sleep. He was wired from the day and really wanted to go for a run. But with his leg still painfully black-and-blue, he knew that wasn't going to happen. Instead, he opted for a drive. He carefully limped his way across the apartment to the front door. Next to it was a wall-mounted cabinet which housed a dozen or more keys. He found the one he was looking for, and quietly slipped out, locking the door behind him. In the elevator, he pressed **G** and rode down past the lobby to the underground garage. When the door opened, the garage was quiet. Most of the residents of the Tower were his parents age or older, so he really wasn't expecting company at this hour.

His parents had eight parking spots reserved for them, and each of them was occupied. They had different cars for different uses, but Jack made a beeline for the red Ferrari F430 Spider. It was his dad's toy, but Jack loved to drive it every opportunity he got. He got in, fired it up, and smiled as he savored the sweet notes coming from the exhaust. He sank a little deeper into the soft beige leather of the seat underneath him. Jack believed every sports car should have a manual transmission. There was no better feeling than accelerating hard, hitting the clutch, throwing the stick from third gear to fourth, and stomping on the gas. But his father had opted for the paddle shifters for "ease of driving," he said. Normally Jack would gripe about it, but with his injured left leg, he wasn't sure how well he could work a clutch right now.

He pulled slowly out of the space, approached the security gate and hit the button on the remote. The gate lifted smoothly and quickly, and soon Jack was out on the streets. He was confident a drone couldn't keep up with a Ferrari, but he intended on checking his mirrors regularly to see if anyone was following him. The air was cool and crisp, and traffic was relatively light. With the top down, he drove several blocks east until he hit FDR Drive, then headed south along the water. He enjoyed the breeze and the view as he wrapped around the southern tip of Manhattan. He kept looking behind him and, so far, it didn't appear as though he was being followed. He drove at a reasonable speed for the most part, but when the opportunity presented itself, he hit the gas and enjoyed the powerful acceleration. He encountered traffic near Greenwich Village, and even more as he neared Times Square. Party's over, he thought to himself, and headed back.

When he returned to the Tower it was dark. There were no lights on in the whole building, and the gate to the garage wouldn't open. A total power outage. That's strange, Jack thought. The Tower had a series of backup generators that engaged instantly in the event of an outage. With many of the residents older, the board had voted unanimously on the generators to provide electricity, light and air conditioning, no matter the situation.

Jack reluctantly parked the Ferrari on the street and limped around to the front of the building. There was a small red light coming from inside the lobby, but it was otherwise dark. Jack went to put his key in the front door, but found it was already unlocked. This door is never unlocked, he thought, and his level of concern began to rise. He slowly opened the door and moved carefully across the foyer, the red light from the emergency exit sign the only thing lighting the way. As he moved past the security desk, he tripped over something big and fell hard to the floor.

From his belly, Jack turned his head to see what he tripped over. It was Lou, the night security guard, sprawled across the floor. His throat had been slit, and there was a large pool of blood under his head. Jack had talked to him a lot before or after one of his late night runs. He'd gotten to know and like him. Lou Embers was a former member of the MARSOC (Marine Corps Forces Special Operations Command). He had conducted countless special operations and was well trained to defend himself and others. There was no sneaking up on Lou, but his pistol was still in its holster. Whoever did this was equally well trained.

Jack reached into Lou's pocket and pulled out his cell phone. He quickly scrolled through the contacts until he found Tommy Mitchell's name. He wrote a quick text that said 'Tower 911 - Jack' and hit send. Jack pocketed the phone as he stood and began to make his way to the stairwell as quickly as possible. He had thought briefly about taking Lou's pistol, but he had very little experience with guns and decided better of it. The pain in his injured leg made every step of the climb up the stairs excruciating, and it got worse with each flight. After what seemed an eternity, Jack finally made it to the top floor. The door from the stairwell to the penthouse level normally required a key, but it sat wide open. Jack eased through the door and quietly made his way to the apartment. He was dripping with sweat, his leg was throbbing, and his heart was pounding from both exertion and fear. The front door of the apartment was also open, but only a few inches.

He pushed it open quietly, just enough to squeeze through, and moved slowly across the dark apartment. Light from the moon was streaming in through the windows and skylights, allowing him to see where he was going. His eyes scanned the apartment while his mind raced. Was the intruder still here? Was everyone ok? Where was Emma? Amy? He heard some scuffling sounds and made his way in that direction. As he got closer, the sounds appeared to be coming from his room. The one he'd left Amy sleeping in when he snuck out. The door was also ajar.

Jack slowly pushed it open. He took one step into the room, then gasped. The man with the scar under his eye was holding Amy and had a straight razor pressed against her throat. He wore blue surgical gloves, black track pants and a black t-shirt. His back was against the wall, next to a window which was now open.

Jack held out his hands, palms facing them. "Please," he said.

"The drive. Now," the man said. He pulled Amy a little tighter, held the razor a little closer. Amy groaned and a small stream of blood trickled down her neck.

"Okay!," Jack shouted. "Stop! Don't hurt her, please."

"Now," he said again. The cold in his voice sent a shiver down Jack's spine.

Jack moved slowly, hands still raised, over to the side of the bed closest to the door. He slowly kneeled down and reached his arm under the mattress. When he found what he was looking for, he began to retract his arm.

"If anything other than the drive comes out from under that mattress, the last thing your wife will see is her blood splattering all over this room. Do you understand?"

Jack nodded. "It's the drive. I swear."

He pulled his hand out slowly and held it up for inspection. He was holding up the sleek, black device. As he started to stand, the man said, "Don't get up. Stay right where you are."

Jack remained on his knees, holding the drive up in the air. He looked at Amy, tears welled in her eyes, pleading for help.

"Please," Jack said. "Take the drive. Just don't hurt her."

Suddenly there was a loud bang which came from the front of the apartment. It was the sound of someone kicking the front door open.

"The drive," the man said. "Toss it on the bed. Do it now."

Jack tossed the drive onto the bed near where they stood. The man with the scar threw Amy down hard onto the bed, scooped up the drive, and was out the window in a flash. His footsteps clanged on the fire escape as he quickly made his way down.

"Jack!," they heard from out in the apartment.

"In here!," Jack shouted, as he rushed to Amy.

Seconds later, Tommy was there, his pistol at the ready as he scanned the room.

"He's gone," Jack said.

Chapter 55

Dr. Linda Norton's office was located in midtown, near the East River. Her time was typically divided between the office and the morgue on the upper east side. Agent Lewis called ahead, so when she arrived at the office, they were expecting her.

"She's just finishing up a call," Dr. Norton's receptionist said. "She'll be right with you. Please, have a seat. Can I get you anything?"

"I'm fine, thank you," Agent Lewis said, and took a seat in the reception area. It was a small space, and understandably so. How many visitors did the office of the Chief Medical Examiner get? According to their website, '*the New York City Office of Chief Medical Examiner (OCME) conducts independent investigations using advanced forensic science in the service of families, communities and the criminal justice system. Our work provides answers for those affected by sudden and traumatic loss, and helps protect public health.*[1] Hopefully there were very few visitors to this office, she thought to herself.

A few days earlier, as the FBI began putting together a file on Dr. Norton, they noted that she had earned a bachelor's degree from NYU in biochemistry, a degree in medicine from Cornell, and a PhD in Cellular Biology and Pathology from the New York Medical College. She was appointed the Chief Medical Examiner of the City of New York in December 2008, and was widely considered one of the best in her field.

Agent Lewis took out her phone and began scrolling through her emails, when the inner office door opened, and Dr. Norton appeared. She was an attractive black woman in her mid-to-late fifties, her hair up in a bun. She wore a dark blue skirt, white blouse, and had a pair of reading glasses hanging around her neck.

"Sorry to keep you waiting," she said.

Agent Lewis stood, removed her ID and badge, and introduced herself. "Special Agent Donna Lewis, FBI. Thank you for taking the time to meet with me."

"Linda Norton. It's my pleasure."

They shook hands, then Dr. Norton gestured Agent Lewis inside her small office and followed after her. With the door closed behind them, Dr. Norton took her seat behind the desk, but only after Agent Lewis had been seated in one of only two other chairs facing the desk. The office reminded Agent Lewis of a college professor's. Small and cramped, with books and papers strewn about and stacked in piles. There were two small windows high on the wall that let light in, but could not be opened.

Sitting back in her chair, with her hands folded on her lap, Dr. Norton said, "So, how can I be of assistance to the FBI today?"

"I'd like to speak with you about an autopsy you performed several weeks ago. The deceased was a Dr. William Holst."

"Ah, yes. I was wondering when someone was going to come and see me about that."

Agent Lewis shifted slightly in her chair. "Why is that?"

"Well after I filed my report, I expected I'd be getting a call or someone would show up at my door. Usually there's an investigation, other doctors review my methods and findings, and then a panel determines if they concur with my original conclusion. Frankly, I'm surprised it's taken this long. But I'll be honest, I wasn't expecting the FBI."

"I'm sorry, I'm a little lost. Would you mind backing up a bit?"

"Sure. What's confusing you?"

"Everything, so far. You said after you filed your report, you were expecting a call or a visit. From who?"

"Well usually it's the NYPD, a detective of some sorts."

"I'm sorry, I don't understand. Why would the NYPD send a detective after you've conducted an autopsy?"

"It's standard operating procedure when it's determined that the deceased was determined to be the victim of a homicide."

Agent Lewis swallowed. "Excuse me?"

"Homicide. If it's determined..."

"No, I get it. Are we still talking about Dr. Holst?"

"Yes."

"What are you saying? He was the victim of a homicide?"

"Without question."

"Hang on a second. What?"

Dr. Norton was slightly taken aback by her reaction. "Forgive me," Dr. Norton said, "but why does it seem like this is new information to you? Are you not here because of my report?"

Agent Lewis shook her head. "No. I've never seen your report. I'm here on a wild goose chase. Or at least I thought I was." She leaned forward, and placed an elbow on the desk. "Would you mind telling me what you found during the autopsy that led you to believe it was a homicide? Please be specific, don't leave anything out."

"Of course," Dr. Norton said, now looking confused herself. She turned slightly to her right, pulled on her reading glasses, and began fishing through a stack of folders on her desk.

"Ah, here we go," she said, as she removed a folder from the pile and opened it. She looked at Agent Lewis and said, "These are my handwritten notes during and about the autopsy. I'll skip to the relevant findings, if that's alright with you."

Agent Lewis nodded.

"The deceased had a number of contusions on his arms consistent with grab marks. These are not uncommon," she said, looking up at Agent Lewis. "Their presence indicates he was grabbed forcibly by his arms and probably led by them." She returned to her notes. "There were numerous bruises on his torso, both front and back, consistent with blunt force trauma. He'd clearly been hit several times, either by an object or a fist. Based on the bruising and blood pooling, the injuries to both his arms and torso were fresh. They occurred on the day of his death."

Agent Lewis listened, mouth slightly agape. She couldn't believe what she was hearing.

"He also had compression marks on his face, primarily across his mouth. Normally this is consistent with suffocation, but in this case, the marks came from someone holding their hand firmly over his mouth as they forced the pills down his throat. He had enough Ativan in his stomach to kill him twice over."

"Ativan? The sedative?"

"Yes. The same pills that were found all over his desk when his body was discovered."

"Is there anything else?," Agent Lewis asked, still in disbelief.

"Yes," she said, looking back at her notes. "He also had hair on the back of his coat, which was determined to be his own. And small patches of hair were missing from the back of his head."

"They shaved his head?," Agent Lewis asked, incredulously.

"No. It appears they grabbed him by the hair and pulled his head back in order to force the pills into his mouth. During the struggle, some of his hair was pulled out."

Agent Lewis sat back in her chair, processing what she'd just heard. After a moment, she said, "Dr. Norton, with all respect, a lot of what you just described sounds very hypothetical. You're assuming the bruises on his arms and body are somehow connected to his death, right?"

"Yes."

"And you're assuming the marks on his mouth came from whoever force fed him pills?"

"Yes."

"And you're assuming they grabbed him by the hair, and some was pulled out?"

"Correct."

"Do you have anything you can prove, and not assume, other than the amount of pills that were in his stomach?"

Dr. Norton closed the folder, placed it back on the pile, removed her reading glasses, and looked at Agent Lewis. "With all due respect to you, Agent Lewis, I've been doing this job for a long time. I know what it looks like when someone is grabbed roughly by the arms. And I know what it looks like when someone is beaten. I know how to connect the very obvious dots in a case like this. Dr. Holst was murdered. He was forced to swallow those pills, and his death was staged to make it look like a suicide. There is no doubt in my mind."

"I appreciate that, Dr. Norton, I do. But in my line of work, I need something concrete if I'm going to open an investigation or arrest someone. What we have here, however, is simply your opinion. An expert opinion, yes, but it sounds like we can't prove any of it."

Dr. Norton nodded slightly, with a soft mm-hmm under her breath. "Well, as you know, my job is to determine the cause of death, in my 'expert opinion', and then write a report to that end. Which is exactly what I did. But for some reason, you're the first person to inquire about it, and you weren't even aware of it until I told you."

"So this is the first time you've written a report in which it was determined the deceased was the victim of a homicide without receiving a call or visit from an NYPD detective?"

"It is."

"Did you call anyone about it? Your superior, perhaps?"

"Agent Lewis, my superior is the Attorney General for the state of New York. As you might imagine, they have a rather full plate. And if you'd care to visit the morgue some time, you'll see that I do as well. I do a lot of post-mortems, and I write a lot of reports. Once they are submitted, I'm on to the next case."

"Where do you submit these reports?"

Dr. Norton gestured towards the computer sitting on the left side of her desk.

"I dictate them into specialized software that converts them to text and auto-populates the report."

"Would you mind showing me the report you submitted on Dr. Holst, and perhaps printing me a copy?"

"Legally, I can't do that without a warrant or subpoena. But I'm sure you already knew that," she said with a smirk.

"I'm more than happy to come back with a subpoena, Dr. Norton, but I was hoping you'd save me the time and effort," Agent Lewis said with a smile. "How about this," she continued. "Show me just the portion of the report where you state, conclusively, that Dr. Holst was, in fact, murdered. Then I'll come back another day with a subpoena and you can print me the entire report. Sound fair?"

Dr. Norton sat back in her chair, thinking. She looked at Agent Lewis and once again folded her hands in her lap.

"Give me something here, Dr. Norton," Agent Lewis said. "If what you say is true, the implications could be huge and potentially far reaching. You're telling me a prominent New York oncologist was murdered, you submitted a report from the Chief Medical Examiner's office, and no one followed up on it. No visits from the NYPD, no investigation opened, no arrests made. Surely you can see how bizarre this all is."

Agent Lewis waited a moment before going on. "Look, you only need to show me a few sentences from the report you submitted. No one will know, and I'll be back tomorrow with a subpoena to make everything nice and legal, ok?"

Dr. Norton sat motionless for a long moment before exhaling audibly. She leaned forward and began pecking away at her keyboard. After a minute, she said, "Well that's odd."

"What's that?," Agent Lewis asked.

"It's not here."

"What's not there?"

"The autopsy report. It's gone. It's like it was never here."

Chapter 56

Bobby barreled into the room, but stopped quickly in his tracks when Tommy whipped around and leveled his pistol at him.

"Whoa!," Bobby exclaimed.

Tommy lowered his pistol on seeing Bobby, but remained on high alert.

"Jesus," Bobby said. "What the hell is going on?," Bobby asked.

Jack gave Bobby a quick rundown of what just happened.

"Dammit. I should have been here," Bobby said.

"You'd be dead if you had been," Tommy said flatly.

"Is that right?," Bobby asked, in a challenging tone.

"Yes, it is," Tommy said, taking a step towards Bobby. "That's a special forces Marine lying down there in the lobby. He was a good friend and a very skilled fighter. Whoever killed him is well trained and would have made quick work of you," Tommy said, looking Bobby up and down, unimpressed.

"Alright," Jack said. "Let's all dial it down a notch."

Bobby turned to Amy, who was sitting next to Jack on the bed, holding a cloth to the cut on her neck. "Are you ok?," he asked.

"Sort of," she said.

"Did you get a look at the sonofabitch who did this?," he said looking at both Amy and Jack.

"A good look, yes," Jack said. "It was the same guy that tried to run me down. The guy with the scar under his eye."

"Wait, where's Emma?," Bobby asked, suddenly concerned.

"She's ok," Amy said. "She's sleeping. I just checked on her. She didn't hear anything." Turning to Jack, she said, "This has to stop."

"I know," Jack said. "Tommy, call the police. Find one of your buddies on the force, someone you can trust. Tell them what happened, and have them take care of Lou. But don't tell them anything about what happened up here. I'll give you our guy's description for them."

Tommy slowly nodded, his head down. He'd known Lou a long time and was both upset and angry at his death.

"What do we do now?," Bobby asked.

"I'm going to call the FBI," Jack said. Everyone in the room looked at him at once. He knew what they were all thinking. "I have no choice. We have to trust someone, and I can't keep putting you in danger," he said, looking at Amy. "They can protect you and Emma."

"What about you?," she said.

"I need to finish this. Once I'm in the hands of the FBI, they may not let me go. For my own protection, they'll say." He shifted towards her on the bed and put a hand on her leg. "I have to do this. For Nate. For you and Emma. For all the other families that lost someone they love."

"What about that thing he took? The drive?," Amy asked, hoping that would mean the end.

"Yeah," Bobby said. "Wasn't that key to this whole thing?"

"Don't worry about that right now," Jack said to them both. "Bobby, go lock the place up. And see if you can figure out how he got in."

"Ok," Bobby said, and reluctantly left the room.

Jack looked at Tommy, who stood motionless, arms folded, still staring at the floor.

"Tommy," Jack said. "Go ahead. Make the call, please."

Tommy nodded, pulled his cellphone from his pocket and went to find some privacy.

Alone in the room, Amy turned to Jack and said, "I don't like this. We need to stay together."

"I know. I don't like it either. But you'll be safer away from me right now. I thought you'd be safe here, but clearly I was wrong. You and Emma are all that matter to me."

"Then stop this!," she said sharply. "They have the drive. It's over. Let's go home."

"It's not over yet," Jack said, a little too harshly. "I'm sorry. We aren't safe at home either, Amy. Not from them, and not from whatever is making you, and Emma, and other people sick. All of this can't be for nothing. Nate's death can't be for nothing. We need to stop these people."

Amy sighed. She saw the look in Jack's eyes. She knew he would never stop looking for answers. He would never stop until he found out why Nate died, why she and Emma were sick, and who was responsible.

"Ok," she said. "For Nate. What's next?"

Chapter 57

The phone rang only once before the call connected.

"I have retrieved the drive."

"Has he seen what's on it."

"I don't think so. We would be reading about it in the papers by now if he had."

"Good. Destroy it."

"And the runner?"

"You didn't take care of him?"

"I was... interrupted."

There was a long silence, and then, "Leave him. We have surveillance on him twenty-four hours a day. Destroy the drive. We'll contact you if we need your services further."

"As you wish."

Chapter 58

"How are they doing this?! How have they figured out how to treat cancer by blood type?," Cheryl asked.

Agent Lewis shrugged. She'd returned from the medical examiner's office empty handed. No report, no proof, just more conjecture. Dr. Holst's body had been cremated at his wife's request, so reexamination was impossible. She sat at her desk, Cheryl across from her.

"I don't know, Cheryl. I'm beginning to think I don't know much of anything. I'm getting stonewalled at every turn, and every time I think I have something, it disappears right in front of my eyes. Let's talk about the surveillance video from your office building."

Before they could, there was a knock on the office door. "Come in!," she said, the frustration obvious in her voice.

The door opened and a female agent Cheryl had never seen before came in. "Agent Lewis, could I speak with you privately?," she asked, eyeing Cheryl.

"Agent Lane, is this regarding Jonathan Aker?"

"Yes, ma'am."

"Then you can say whatever you need to say in front of her," Agent Lewis said, gesturing to Cheryl. "She's a material witness in this case. If there is a case..."

"Yeah. About that..."

"What now?"

"Mona Aker, the wife of Jonathan Aker, and their son Riley are sitting in Conference Room A."

"Why do I not like the sound of this?," Agent Lewis said. She folded her hands and placed them on the desk. "Go on..."

"Unfortunately," Agent Lane reluctantly continued, "Mr. Aker was shot and killed during a home robbery last week."

"What?!," Cheryl blurted out.

"Goddammit!," Agent Lewis said, slamming her hands on the desk. She took a second to compose herself before asking, "And what did they take during this alleged 'home robbery'?." She made air quotes with her fingers as she said the words home robbery.

"According to the police reports, all the computers in the house were taken, and his iPad and cellphone was missing."

"That's it? No cash, no jewelry, no TVs?"

"Not according to the report. And Mrs. Aker has confirmed that."

"Of course," Agent Lewis said, sarcastically. She ran both hands through her hair with a frustrated sigh. She stood, turned to Agent Lane, and said, "Tell Mrs. Aker I'll be in to speak with her in a moment."

"Yes ma'am," Agent Lane said, and left the office, closing the door behind her.

"Like I said, stonewalled at every turn."

The intercom on her desk phone beeped.

"Yes," she said, pressing the appropriate button.

"There's an urgent call for you. Line 2."

"Thank you," Agent Lewis said. Still standing, she picked up the receiver and pressed the blinking red light on line two. "This is Special Agent Lewis..." She listened intently, not saying a word. A minute later she hung up the phone and plopped back into her chair.

"That was Jack," she said, with a blank look on her face. "The man with the scar under his eye strikes again. He broke into their apartment and attacked Jack's wife. She's ok, but he's having her and his daughter brought here for protection."

"Good," Cheryl said. "What about Jack?"

"He's not coming in."

"Why not?"

"I have no idea. He hung up before I could ask. But I don't know what more he can do at this point."

"What do you mean?"

"Dr. Holst's drive was taken. It's over, Cheryl."

Chapter 59

Tommy got in touch with a Detective Mark Davies of the NYPD. They served together for more than a year and Tommy fiercely vouched for him. Davies met them in the lobby of the Tower with the coroner in tow. The power had been restored and the lights were back on. The scene on the floor was gruesome. Lou was lying in a massive pool of his own blood, his throat having been slashed by the same straight razor that was held to Amy's.

Davies was easily six-four, pushing two-hundred-and-fifty pounds, and looked like he worked out every day of his life. He normally wore a suit to work, he told them, but due to the early morning hour, he was in sweats and a tight t-shirt that was straining at the seams. He and Tommy embraced, and then Tommy introduced Jack. They told him what they knew about the killer, without sharing any more than was necessary, and Jack gave his best description of the man with the scar under his eye. Davies wanted Jack to come down to the police station and give his description to a sketch artist, but Jack refused. I need to be here with my family right now, he said.

"This was not your average burglar," Tommy said. "The guy who did this," gesturing to Lou laying on the floor, "was well trained. Former military, if I had to guess. Maybe even special forces. Lou was no slouch and he didn't even get his pistol out."

Detective Davies was taking notes as he looked and listened. "Did you get him on video?"

"No," Tommy said. "He killed the power to the whole building. He even managed to ensure the generators didn't kick in. The place was a total blackout."

One of Davies's colleagues finished dusting the front door for fingerprints, and was making his way to the security desk.

"You're not going to find any fingerprints," Jack said. "He was wearing gloves. Blue ones. The kind surgeons wear."

"Awesome," Davies said, sarcastically. "You guys really aren't giving me a lot to go on. You know that, right?"

Tommy and Jack both nodded.

"Well, for now I'll see what I can find with the neighboring buildings. If the other buildings around here still had power, their cameras may have seen something.

"I doubt it," Tommy said. "This guy is good. He breached a lot of security measures here without breaking a sweat. He killed Lou with no apparent fight. And he got into the penthouse without raising any alarms. He's not the type that makes mistakes. You're not going to find anything on video."

"You never know," Davies said. "Everyone makes mistakes."

"Not this guy," Tommy reiterated.

While they talked, the coroner's office took pictures of Lou, inventoried his things, collected what little physical evidence they could find, and zipped him into a body bag. They loaded him onto a gurney and wheeled him out the door.

"Is there anything else you can tell me about the assailant?," Davies asked, more to Tommy than Jack.

Tommy shook his head no. "Sorry buddy. I wish we had more."

"Me too," Davies said. "Well, if you think of anything else, you know how to reach me."

He folded up his notepad and put it in his pocket. He shared a quick embrace with Tommy, and started to walk away.

"Detective," Jack said after a moment. Davies stopped and turned. "There is one other thing."

Davies walked back to stand in front of Jack.

"He'll be back," Jack said. "The guy who did this."

"What do you mean?," Davies asked, perplexed. "Why in the world would you think would he come back?"

"Because he didn't get what he came for."

Chapter 60

The top story in the New York Journal the next morning was the death, and apparent suicide, of Dr. Linda Norton, Chief Medical Examiner for New York City. Her body was found floating in the East River. An eye witness, who refused to give his name, told authorities Dr. Norton jumped from the Queensboro Bridge in the early hours of the morning and fell to her death.

Agent Lewis slammed the paper to her desk. Of course he refused to give his name, she thought. Because he's full of shit. After their meeting, she had considered putting an agent on Dr. Norton for forty-eight hours. There was mild concern for her safety, but she also wanted to see who else turned up regarding her findings. But with the autopsy report having mysteriously disappeared, she thought she might be overreacting. Clearly, she was not.

There was a soft rap on her office door.

"Come in," she said.

Cheryl peeked her head inside. "Good morning."

"Is it?," Agent Lewis asked sarcastically.

"I take it you've seen the paper."

Agent Lewis waved a hand over the newspaper strewn across her desk.

"We need to get the flash drive from my apartment. Today."

"Why?," Agent Lewis asked with a sigh.

Cheryl was slightly taken aback. She came the rest of the way into the office and closed the door. "What do you mean 'why'?"

"I mean 'why', Cheryl. What is it going to show us? The man who has been terrorizing Jack and his family? Probably the same man who's been going around killing anyone even remotely involved in this case. We'll run his face through our database, and maybe even get an ID. Then what? We can't prove he's actually done anything. We can't arrest him for anything. We have no witnesses to any crime he's committed, other than Jack and Amy. But I'm sure he'll have an excellent alibi, one that will be corroborated by any number of upstanding citizens." The frustration and defeat in Agent Lewis's voice was apparent.

"What are you saying? So we just give up? We let everything that's happened be for nothing?," Cheryl asked, indignant.

"Cheryl, sit down, please."

She took a seat across the desk from Agent Lewis.

"Let's recap, shall we?," Agent Lewis began. "The reporter, your friend, who discovered that EBF-14 is targeting specific cancer patients is dead. The oncologist who he was going to meet with, who prescribed more EBF-14 than anyone, is dead. Who knows what he was going to tell Matt. His drive with who knows what on it is gone. The young Dr. Aker, the whistle-blower at AstaGen who created EBF-14, is dead. His wife doesn't know anything about anything. The medical examiner for the city of New York

226

who was convinced Dr. Holst was murdered is dead. We're out of witnesses, out of leads, and your friend Jack seems determined to get himself killed. Did I leave anything out?"

Cheryl's disappointment and anger grew as she listened to Agent Lewis talk. She stood up at the desk, put both hands on it, and leaned in. "Yes, you did leave something out. You left out the death of Nate Turner, Jack's twelve-year-old son. You left out his wife, Amy, his daughter, Emma, my sister, Brenda, my niece, Lily, and the countless others who are dying from this cancer. A cancer that apparently sprang up out of nowhere that AstaGen conveniently has a treatment for. You left out Andrea Aker, recently widowed and left to raise two kids by herself. You left out all the lives that have been and will be lost because of Omnicarcinos. You left out all the families that are being torn apart by financial struggles, illness, grief, and death because of this cancer. Did *I* leave anything out?!"

Agent Lewis sat back in her chair and sighed. With her hands up, she asked, "What would you have me do, Cheryl? I wasn't being callous before, I was being honest. We have no witnesses, no documents, no proof of anything. We continue to operate on nothing but conjecture, opinion, and he-said she-said. And Jack just lost the one thing that might have had the evidence we were looking for. So I ask again, what would you have me do?"

"Let's get the video, find out who this asshole with the scar under his eye is, and bring him in. Amy's statement and her positive ID of him should be enough to hold him, right? Then maybe you can work some FBI magic and get him to talk. Find out who's giving the orders."

"Just like that, huh?"

"It's worth a shot. It's better than another day of sitting here on our asses doing nothing. And it's certainly better than giving up."

Agent Lewis stared at Cheryl. She admired her spunk and her tenacity. Plus, they had nothing to lose.

"Where did you hide the flash drive?"

Chapter 61

He turned the drive over in his hands. His orders were to destroy it. But something was eating at him. Something just didn't feel right. He needed to know. He drove slowly, and when he saw the computer store, he stopped the car, and double-parked in the middle of the street. Ignoring the honking, he walked up onto the sidewalk and strolled into the store.

"Can I help you find something?." A young employee, probably a college student, sporting a bright blue polo shirt and a smile approached him. His name tag read 'Randy - Sales Associate'.

"Yeah. I think this hard drive might be broken. Can you help me check?"

"Absolutely," Randy said eagerly. "Come right over here." He led him to a bank of desktop computers, each of them powered up, their screen savers flowing brightly. "May I see the drive?"

The man with the scar under his eye passed the drive over. Randy looked at it for a few seconds, and then opened a drawer under the computer table. The drawer was full of cords and cables, and Randy quickly found the appropriate one. He attached the cable to the back of the drive and plugged the other end into a USB port on the nearest computer. The man with the scar under his eye folded his arms, waiting impatiently. Randy fiddled with the mouse, and a few clicks later said, "Nope, not broken. Looks like it works fine. In fact, it's brand new."

"How do you know it's brand new?"

"It's empty," Randy said. "All four terabytes of storage space are available."

"Motherfucker!," the man with the scar under his eye shouted. Several startled customers looked in their direction. He turned and headed for the door.

"Wait, don't forget your drive!," Randy called after him.

"Keep it," he said, and stormed out the door.

Chapter 62

"What do you mean a 'fake drive'?," Tommy asked. They were back up in the apartment sitting at the kitchen table. Morning had come and the sun was streaming in through the windows. Tommy and Bobby were sitting across from Jack and Amy. Jack's parents had taken Emma to the park across the street, shadowed, unbeknownst to them, by a friend of Tommy's. Michael, Laura and Emma were completely unaware anything happened last night. They didn't hear or see anything. The advantages of a very large apartment.

All eyes were currently on Jack, waiting for an explanation.

"The night I snuck out, the same night I realized I was being followed by a drone, I went to an electronics store. I needed to replace my burner phones. I was a day late updating them and I needed to get in touch with Cheryl. To make sure she was ok. I ditched the drone long enough to duck inside the store. I bought three burner phones, because I wasn't sure if or when I would be able to get more. I still have them."

Everyone was nodding along with the story. They all knew most of what he was telling them already.

"While I was there, I also bought a duplicate of Dr. Holst's hard drive. I didn't know if I would need it, but it turns out I did. That's what I hid under the mattress, and that's what I gave to the man with the scar under his eye."

Amy smiled with a small sense of pride, but Tommy and Bobby were not as impressed.

"Jack," Tommy began, "how long do you think it's going to take him to realize you gave him a bogus drive?"

Jack sat with his hands folded on the table. "Well, if we're lucky, he'll destroy it without ever looking at it."

"Right," Bobby chimed in. "Because our luck has been so stellar up until this point." His comment was dripping with sarcasm, but his point was well taken.

"Yeah. That's why I expect him back." He turned to Amy. "And that's why you and Emma will be under the protection of the FBI by lunchtime."

"Where is the actual drive? Dr. Holst's?," Tommy asked.

"It's safe," Jack said. "I'd rather not say, in the event that any of you are put in a compromising position. It's better that you don't know... for now, anyway."

Bobby began to protest when the front door suddenly flew open, startling the four of them. Jack's parents came bursting through the door, out of breath. His father's shirt was ripped, he had a cut above his eye that was bleeding, and blood ran down the side of his face. His mother's blouse was missing a sleeve and her right cheek was swollen.

"Jack!," his father, Michael, shouted.

Jack and the others leapt up from their seats and rushed over to them.

"What happened?!," Jack asked. Before he got the words out, Tommy sprinted past them, and out the open front door.

"They took Emma!," Jack's mother, Laura, screamed.

"What?! Who took Emma?!," Amy shrieked.

Laura held Jack's arm as he led her to one of the chairs they had just vacated at the kitchen table. Michael sat down next to her. Amy was quick with a cloth for the cut over his eye, and some ice for them both.

"A man jumped us from behind in the park," Michael said, still visibly shaken. "He tried to grab Emma. I fought with him, we both did. Another man was running towards us. I didn't know him, but he looked like he wanted to help." Must have been Tommy's friend, the one that was supposed to protect them, Jack thought. "But the guy who took Emma pulled a gun. It had a silencer on it. He shot the other guy before he could get to us. Shot him right in the head. Then he pointed it at us. I told Emma to run, but she was frozen with fear."

"What happened to Emma?! Where's Emma?," Amy screamed.

"He took her," Laura said, slumped over, crying.

"We couldn't stop him, Jack. I'm so sorry," Michael said, holding an ice pack to his eye.

Amy was crying hysterically. Jack held her tight. "Dad," he said. "What did he look like? The man who took Emma..."

Michael thought for a second and said, "He was about six feet tall, white guy with brown hair, and very strong. He threw me around like I weighed nothing."

"Did he have any distinguishing marks," Jack asked. "Like a tattoo, or maybe a scar on his face?"

"A scar, yes!," Michael said. "Just below his right eye! How did you know?"

Chapter 63

The flash drive was surprisingly easy to obtain. It was right where Cheryl said it would be, at the bottom of a cereal box in her kitchen pantry. The agent sent to retrieve it encountered no resistance, did not report being followed, and was in and out of Cheryl's apartment in under five minutes. He returned in less than an hour and handed over the flash drive to Agent Lewis.

The video quality was not great. It was apparent the New York Journal did not invest in top of the line surveillance cameras. Considering they were forced to install them, it's not really surprising. A mandate came from Human Resources the day after an intern got high, fell down the stairs, and broke her ankle. Within a week, the cameras were going up. How often would they ever have to review the recordings? Not often, they were betting. Hence the cheap equipment and poor video quality.

Lonnie, the FBI's in-house tech guy, was on the job. Sitting at his terminal, he worked on the video, adjusting resolution and contrast, refining pixilation, zooming in, and attempting to create a decent still shot of the man with the scar under his eye. The goal was to have an image that could be fed into the FBI's facial recognition software and, hopefully, find out who he is.

For most of the video, the man's back is to the camera. It was mounted in the upper corner of the stairwell wall, where one floor ended and the next began. So the angle of the video was mostly from behind and to the side. Lonnie managed to grab two decent still shots. One from the side, and one straight on as the guy with the scar under his eye appeared to be looking around to make sure he was alone.

Cheryl and Agent Lewis each leaned in over a shoulder as Lonnie worked. When the printer spat out the images, they looked at them together. They were grainy, but passable.

"So that's our guy...," Agent Lewis said. "Lonnie, let's get these loaded into the NGI right away."

"You got it," Lonnie said.

Agent Lewis took out her cell phone and began typing. Not wanting to interrupt, Cheryl leaned in to Lonnie and said softly, "NGI?."

"Yeah, the Next Generation Identification system," Lonnie said. "The FBI spent like a billion dollars on it a few years ago. It gives us, and the rest of the law enforcement community, access to the world's largest electronic warehouse of biometric and criminal history information."

"Wow," Cheryl said. "And it can give you an ID from those pictures?"

"Hopefully. These pictures aren't the greatest quality, but I've seen worse. If anything can do it, this baby can," he said, as he patted a piece of hardware situated next to his terminal like a proud father. "Part of the NGI is the IPS, the Interstate Photo System. Through facial recognition, the IPS allows us to search millions of criminals' photos, data the FBI has collected for decades, and generates a list of candidates as potential leads and ranks them by probability.[2] The database includes more than 52 million faces, up to one-third of Americans."

"That's amazing!," Cheryl exclaimed. "How long does it take?"

Lonnie continued to work as he talked, preparing to upload the images he'd captured into the software.

"Normally we can match a single face from a pool of more than 50 million mug shots or passport photos with an accuracy above ninety-percent in about thirty seconds, give or take."

"Holy crap!," Cheryl said.

"Keep in mind, that's when the images are static and well lit, like when you take a passport photo. These images are not that. So it may take a little longer for the system to try and identify, and then match, the different facial features and distinguishable landmarks."

Cheryl shook her head in amazement.

"Where are we?," Agent Lewis asked, rejoining the conversation.

"Uploading the images now...," Lonnie replied. A few mouse drags and a couple of clicks later, and the software was up and running. Faces began flashing across the screen, so many and so fast it was impossible for the human eye to keep up. They all watched intently as the images flashed by, waiting for a positive ID. As promised, in less than a minute the search was complete. The screen displayed its findings.

0 Results

"What?!," Agent Lewis said, exasperated.

"What does that mean?," Cheryl asked.

"Run it again," Agent Lewis said, ignoring Cheryl's question.

Lonnie reset the software, uploaded the images and launched the search again. Less than a minute later the display read...

0 Results

"Goddammit," Agent Lewis said. "Is it the images or something else?," she asked Lonnie.

"I don't think it's the images. They're not great, but I've matched up plenty of faces with worse. This guy doesn't exist. Not in our database, anyway."

"How is that possible?," Cheryl said, asking no one in particular.

"It's not. A guy like this has a file, there's no doubt about it. Or did, anyway." Agent Lewis sighed. "If he's well connected, it's possible his facial biometrics have been deleted from the system."

Lonnie turned in his chair and looked at her sideways. "That would require some serious hacking," he said.

"Not if someone was ordered to delete it," she replied. Everyone took a moment to absorb what that could mean, particularly Cheryl. "Keep trying. Maybe we'll get lucky. Let me know if you find anything."

Cheryl followed her back to her office and they both sat, frustrated. "Well that did not go as expected," Agent Lewis said. "I figured we'd at least get an ID, even if we can't locate him yet."

An older woman shuffled into the office holding a package. She couldn't have been more than five feet tall, and was stooped slightly, making her look even shorter. She placed the package on the desk and said, "This just arrived for you. It's marked urgent."

"Thank you, Ruth," Agent Lewis said.

Ruth nodded and slowly backed out of the office.

"She's been here forever," Agent Lewis said to Cheryl, as she turned her attention to the package. It was a white padded envelope with no return address on it. She opened it carefully and removed the contents. She slid a small, thin, opaque plastic case out, on top of which was a handwritten note on paper from a yellow sticky pad. Agent Lewis smiled as she read it, and then passed the note to Cheryl.

"*Inside you will find blood, hair, and skin samples from our friend with the scar under his eye, courtesy of my parents! Have fun! - Jack*"

Cheryl looked up at Agent Lewis and they both smiled.

"The sonofabitch won't be able to hide from his DNA!," Agent Lewis said. She pushed herself away from the desk and hurried out of the office, package in hand, Cheryl close behind.

Chapter 64

The Turner's penthouse apartment was a flurry of activity. After being attacked, and having Emma taken from them, Michael and Laura had to be brought up to speed. Jack had no choice. He told them everything. They were currently screaming in his ear about calling the police, the FBI, and any other law enforcement agency they could think of. Jack tried to assure them that he was in constant communication with the FBI and, through Tommy, the police and even the military. But this was all new to them so they were having trouble adjusting to the level of trouble Jack had been dealing with for months.

Not long before his parents laid into him, Amy had given him an earful, having refused to go into protective custody with the FBI. "I'm not going anywhere without Emma!," she shouted. Jack knew there was no arguing with her, and he really couldn't blame her.

Tommy had returned to the apartment and confirmed that his friend, Marco, was, indeed, dead. A single shot through the eye socket into the brain cavity. And that was from twenty yards out while he was in a full sprint while the shooter was struggling with Michael and Laura. "First Lou, now Marco. If I ever get my hands on this motherfucker...," Tommy said. "This guy's a pro, Jack. That's not an easy shot for anyone."

Jack tried not to be impressed with the killing prowess of the man that currently held his daughter hostage. "Did you deal with the police?," he asked, changing the subject.

"Yeah," Tommy said. "I called Mark Davies. He was surprised to hear from me again so soon."

"I bet," Jack said.

"He'll take care of Marco, and file the report we want him to," Tommy said.

"Good," Jack said. "We don't need any attention right now."

Tommy nodded.

"So listen," Jack went on. "They have Emma. We know what they want. It's only a matter of time before we get the call and they demand a meeting to make the exchange. We need to get into Dr. Holst's drive as fast as possible. How long until your guy gets here?"

"He's already on the way. He should be here any minute," Tommy said.

"Good," Jack said.

Tommy's guy was Ian Frather, also known as Prowler, a computer hacker Tommy met in the service many years ago. According to Tommy, Prowler's claim to fame took place about ten years ago when he hacked the FAA's National Flight Data Center and suspended every flight nationwide. Every flight on every board in every airport across the country had a DELAYED status for fourteen minutes until they got it all sorted out. When asked why he did it, Prowler said, "Because I could."

Neither Tommy nor Prowler could say what agency he was currently working for, but according to Tommy he is the best at what he does. When he arrived at the penthouse, he had surprisingly little with him, just a computer bag slung over his shoulder. Jack expected tons of hardware, cords everywhere, and computers as far as the eye can see. "Nah, bro, I have everything I need right here," he said, patting his bag.

After quick introductions, Prowler commandeered the dining room table and it quickly became his workstation. "He's not really a people person," Tommy said quietly in Jack's ear. Prowler took position at the head of the table, opened his laptop, set up his own router for high speed internet access, and powered everything up. While he was waiting, he pulled out four cans of Red Bull from his bag, and placed them on the table. Then he sat up, cracked his knuckles, and looked at Tommy and Jack.

"So, whadda we got?," he asked.

Jack pulled Dr. Holst's external drive from his pocket. He'd retrieved it from its hiding place when he heard Prowler was en route. He handed it over and said, "We need to know what's on here. Everything. It's extremely important. When I say it's literally a matter of life and death, I'm not exaggerating."

"Security?," Prowler asked.

"Blowfish encryption," Jack said plainly. He wasn't sure if that was a big deal to Prowler or not. And he couldn't tell by his reaction, or lack of one, either. He simply took the drive, plugged it in, and started clicking away. His screen read Kali Linux, but Jack had no idea what that meant.

"How long do you think it will take to get in?," Jack asked gently. He didn't want to rub this guy the wrong way and create friction right off the bat.

"Depends."

Tommy and Jack looked at each other.

"On...?," Jack said.

"On how much security this thing has, and how long you plan on standing there yapping in my ear," he said, staring at them. They took the hint and walked away.

When they were out of earshot, Tommy said, "We need to talk about the drop," already thinking ahead.

"Let's wait for the call first. Who knows what this guy will ask for."

"Jack, I can't let you go alone. You know that's what he'll say. This guy could kill you, kill Emma, take the drive and disappear. And there would be nothing you could do about it." Tommy's face was serious with an intensity Jack had not seen before.

"Believe me, the last thing I want is to be alone with this guy. Especially when he has my daughter. Let's just wait for the call. Once we know what we're dealing with, we'll talk it out. Ok?"

"Ok," Tommy said reluctantly. "Just remember what I said."

"Tommy, I already lost Nate. I'm not going to do anything that puts my daughter's life at risk. Do you understand?"

Tommy nodded. He put a hand on Jack's shoulder, trying to reassure him, when the phone in Jack's pocket buzzed. He pulled it out and they both looked at the screen. Neither of them recognized the number, but they both knew who it was.

Chapter 65

The DNA Casework Unit (DCU) provides forensic DNA analysis for the FBI and other law enforcement agencies. They are comprised of a unit chief, forensic examiners, biologists, DNA technical specialists, DNA program specialists, management and program analysts, and contracted employees. The DCU utilizes forensic serological, mitochondrial DNA, and nuclear DNA methodologies to provide critical information in criminal, missing persons, and intelligence cases through evidence testing.[3]

Cheryl was both amazed and baffled as she browsed the DCU website. She was in a small conference room no one ever used, on a laptop Lonnie had provided. It was an older refurbished model that had been collecting dust on his desk. No one is going to miss it, he said. Agent Lewis had told her how the DNA analysis process worked, and she was fascinated by the whole thing. She was also excited that they would finally be able to put a name to the face. But when she learned the DCU was 260 miles away, in Quantico, Virginia, and the DNA results wouldn't be known for twenty-four to seventy-two hours after they received the sample, she was not happy. The man with the scar under his eye was still out there and Jack was in constant danger. She had foolishly hoped DNA testing would be as fast as the facial recognition search. But upon reading how involved the testing and identification is, she realized just how foolish she'd been.

The samples Jack provided were on a jet to Quantico and given the highest priority. As the Special Agent in Charge, Agent Lewis was beginning to flex her FBI muscle to ensure things happened fast. But not fast enough, in Cheryl's opinion. Lonnie had tried and failed repeatedly to get a hit on the images he uploaded into the facial recognition software. No matter what adjustments he made to improve the image quality, he kept coming up empty. The DNA was their only hope of getting a positive ID. Cheryl couldn't help but wonder what the FBI would do once they had a name. Would it help them in any way? Would they be able to find him any easier? What good is knowing his name, other than being able to dig into his background?

While Cheryl was mulling this over, Agent Lewis interrupted her thought. She was standing right next to her, though Cheryl didn't even hear her enter the room.

"It's for you," she said, holding out her cell phone. "This is an FBI issued phone. No one has this number," she said with a mix of anger and concern.

Cheryl took the phone, not really sure what to say to that.

"Hello?," she said, tentatively.

"Aunt Cheryl?." It was her niece Lily, but she sounded strange.

"Lily? Are you ok? What's going on?"

There was a click, and the line went dead.

"Lily? Hello?," Cheryl said, then held out the phone to see what happened. As she looked at the screen, it rang again. This time it read 'Private Number'. She handed it back to Agent Lewis, who eyed the phone suspiciously, then answered.

"Special Agent Lewis...," she said.

"Hello Special Agent Lewis. Nice to meet you. Is Cheryl still there?"

"Who is this?"

"I think you know who this is. Why don't you put the phone on speaker so you can both hear me."

"How did you get this number?," she asked.

"I'm really not a patient man, Agent Lewis. Put me on speaker now please."

She pushed the speaker button, and there was a small staticky click.

"Go ahead," she said, handing the phone to Cheryl.

"Thank you," he replied. "Hello Cheryl, how are you?"

"Who is this?," Cheryl asked.

"My name is not important, Cheryl. What is important is that we have your niece, Lily."

"No!," Cheryl shouted. She jumped up from her chair at the table and looked at Agent Lewis with fear in her eyes.

"Oh, I'm afraid so. Very sweet girl, from what I understand. I believe you just heard from her."

"Why Lily?! What do you want?!," she said with obvious panic in her voice. Cheryl had been safe and sound in the protective custody of the FBI. Jack and his family were here in New York. She never once thought her family back home, away from all of this, was in any danger. But now they had Lily, and her guilt began to immediately consume her.

"I'm glad you asked, Cheryl." There was a cold calmness to his voice that was frightening. "Not long from now, I'm going to meet with your friend, Jack. He has something I want, and I have something he wants. Hopefully this exchange goes smoothly. If it does, and I get what I want, Lily will be back home with your sister before supper. But if it does not, and I don't get what I want, poor Lily is going to have to pay the price. And if he really pisses me off, I will personally make a trip to visit your sister, Brenda. Am I making myself clear?"

Tears were welling in Cheryl's eyes. She couldn't live with herself if something happened to Lily or Brenda because of her. She pictured Lily tied up somewhere, tape over her mouth, crying, and her heart ached. She couldn't imagine what Brenda was going through right now.

"What do you expect *me* to do?!," Cheryl shouted.

"I expect you to motivate him, Cheryl. Make sure Jack behaves himself, that he follows my every instruction to the letter, and that he and his buddies don't do anything stupid. Lily's life literally depends on it."

"How am I supposed to do that?!," she shouted. But he was already gone.

Cheryl looked at Agent Lewis with tears in her eyes. For a moment, neither of them spoke. Then Agent Lewis grabbed the phone from Cheryl and pulled out a piece of paper from her pocket. Written on it were the numbers Jack had given them for his burner phones. In case of emergency, he'd said. She dialed each of the three numbers, all with no answer.

She spun around and hurried out of the conference room, Cheryl running right behind her. When they got to her office, Agent Lewis grabbed the phone on her desk. She hit a button and spoke into the handset.

"I need the number for Michael and Laura Turner here in New York, right away."

She replaced the handset and remained standing behind her desk, waiting. Cheryl stood across the desk, her heart pounding. Less than a minute later, a secretary whisked into the room and handed Agent Lewis a piece of paper. She left as quickly as she came and Agent Lewis began dialing.

"Hello?," they heard over the speakerphone.

"This is Special Agent Lewis with the FBI. To whom am I speaking?"

"This is Laura Turner. Is this about Emma?! Did you find her?!"

"Oh no!, Cheryl said. She and Agent Lewis exchanged worried looks. Cheryl ran her hands through her hair and began to pace back and forth in the small office.

"I'm afraid I don't have any new information about that. But it's urgent that I speak to Jack right away."

"Oh," Laura said, disappointed. "He's not here. He went to meet that lunatic who took Emma. He wants something Jack has."

"Did he go alone?"

"I think so. He was supposed to, but a couple of Jack's military friends left a few minutes after he did."

"Ok, thank you Mrs. Turner. I'll be in touch."

Cheryl fell back into a chair. "Oh my god...," she said, then buried her face in her hands. Not a minute later her cell phone rang. The caller ID told her it was Brenda. Cheryl gasped. With tears in her eyes, she said blankly, "What am I supposed to say?"

Chapter 66

Prowler had been unable to crack the drive. He uncovered multiple layers of unexpected security and simply did not have enough time to break through. But he was impressed with the level of sophistication that was protecting the drive's contents. "There's no way the doctor did this," he said. "Whoever helped him was serious about protecting this information. Honestly, even with enough time, I don't know if I'd get in."

Jack couldn't believe he had to give up the drive without knowing what was on it. And he was pretty sure the man with the scar under his eye was going to kill him in a few minutes. Why wouldn't he, Jack asked himself. He was supposed to meet him in Central Park at noon, by a specific red bench. Hopefully a crowd would double as his security blanket, Jack thought. But either way, everything was going to end today.

"So, listen," Prowler went on. "I may not be able to crack the drive, but there is one thing I can do that might help. I can embed tracking software on it, so we can monitor its location."

Tommy and Jack both looked at him quizzically.

"Kind of like LoJack, or the Find my iPhone software, but much more sophisticated," he said, hoping the simple example would clarify his meaning.

"What kind of range would it have?," Tommy asked.

"It's satellite based software, so unless they take it into a cave, the range is really unlimited."

"Do it," Jack said. "How long do you need?"

"Not long. Pack your gear, get ready to go, and it'll be ready before you leave."

"What gear?," Jack asked. "All I need is the drive. He told me not to even bring a phone."

Tommy caught Prowler's eye and shook his head slowly.

"Oh, right," Prowler said. "Never mind. Just give me a few minutes and it'll be ready."

There are over nine thousand benches in Central Park. Placed end to end, they would stretch out for more than seven miles. The bench Jack was looking for was at the edge of a large field currently brimming with activity. People picnicking, kids playing, dogs running, Frisbees flying. It was a beautiful, clear day, the sun was shining and there was a large crowd enjoying it. Jack couldn't understand why this was the chosen spot, but he welcomed the sight of so many witnesses. As he approached the bench, there was a woman sitting on it, eating a yogurt and talking on her cell phone. Jack casually sat down on the opposite end of the bench.

As he had been instructed to do, he reached underneath the seat and felt around. He found a piece of paper taped to the underside of the seat. It was folded over, with a bulge in the middle. He removed it, brought it to his lap, and unfolded the paper. Inside was a small earpiece, and the note read 'Put this in your ear'. He picked it up and inspected it briefly. It was small enough to be invisible inside the ear, and had a tiny antenna protruding from one side. He wasn't sure if it mattered which ear, but he put it in his left and it fit perfectly.

"Hello, Jack," he heard, immediately after inserting the earpiece. He recognized the coldness of the voice. The audio was so clear, it was like the man with the scar under his eye was standing right next to him. "You can speak, Jack. I will be able to hear you just as well as you can hear me."

"Where's Emma?"

"You'll see her in just a minute, Jack. Now, here's what I want you to do..."

"No," Jack interrupted. "I'm not doing anything until I know Emma is ok. Let me hear her voice."

Silence. Jack heard nothing but the sounds of the park around him. He was hoping Emma's would be the next voice he heard, but it was not.

"Listen to me very carefully, Jack. You are in no position to give orders. If you interrupt me again, you will never see Emma again. If you don't do what I tell you, you will never see Emma again. And if you do anything stupid in the next few minutes, Emma will die. Amy will die. You will die. And your parents will die, just for the trouble you've caused me. Am I making myself clear?"

"Yes," Jack said weakly.

"Good. Now stand up and walk down the path to your left. When you cross over the bridge, go left again through the trees. Follow the tree line for fifty yards. There will be a small opening. That's where you will find us."

"Us?," Jack said, standing up from the bench.

"Yes. Me and Emma. Us."

Jack followed the path to his left. His leg still sore and achy, he moved slowly. He avoided two young boys tossing a football, and made his way over the small bridge. Once across, he turned left into the thick brush and followed the tree line. As he walked, all sounds of the park faded away until he was left with nothing but the sound of his own footsteps. He soon emerged into a small clearing. He looked around. The opening in the trees was circular, about twenty-five feet around. It appeared man-made, and very recently.

"Hello, Jack." The voice came not from the earpiece, but to his right. Jack turned and there he was, standing just inside the clearing. Hatred and fear welled inside Jack as he stood there looking at the man who had caused him so much grief.

"You can take out the earpiece. I've deactivated it."

Jack removed the earpiece and tossed it into the woods.

"Where is Emma?," he said.

"Right there," the man said, pointing to his right, to the trees directly across from Jack. Squinting in the sun, he saw her. She was tied to a tree in the shade, her mouth taped. She look scared, but unhurt.

"Do you have something for me, Jack?"

Jack nodded and slowly moved towards him.

"Remember what I said, Jack. Don't try anything stupid."

When just a few feet remained between them, Jack stopped. He slowly removed the drive from his back pocket and handed it over.

"This better be the real thing, Jack, or we'll just start the game all over again."

"It is," Jack said.

"Have you seen what's on it?"

"No. I tried, but it's encrypted."

"You mean your hacker buddy couldn't get in?"

Jack looked at him and stared blankly.

"That's right, Jack. I know about all your pals. I even know they followed you here to the park. I told you to come alone. Instead you bring a sniper with you. Was he planning to shoot me? That's really not very nice, Jack."

"No!," Jack shouted. "I didn't know, I swear!"

"Relax, Jack. I believe you. Besides, it doesn't matter now, does it? It's over. I have what I want, and you have what you want," he said, gesturing to Emma.

"Just like that?," Jack said suspiciously.

"Just like that," he replied with a wink. And with that, the man with the scar under his eye rapidly drew a silenced pistol from his waistline and shot Jack twice in the chest.

Before Jack even hit the ground, the man disappeared into the woods, drive in hand. It was several minutes later before Tommy emerged through the trees. His pistol was raised and at the ready, but he lowered it quickly when he saw Jack's body on the ground. Emma, still tied to the tree, was sobbing softly.

Chapter 67

His name was Simon Gabriel. A former Navy Seal, he had tours in Grenada, Bosnia, Afghanistan, Pakistan, Yemen, and the Horn of Africa. He was considered to be an expert in martial arts, skilled with explosives, and a master of weapons and tactics. During his time in service, he was awarded the Silver Star, the Navy Cross, a Purple Heart (thanks to an improvised explosive device (IED) that gave him the scar under his right eye), and the Congressional Medal of Honor. He was a war hero of the highest merit.

On his last mission, bad intelligence led his team into an ambush. He was the only one to survive. After days on the run, he was finally picked up by search and rescue. When he returned to base, he pointed his weapon at a superior officer, said some rather choice words, and threatened to kill him. He was taken into custody and dishonorably discharged. He hadn't been seen or heard from in two years. Now, for some reason, he was terrorizing the same people he served to protect for nearly two decades.

"My god," Cheryl said. "How are we supposed to stop a guy like this?"

"YOU are not," Agent Lewis said. "We are. Now we know who he is. We know what he looks like. We will notify every law enforcement agency in the country. We'll start scanning digital frequencies for his voice print and his facial recognition. It's only a matter of time before we locate him."

Cheryl couldn't help but wonder why they hadn't been doing that already. "And then what?," she asked.

"Then we bring him in for questioning. We'll find out who he's working for, and why."

Cheryl picked up the dossier Agent Lewis had just been reading off the desk.

"With all due respect to you and the FBI, this doesn't sound like the type of guy that's going to come quietly."

"We have some pretty skilled people too, Cheryl. Don't worry."

But worry was all Cheryl could do. Lily was missing. Emma too. Jack hadn't been heard from since he went to meet with Gabriel. It felt weird calling him by name, Cheryl thought. She had gotten used to thinking of him simply as the man with the scar under his eye. Now they knew who they were dealing with. And it was so much worse than expected.

Was Jack dead? If he went to meet with Gabriel on his own, the answer was probably yes. That meant the drive was gone and so was any chance of exposing AstaGen.

"We need to find Jack," she said to Agent Lewis.

"We have agents combing the park now. They'll report back to me as soon as they know something."

Cheryl sat down. She thought getting the DNA results would make her feel better, but she couldn't have been more wrong. This guy was the *last* guy you wanted to mess with. And now he had Lily.

Brenda had been hysterical on the phone. Two men had grabbed Lily right out of her hands as they walked to their car from dance class. They shoved Brenda down, grabbed Lily, threw her into the back of van, and sped off. It didn't take Brenda long to make the connection and call Cheryl. No apology, no words of remorse were sufficient. Brenda was irate and Cheryl was taking the brunt of the blame. She tried to make Brenda see the bigger picture, that there were larger issues and others more deserving of her wrath, but she wasn't hearing it.

"Ever since you came here and started asking questions... I knew this would happen!," she said. "You stirred up something and now Lily is missing!"

Her anger was understandable. Cheryl wanted to remind Brenda that her family, and many others, were affected by Omnicarcinos, a very new and suspicious form of cancer, and that there was a lot more to it than just chance or bad luck. But now wasn't the time. She did what she could to soothe her, but Brenda was out of her mind with worry. When they hung up, Cheryl felt about as awful as one can feel. Guilt, grief, anger, fear... it was all piling up.

She had to take her mind off of Brenda, Lily, and Jack. She needed a distraction, to focus her energy elsewhere. She decided to do what she did best. Research. She was going to dig in and find anything and everything she could about the cancer and the people who had it. Cheryl first learned that Omnicarcinos, loosely translated from Latin, meant 'cancer everywhere'. But what she needed to know was who else had it and where they were. There were over 35 million Americans with a blood type of B and she prayed the final number of patients diagnosed with Omnicarcinos was much smaller.

Back at the table in the small, rarely used conference room, Cheryl attacked the laptop she borrowed from Lonnie. She referenced every site she could find, reached out to every contact she could think of, used every trick Matt had taught her. She thought about Matt. It was hard to believe he was gone, and she never got the chance to explore what might have been. His death was just one more brick on the house of guilt Cheryl was quickly building for herself.

There was more to this than they had previously considered, she knew it. And she was determined to uncover all of it. Not one more person would die from Omnicarcinos if she could help it.

Chapter 68

"That hurt like a bitch! You didn't tell me it was gonna hurt like that."

"Don't be such a baby," Tommy said, peeling back a velcro strap on the bullet proof vest Jack was wearing. Two slugs protruded slightly from the kevlar. "You're lucky. Back in the day, these things didn't have the ceramic plates to help distribute the impact of the bullet. Those *really* hurt. Left bruises the size of my fist. You'll be sore for a few days, but you'll live."

Jack nodded as Tommy spoke. They were in the back seat of Tommy's SUV pulling into the underground parking garage of the Tower. His friend, Alex, was driving. Tommy found Jack unconscious in the clearing, but he was pretty sure he was alive. He reached down for a quick check of his pulse just in case before running over and freeing Emma. A couple of slaps to the face and Jack was awake. Tommy hurried them from the clearing in case the man with the scar under his eye decided to return. Emma was dirty and shaken, having just seen her father shot, but otherwise unharmed. They avoided any undue attention as they hurried through the park to Tommy's waiting car. Jack's chest throbbed, but he managed to walk without attracting any strange looks. Emma was still upset, but Tommy carried her and assured her everything was going to be ok. Once they reached the SUV, everyone felt a little better.

"Hey," Jack said, "here's a question I probably should have asked earlier..."

Tommy looked at him with one eyebrow raised as he removed the vest.

"What if he shot me in the head?"

"Yeah, that would have been bad," Tommy mocked. "Honestly, I'm surprised he didn't. I would have. Quickest way to make sure."

"Great."

"Don't worry about it. It's over," Tommy said.

Jack rubbed his chest. Definitely gonna feel that tomorrow, he thought to himself. He put an arm around Emma.

"You sure you're ok, honey?"

"I'm ok, Dad. Are you?," she asked, looking at the red welts slowly expanding on his chest.

"Yeah, I'll be ok. I'm just glad you're back and you're safe. Mom is gonna be so excited to see you."

They parked the SUV in one of the employee parking spots and took the elevator to the penthouse level. Each of them couldn't help looking around as they walked from the car to the elevator. Their alert level would be on high for a while. When they walked into the penthouse they were swarmed by Amy, Jack's parents, and Bobby. Amy scooped up Emma, hugging and kissing her and asking a thousand questions. After Laura and Michael had a turn with her, Amy whisked her away to get her cleaned up and fed. Jack's parents followed close behind to make sure Rosie had food ready when Emma was ready to eat.

"Holy crap, you're alive! I can't believe that worked!," Bobby said once Emma was out of earshot. "I would have bet money you weren't coming back."

"Gee thanks," Jack said with a smirk. He knew Bobby long enough to know he didn't mean anything by it. He always spoke his mind. They made their way to the kitchen headed for the island table.

Jack turned to Tommy and Alex as they walked, and his tone changed. He gave Tommy a nudge and said, "What the hell were you guys up to? Were you trying to get us killed?"

Tommy stopped walking and put a hand on Jack's shoulder. He was a few inches taller than Jack, and a lot bigger. "Jack, relax. Alex was positioned to take the shot, but only if we knew it wouldn't put you or Emma at risk. And he doesn't miss. But when you walked into the trees, away from our position, we knew the plan was out the window."

"He knew you were there!"

"How could he possibly have known we were there?"

"I have no idea. But it would be nice if you kept me in the loop, especially regarding things that could put me or my family in danger, ok?" Jack said, taking a seat. Tommy sat next to him, Alex and Bobby on the other side. Rosie was putting food out as they talked. Bobby was already diving in.

"You're right, Jack, I'm sorry," Tommy said. "We won't take any action without first discussing it with you."

"Thanks. But I don't think you need to worry about that anymore. The drive is gone. Even if we *could* get it back, we still can't open it. Prowler said he can't get through its security. And if he can't, who can? Without the password, it's useless to us."

There was a silence among them. They all knew what Jack said was true. Without the information on the drive they had nothing.

"What about the doc's office?," Bobby proposed. "Is it worth having someone go back there to see if the password is there?"

Jack scratched his head before saying, "I thought about that. But I'm sure they're watching the place closely. I wasn't looking for it the first time, but I didn't see anything when I was there. He'd have been foolish to keep them in the same place. He was smart to move the drive and hide it in his car. Who knows what he did with the password. For all we know, it's not written down anywhere, and it died with him."

"True," Bobby agreed.

"Jack," Tommy said, "I think we should give Prowler another crack at it. He said he *might* not be able to get in. But that's not for sure. Maybe he'll get lucky."

"The drive could be anywhere right now," Jack said. "We can track it, and I'll bet when we do we'll find it's someplace secure, if it hasn't already been destroyed. I don't think going after it is a risk we can afford to take unless we know for sure we can access it once we have it. I can't risk anyone else's life for 'maybe'."

Tommy nodded. They all nodded.

"Wait, you just called me Jack, didn't you?," he asked, looking at Tommy with a smile.

"I did. Been doing it for a while now, but it's nice that you noticed," Tommy said with a wink.

"So no more 'Mr. Turner'?"

"I think we're beyond that now, don't you?"

Jack nodded with a smile.

They talked for hours looking for any other options. But they kept arriving at the same painfully obvious conclusion. Without the information on the drive they had nothing. And even if they somehow managed to get it back, they still had no way to find out what was on it. Bobby insisted there must be something they could do. But no ideas or suggestions worth pursuing were offered by anyone. As the sun went down, and all the food was gone, each of them arrived at the same conclusion.

It was over.

Chapter 69

The FBI found shell casings in the park, but no blood, no body, no witnesses, and absolutely nothing to go on. Lily had been released and was safely back home with Brenda.

Jack, Amy, and Emma flew back home despite his parents' best efforts to keep them around. He thanked them for their hospitality, apologized profusely for what he'd put them through, and assured them it was over.

Tommy remained on watch at the Tower. He had saved Jack's life twice, at least, and Jack knew he'd never be able to repay him. He insisted on knowing the moment Jack learned anything new, particularly regarding the man who killed two of his friends. Lou and Marco's deaths would not go unanswered.

Bobby was back at Keeler Locks and Bolts, surly as ever. He seemed more annoyed than any of them that the dead end they reached appeared final. Jack was grateful for his help, and continued to pitch in around the shop a few days a week, learning from the master.

Cheryl, released from the FBI's protective custody, returned to the New York Journal. She was sticking to her promise, spending her every moment at work on Omnicarcinos. Her boss was glad to have her back, and she was excited to have a purpose. Matt's death left both a void in her life and an opening at the paper. Cheryl had been promoted from researcher to writer. It was a bittersweet promotion for her.

She had no fear of pursuing the story that ultimately led to Matt's death. Every material witness was dead, any hard evidence they had was gone. All she could do was dig up facts and statistics, and speculate their possible meaning. She couldn't prove anything, the Journal wouldn't print anything she couldn't confirm, and AstaGen knew it. She was no threat to them. They knew she had nothing. But she would keep digging.

Agent Lewis promised to keep in touch with any new developments. She was opposed to Cheryl's departure, simply going home, unprotected. Same for Jack and his family. But she couldn't argue with their logic. They had nothing. None of them did. No leads, no evidence, no proof of anything. And as such, they were no longer any threat to AstaGen. And probably not in any danger. She vowed to continue the search for Gabriel, but they all silently knew she'd never find him. She also promised to keep looking for any connections between Omnicarcinos, EBF-14, and AstaGen.

Jack, Tommy, and Bobby had been told the identity of Simon Gabriel. His resume was both impressive and frightening. How does a guy like that go from accomplished war hero to hired goon, Jack wondered. He was relieved Gabriel was out of his life, hopefully for good. He thinks I'm dead. Or at least, he did. Was AstaGen still watching, still listening? Jack assumed they were, which meant they knew he was still alive. Would they come looking for him? He doubted it.

Cheryl filled Jack in about her new position with the Journal. She promised to keep in touch, and she would be sure to stop in when she flew in to visit Brenda and Lily.

Everyone settled back into their routines. Amy went back to her books, Emma went back to school, and Jack, his leg finally healed, started running again. It was slow going at first. He was tight, sore, and out of shape.

Weeks went by and Jack ran every day. It was cathartic for him. He stewed over how things turned out. They were right back where they started, no closer to an answer. Amy and Emma continued to take EBF-14 because it was the only thing keeping them alive. They checked in with Dr. Bosh, who was miraculously still alive. He had uninvolved himself in the matter quickly enough to avoid attention, but he admitted to being followed and was certain someone had been listening in on his calls.

What bothered Jack most was that he still didn't know how Amy and Emma got sick. They were both B blood type, but that still didn't explain why they had cancer. He knew he was missing something. Amy kept telling him to let it go. They were lucky to be alive after everything they'd been through, and she didn't want to take any more chances. But Jack simply couldn't accept the fact that he was going to lose his wife and daughter. He still ached for Nate every day. He sat in his room often, missing him and crying. He wouldn't allow another empty room in his house. But he had no idea how to prevent it.

He had trouble sleeping, nightmares coming almost every night. He saw Gabriel charging at him, sometimes with a gun, sometimes a straight razor. Most of the nightmares ended with Jack being shot in the chest and waking with a jolt. Amy tried to comfort him, but she knew what troubled him. He was not going to rest until this was over, one way or the other. As much as she wanted him to let it go, she didn't want to die. And she certainly didn't want Emma to die. She knew that's what giving up meant. It was only a matter of time.

She secretly wanted Jack to find the answer, for Emma's sake. But she couldn't tell him that. She feared for him, for all of them. But she decided she'd rather take her chances with the illness and the medication than these people. She was thrilled AstaGen was out of their lives.

Jack took to the streets at all hours of the night when he couldn't sleep. He was finally feeling more comfortable running and his endurance was slowly returning. He ran through town, subconsciously listening for the sound of a drone. He never heard one. He looped around the lake enjoying the cool fall breeze and the quiet of the night. The rhythm of his footsteps soothed him and he relaxed.

As he neared the water station, he saw it again. The same truck he'd seen months ago, the one that nearly ran him over. It was pulling out through the same gate as before. There was little light, but enough for him to see clearly what was printed on the side of the truck. *Sagante'*. He remembered when he saw it the first time thinking it sounded like a Spanish wine. He stood in the darkness as the truck pulled out and drove off, away from town, towards the highway. He remained there for a moment as the truck drove off.

It hit him like a ton of bricks and suddenly everything fell into place. The water! Jack ran his hands through his hair as he put it all together. Oh my god, the water, he thought. He could hear the sound of the truck fading in the distance. Why was a tanker truck making regular stops at the water station? He thought about the truck and saw the word in his mind. Sagante'. It couldn't be. He carefully rearranged the letters in his head... AstaGen.

Chapter 70

Cheryl was at her desk, where she could be found most days. Despite being promoted from researcher to writer, she still spent a majority of her time in front of her computer, pecking away in search of information. She had poured over documents, studies, medical articles, and scientific journals of all kinds, but found very little new information relevant to Omnicarcinos.

She rested her left elbow on the desk, leaning her head against her hand, drumming her fingers on her desk. She was at a dead end and had no idea where to turn next. She leaned back into a stretch and yawned when her phone dinged, notifying her of a new email. She picked it up, clicked the notification, and saw one new message to her work address. The subject read simply *Clinical Trials*, and the sender was *Anonymous*. She was reluctant to open it, but her curiosity got the better of her. The email was short. "Rh factor." That's all it said. There was no signature.

Cheryl stared at the email. Clinical trials, Rh factor. She had no idea what any of that meant, nor did she know who sent it. But it was the only thing she had to go on right now, so even if it turned out to be nothing, it would give her something to do. She had downloaded the clinical trials of EBF-14 weeks ago, but hardly understood much of what she read. Little mention was made of blood type, but it did confirm in fine print that all subjects were a blood type of B. She missed it the first time she read it, but when they got Matt's video, she looked again. She initially wanted to believe it was a coincidence, but she knew better.

She opened the file and started reading the clinical trial report again. With all the medical jargon, tables, graphs, and statistics, it was just as hard to get through this time as the others. When she got to the fine print about blood type, she noticed a tiny superscript that indicated a footnote. In even smaller print at the very bottom of the last page, wedged in between the comments and references, she found it.

"All subjects Rh-negative."

It took her three passes to find it. She never would have seen it had she not been looking specifically for it. "What the hell does that mean?," Cheryl asked aloud to no one. A quick Google search answered her question.

Each person's blood is one of four major types: A, B, AB, or O. Blood types are determined by the types of antigens on the blood cells. Antigens are proteins on the surface of blood cells that can cause a response from the immune system. The Rh factor is a type of protein on the surface of red blood cells. Most people who have the Rh factor are Rh-positive. Those who do not have the Rh factor are Rh-negative.[4]

Several more keystrokes and Cheryl learned that approximately fifteen percent of Americans are Rh-negative. That figure is even lower in the Asian and African American population. But only two percent of the U.S. population have a blood type of B and are Rh negative. Cheryl opened the calculator on her phone. Two percent of 324 million was nearly 6.4 million people.

That number still sounded high. She pulled out the notes she'd taken a few months ago to see if she was right. According to the CDC, less than 0.3% of Americans had been diagnosed with Omnicarcinos. Less than a million people, far fewer than she calculated. Was it possible that more than five million people had been incorrectly classified? She doubted it. Maybe not all B-negative people were sick? That seemed more likely. But the numbers were way off.

Why was this even important, she wondered. Whoever sent her that email wanted her to know the numbers, but why? She stood up from her chair and started pacing slowly around her office. Hands on her hips she stared at the ceiling. Why would the numbers matter, she asked herself. Who would care about the numbers? And then she answered her own question. She knew exactly who would care about the numbers. She raced over to her desk and grabbed the calculator again. If the CDC's estimates were correct, just under one million people had been diagnosed with Omnicarcinos. The twelve-month cost of EBF-14 is $300,000. Even if only half of the patients were able to afford it, either privately or through insurance, that's an annual windfall of nearly $150 billion to AstaGen. From one drug.

Cheryl sank back down into her chair. She finally understood. AstaGen had somehow created a new form of cancer. That would explain how it suddenly appeared out of nowhere just a few years ago. They also must have found a way to infect people of a certain blood type. A small percentage of the population, so as not to attract too much attention. What were the chances that everyone in the clinical trials were B-negative by accident? None. These people were handpicked. AstaGen developed a drug to treat their new form of cancer. Maybe they already had the drug, and all they needed was the disease.

That must have been what Jonathan Aker wanted to tell them before he died, Cheryl thought. He was the lead scientist on the EBF-14 team, so he knew what AstaGen was up to. According to Matt, Aker had some kind of crisis of conscience. Initially, Aker was so excited with the idea of seeing if he *could* do it, that he never stopped to think if he *should*. But he intended to tell Matt what they'd been doing, so they killed him. They all knew AstaGen was trying to protect their product and their profit, but Cheryl didn't realize just how big it was until right now. Billions of dollars were at stake.

Cheryl was in disbelief. She thought about Nate's death. About Lily's seizure. About Brenda's illness. And about all the families out there who were living with, or dying from, Omnicarcinos. All so AstaGen could turn a profit. A man-made cancer so they can sell their drug. She didn't want to believe evil of this degree could exist in the world. Matt had always called her naive, and he was right. She sat back in her chair, put her face in her hands, and started to cry.

Chapter 71

Jack's mind was reeling. He stood motionless in the shower, letting the hot water wash over him. The water. For years they had been so careful about everything they ate. Amy had insisted. Never once did they consider the possibility that it might be the water. They had a double filtration system in the house to remove particulates, chemicals, and other harmful substances. But clearly there was something else in the water that was getting through, causing people to get sick. And it was deliberate, Jack was sure of that now.

He got out of the shower, toweled off, and pulled on shorts and a t-shirt. It was one in the morning, Amy and Emma were both sound asleep. Jack was silently relieved Amy was not awake. He didn't want to tell her. But after New York, he promised no more secrets. He laid down in bed next to her and listened to her breathe. He was terrified of losing her and Emma. He watched her sleep for a long time.

He remembered the first time he watched her sleep. It was during their honeymoon. They'd gone to Maui, a gift from Jack's parents. After a day of fun in the sun, they returned to their hotel, the Ritz-Carlton, Kapalua. After a shower and a quick dinner, they returned to their room and Amy fell fast asleep. She had the uncanny ability to fall asleep seconds after she closed her eyes, sometimes in the middle of a conversation. Jack envied her for that. He had always been a light sleeper, waking at the slightest of sounds. And it took him time to fall asleep. Time for his mind to quiet down. Some nights that never happened. Tonight would be one of those nights.

He used the quiet time in the dark to formulate a plan. He needed proof. If the FBI was ever going to step up and take action, they needed something solid. Evidence they could pursue and build a case around. Agent Lewis had told them as much. He was going to need some help to make his plan work. Amy most certainly wasn't going to like it. But he would rather upset her than lose her, so he intended to move forward with or without her blessing. For her sake, and for Emma's.

Morning came and when Amy woke, Jack was already in the kitchen making breakfast. Once Emma was off to school, Jack sat Amy down and told her everything. The water station, the truck, and what it all meant. She didn't take it well. She rushed from the table over to the kitchen sink, and threw up. She thought about all the times she took her EBF-14, swallowed it down with the very water that caused the cancer. She grabbed the coffee pot and, with a scream, smashed it against the wall, coffee and glass spraying everywhere. How many pots of coffee had she made with that water. Jack grabbed her and held her tight. She thought of all the pitchers of water she filled, the glasses she poured for Emma, and started to cry.

"Promise me we'll get them, Jack," she said softly through her tears. "Promise me. I don't care what it takes." She leaned her head against Jack's chest and sobbed.

He stroked her hair and rocked her slowly. "I promise," he whispered, and kissed the top of her head. They stood there quietly for several minutes. When she calmed down, Jack told her about his plan as they cleaned up coffee and broken glass. She wanted this to be over and was now behind him one hundred percent.

"Whatever it takes," she said. He kissed her, told her he loved her, and was out the door.

He jumped in the car to put phase one of his plan into action. When he pulled up to Keeler Locks and Bolts, Bobby was already inside, busy dismantling something on his workbench. It was still early in the day so the shop was empty. Jack locked the door behind him so they weren't interrupted. "We need to talk," Jack said.

"Uh oh," Bobby replied. "What now?"

Jack told him his theory about the water. He told him about the truck he'd seen twice now, and his word scramble of Sagante' to AstaGen.

"Holy shit," Bobby exclaimed. "What are you saying? They're poisoning the water supply in order to give people cancer?" Bobby had an incredulous look on his face.

"Yup," Jack said flatly. "And then they sell them EBF-14. It's the perfect business model. They are literally creating customers for their product."

The weight of what Jack said hit Bobby hard, and he took a seat on his stool. Bobby was born and raised here. Generations of Keeler's lived here all their lives. He couldn't believe something like what Jack was suggesting could happen here. But after what happened in New York, very little was hard to imagine.

"The water? Really?," Bobby asked, still in disbelief.

"It has to be," Jack said. "It's all that's left. And that truck is the key."

"What's in the truck?"

"That's what we need to find out."

Jack laid out his plan and explained Bobby's role in it. The details hadn't been finalized, but Jack laid out a rough outline for him. Bobby nodded along, and understood his part. When Jack was done talking, they exchanged a few ideas, Jack answered Bobby's questions, then headed out.

As he approached his car, Jack spotted something sticking out from under the driver's side windshield wiper. It looked like a piece of paper. He walked around to the side of the car, and pulled it out, looking around. Activity on the street was beginning to pick up, but Jack didn't see anyone suspicious. He unfolded the note and read it.

"*Andy's, right now*," it read.

Andy's was a local diner that had been in business for more than forty years. Andy Yerger was the original owner and still ran the place. Easily the best breakfast plate Jack had ever had. He looked at the note, turned it over, held it up to the sun. There were no marks on the paper, and he didn't recognize the handwriting. Since he'd had enough surprises for a while, he walked back into the shop and showed it to Bobby. He locked up the shop and, together, they walked down the street to Andy's. Once inside, they looked around, and there was only one face they didn't recognize. He was sitting in the back, in a corner booth. He stood as they walked towards him. He was a young man, early thirties, wearing jeans and a tight t-shirt, his muscular arms at his side. As they approached, he held out his hand in greeting.

"Hi fellas. Matt Cunningham. Pleased to meet you."

Chapter 72

Déjà vu set in as Cheryl took the three steps down from the puddle jumper onto the tarmac. Welcome back to Mayberry she thought to herself once again. It was nearly noon and the sun was shining high in the sky. The turbulence coming in was rough on the small plane, ending

Cheryl's short, but prized no-vomit streak. Once inside the terminal, she headed straight for the bathroom. She rinsed her mouth, brushed her teeth and splashed some cold water on her face. The terminal was busier than her last trip, but then again, it was the middle of the day now.

Brenda was there waiting for her at the curb, sitting inside her Explorer, engine running and windows down. Cheryl rolled her suitcase up, threw it in the back and hopped in. They shared a quick, awkward hug in the front seat and drove off. They chit-chatted about nothing, catching up on mundane things for the drive back to Brenda's place. When they got back to the house, Cheryl wheeled her bag into the den/guest room and joined Brenda in the kitchen.

"I wasn't expecting you so soon," Brenda said. "Lily will be excited to see you."

"How is the munchkin?," Cheryl asked, still feeling guilty about Lily's abduction. Even though she knew it wasn't her fault, she still felt a degree of responsibility about what happened. And Brenda's words from the last time they spoke still stung.

"She's great," Brenda assured her. "She's feeling good, no worse for wear."

"That's awesome. I'm happy to hear it."

Brenda nodded and gave her a half-smile. "So you want to tell me what you're doing here? I know you're not just here for a visit."

Cheryl looked at her younger sister. The five-year difference in age created a distance between them growing up. They were not very close as kids. But the age difference mattered less as they got older, and they became closer with time. Right now, however, Cheryl felt worlds apart from Brenda. They led such different lives, and what Brenda has had to deal with over the last two years, Cheryl couldn't even imagine.

Cheryl took a seat on the couch and patted the cushion next to her. "Come sit with me. We need to talk."

Brenda sat down and they both angled their bodies towards each other. Cheryl had been dreading this conversation since she took her seat on the plane in New York. She took a deep breath and laid out everything for Brenda. The sudden appearance of Omnicarcinos a few years ago, the rapid development and approval of EBF-14, the incredible clinical trial results, all the subjects with B-negative blood, the number of people estimated to have Omnicarcinos, the value of each patient to AstaGen, and the massive amount of money they were making from this disease. Tears formed in Brenda's eyes as Cheryl spoke.

"You mean they're doing this on purpose? They did this to us on purpose?!," she asked, getting louder.

"Yes," Cheryl replied, taking her hand. "They created both the disease, and the drug to treat it."

"Why?!," Brenda asked, crying now.

"I just told you why. We're talking about billions of dollars, every year."

"But why?! Why would they do this to people? Don't they know people are sick, that people are dying?!"

Cheryl couldn't help but think for a split second that her naiveté was matched only by Brenda's. "They know, Brenda. They don't care. All they care about is their bottom line. And they found a way to create billions of dollars in new income on a yearly basis. They don't care about you, they don't care about Lily, or anyone else that's sick. They will keep you alive and on their medication for as long as possible, so they can make as much money as they can."

Cheryl's words were harsh, but Brenda needed to hear them. Cheryl would need Brenda's help before this was all over, and Cheryl needed her to be upset, angry and willing to help.

"How are they doing this?," Brenda asked softly between sniffs.

"I don't know yet. I don't know how they created the disease. I don't know if they already had the drug. I don't know how they are infecting people... I don't have all the answers yet, Brenda. But I will, I promise. And then we will expose these people for what they are."

Brenda's wall had come down as they talked. She knew deep down her big sister was looking out for her and Lily. She only wanted to protect them. They hugged and held on to each other for a while. When they separated, Cheryl said, "I have to go. There are things I need to do while I'm here. I promise you I won't do *anything* that will put you and Lily in any more danger, ok?"

Brenda nodded as she wiped her nose with a tissue.

"Would you mind if I borrowed the truck for a bit?," Cheryl asked.

Brenda stood, walked over to her purse sitting on the end table near the couch and found the keys. She held them out. Cheryl stood, took the keys, and hugged her sister again.

"I'll see you later. We'll go out for dinner, the three of us. My treat," she said and headed out.

Cheryl climbed into the front seat and let out a deep breath. She felt bad for emotionally manipulating her sister, but she needed her to be on board, and she needed her to be upset. She started the truck, put it in gear and drove off. Ten minutes later, she pulled up in front of Keeler Locks and Bolts, parked, and jumped out. She knew Jack only worked part-time, but she was hoping to get lucky. Inside, the store was empty. There were no customers, and no sign of Jack, or anyone else for that matter.

"Hello?," she said as she walked towards the unmanned counter.

A moment later, a door near the back of the shop opened, and Bobby stepped out, closing the door behind him.

"Can I help you, darlin'?," Bobby asked, mustering up as much southern charm as he could.

"You must be Bobby. I'm Cheryl Anderson, a friend of Jack's. Is he here today?"

A giant grin spread across Bobby's face. "He is indeed, young lady. Would you follow me this way?," he asked, gesturing towards his office.

"Why are you smiling like that?," Cheryl asked, smiling a little herself.

"We have a little surprise for you," he replied.

"Oh?," Cheryl said, intrigued. How could they have a surprise for me, Cheryl wondered, since they didn't even know I was coming.

Bobby smiled again. He lifted the divider so she could come behind the counter. She obliged and followed him to the back of the shop. When he got to the door, he put his hand on the knob, smiled at her again, and then opened it. Inside, she saw Jack sitting facing the door, talking to someone with his back to her. Jack smiled when he saw her, then gave a slight nod to the guy he was talking to. Jack's friend stood and turned around to face her. She knew his face instantly.

"Matt!," she exclaimed. Without thinking she rushed over and hugged him hard.

"Hey, Cheryl," he wheezed, as she crushed the wind out of him.

Chapter 73

"Did you get my email? The one about the Rh factor?"

"That was you?!" Cheryl asked.

"It was indeed," Matt replied.

Cheryl was reeling as she struggled to get a handle on this new reality. "How is this possible?!," she asked again, still holding on to Matt. She was overwhelmed with emotion from seeing him. In her mind, he'd been dead for months. That was the idea, he said. A rush of unexpected feelings had washed over her when she saw him. She missed him more than she realized, and she was overjoyed that he was still alive. It took her several minutes to catch her breath as her heart pounded in her chest.

They all took a seat in the office, with the door closed, and Matt retold the story he had already told Jack and Bobby. The murder of Dr. Holst freaked him out. He was worried he'd be next. He was being followed, threatened, his phones were tapped... it was only a matter of time. If he took one wrong step, he was dead. He needed to disappear.

He spent several days hiding out at the gym. John Stirling, the owner, was nice enough to let Matt sleep on the couch in his office. When he was certain no one was watching, he slipped out in the middle of the night. He borrowed some money from John, and paid cash for a bus ticket to Miami. He figured he would blend in nicely with all the shirtless gym rats congregating on the beach. And he was right. He was hidden in plain sight, and no one seemed to notice. And more importantly, no one appeared to be following him. He made friends at a bar on the beach, and they let him crash at their place for a few weeks.

John Stirling told everyone at the gym that Matt had disappeared. That he was genuinely worried about Matt's safety and feared the worst. Anyone that came around asking questions heard the same story. Matt's ruse with the FBI worked flawlessly. John delivered the package containing Matt's phone to Agent Lewis just as he was instructed, and right on time. He had convinced them he was dead and they took it at face value. It didn't occur to Agent Lewis or Cheryl that Matt would have faked his own death.

The only person who knew, other than John Stirling, was Lucas Perth, his boss and editor at the New York Journal.

"What?!," Cheryl said, a little too loud.

Matt shrugged, and with a rather guilty look managed a feeble, "Sorry."

"Sorry? That's the best you can do?"

"I couldn't tell you, Cheryl. Think about it. It would have put you in a compromising situation if anyone asked. Especially if the wrong people asked. And you got snatched up by the FBI before I even made the decision to disappear. Besides, I didn't want Lucas giving my job away," he said with a wink.

"Too late," Cheryl said in a huff. "He's already promoted me from researcher to writer." She folded her arms in a huff and turned her head away.

Everyone chuckled, including Matt. She was behaving like a petulant teenage girl trying to hide her feelings. It wasn't working.

"I know," Matt said with a smile. "I saw your byline on the website. Congrats."

Cheryl started to respond, but Bobby jumped in before she could. "I hate to break up this little soap opera," he said, "but we need to talk about what's next."

"You're right," Jack said.

"Hang on," Cheryl interrupted. She turned to face Matt. "Why did you come back? Why are you here?"

"Because I knew you missed me," he said with a smirk.

"Really? You think sarcasm and glib is the way to go right now?," she replied flatly.

Matt smiled and shrugged. "It's kinda what I do," he said, looking around at each of them. "I came back because I had to know, Cheryl. We are looking at a massive conspiracy, maybe the biggest ever. If we can prove what AstaGen has been doing, we can make them pay. And we can send notice to any other corrupt drug makers that they can't pull this shit. Not on our watch."

There was a short pause as everyone considered the magnitude of what Matt said. He was right. They were going up against a multi-billion dollar company that was perpetrating one of the largest conspiracies in U.S. history. And how high up it went was anyone's guess. Poisoning people for profit. The idea was terrifying.

Jack broke the silence. He told them about the truck he'd seen at the water station, and his theory about the water. How he believed it to be the source of the disease, and that AstaGen was chemically altering it to create cancer in people with B-negative blood. Bobby had heard it once already, but still couldn't wrap his mind around it. Cheryl and Matt both responded with similar looks of astonishment.

"Oh my god," Cheryl said. "The water...." She looked at Jack as tears welled in her eyes, and he nodded. Cheryl was conflicted by the mixed emotions she was feeling. In part, she was relieved. They finally had an idea of how AstaGen was getting people sick. But she was also angry and horrified. The water! Suddenly it all felt very real. She dreaded telling Brenda.

"Wow," Matt said, shaking his head. "It's official. There's nothing safe left to eat or drink."

Cheryl composed herself, and then piled on. She shared the numbers and stats she'd learned. The data from the clinical trials, the statistics regarding blood type, the estimates from the CDC, the dollars at stake. How AstaGen had manufactured a disease so they could sell the drug to treat it. And now, it seemed, they were using something as normally benign as water to contaminate their victims.

Jack and Cheryl looked at each other. They had arrived at the same conclusion from different directions, but they both knew they were right. Now they just had to prove it.

"If they find out we're even talking about this, we're all dead," Bobby submitted, fear creeping into his voice.

"Right now," Jack said, "we can't prove anything. And they know it. They have the drive, they've eliminated anyone that would talk to us, and they sent us packing. They think Matt is dead, and that we've given up. They're counting on our fear to keep us quiet. But before this is over, I will see AstaGen exposed for the monsters that they are, or they will kill me. My son is dead, my wife and daughter are dying, and there are people out there that will be held responsible."

The others nodded their heads in agreement. None of them were willing to just sit back and accept what was happening. Letting AstaGen get away with murder for profit wasn't an option. They all silently committed to seeing this to the end, no matter how it turned out.

Jack laid out his plans. He and Bobby had already begun implementing phase one, but he would need everyone's help before it was over. They were all on board, and eager to get going. But they also knew a LOT of things would have to go their way, and they'd need a good amount of luck to boot. Something that had not been on their side much, but they were due.

Chapter 74

"Make the call," Jack said. They huddled around the table in Brenda's kitchen.

Brenda had taken Lily to the park, giving them the place to work. As much as she wanted to see AstaGen pay, she wanted little to do with what they were up to. But she wouldn't be able to remain uninvolved much longer.

Cheryl pulled out her cell phone and dialed. Once it began to ring, she put it on speaker, and placed the phone on the table. Jack, Bobby and Matt were standing quietly nearby, listening in.

She picked up after three rings. "Special Agent Lewis...."

"Agent Lewis, it's Cheryl Anderson."

"Ah, Cheryl. I wondered when I would hear from you again."

"Have you learned anything new about Gabriel? Have you found him?"

"I'm afraid not, Cheryl. The guy is a ghost."

"Yeah," Cheryl replied.

"What about you? What's going on on your end? Anything new?"

"A lot, actually. We have proof that AstaGen has been contaminating the local water supply with a carcinogen in order to give people with B-negative blood cancer. Then they swoop in like heroes with EBF-14, and sell their newly acquired patient their wonder drug. We have pictures, video, paperwork, even an eyewitness that's willing to testify."

There was a short silence before Cheryl got a response.

"And how did you manage that?," she asked flatly.

"I thought you'd be a little more excited," Cheryl said, looking at Jack.

"Yeah, sorry," Agent Lewis replied. "I am. I guess I'm just a little shocked. This is not what I was expecting today. How did you manage all of that?"

"Jack saw an AstaGen truck at the water plant a few times..."

"An AstaGen truck?," Agent Lewis interrupted. "What does that mean?"

"When Jack was out for a late night run, he saw a truck pulling out from the water plant. He saw it a couple of times, actually. It said *Sagante'* on the side."

"What does that mean?"

"I don't think it means anything. But when you rearrange the letters, it spells AstaGen."

"C'mon, Cheryl, seriously?"

"I didn't believe it at first, either. But it all adds up. Anyway," she continued, "it didn't take Jack long to figure out what was happening. So when the truck came back, we were ready. We took pictures and shot some video. After it left, Jack and Bobby broke into the water plant...."

"Excuse me?!," Agent Lewis interrupted again.

Cheryl looked over at Jack again, and he smiled.

"It's ok. There was very little security, and only a couple of people working at that hour," Cheryl went on. "They made their way to the office, found the paperwork they were looking for, took some more pictures, and started to make their exit. But on their way out, they saw the guy who had been talking with the driver when the truck was there. The one that signed whatever paperwork he'd been given. Anyway, they cornered him and got him to talk."

"How?," Agent Lewis asked.

"Bobby had his gun, and they threatened him."

Agent Lewis audibly sighed through the phone. Bobby had a hard time holding his laughter in.

"He confirmed everything, Agent Lewis," Cheryl went on. "In fact, he was very cooperative, eager to talk. Turns out the guy isn't very happy about what AstaGen is doing in his hometown. He has family here that's sick."

"I've heard enough. We need to meet, Cheryl. I need to see what you have. I want to see the pictures, the video, the paperwork. Bring everything. And I want the name of the guy they spoke to at the plant. I want to know exactly what he told them. You got that? Exactly." There was a lot more energy in Agent Lewis's voice now than at the start of the call.

"Got it," Cheryl said.

"Jack needs to come too."

"Of course," she said, exchanging a glance with him.

"Who else knows about this?"

"Just Bobby," Cheryl said looking at him, and Bobby winked at her.

"Good. Keep it that way," Agent Lewis instructed.

"Of course," Cheryl said.

"You're all in serious danger now, Cheryl. If anyone saw Jack or Bobby at the plant... If AstaGen finds out what you've learned... If the guy they talked to has a change of heart... You know where I'm going with this, right?"

"I do," Cheryl said.

"Good. You and Jack gather up all the evidence you have and get on the first plane to New York. Call me when you land and I'll tell you where to meet me."

"You don't want us to come to your office?"

"No. At this point, I don't know who we can trust. I don't want anyone to see you traipsing through the office. They'll know something's up. I don't even want anyone knowing about this conversation. Call me when you land and I'll give you the location, ok?"

"Ok, no problem."

"Not a word about this to anyone, Cheryl. Are we clear?"

"Crystal."

With that, they hung up. Cheryl picked up her cell phone, made sure the call was ended, and put it in her pocket. She turned to Jack, who stood up straight with his arms folded and a grin on his face.

"Phase two complete," he said, smiling.

Jack pulled out his own cell phone, dialed, and put it to his ear.

"Tommy, it's Jack..."

Chapter 75

After their flight landed at LaGuardia Airport, Cheryl immediately called Agent Lewis again. As they walked through the terminal, she listened intently to the instructions as Agent Lewis gave them.

"Red Hook Grain Terminal, Brooklyn. Got it," she said aloud, more for Jack's benefit than anything else.

Jack jumped on his phone, and began typing away.

"No, just the two of us," he heard her say. "Yes, we have everything. Ok, see you in an hour or so."

Outside, they waited on the taxi line and talked quietly amongst themselves, hoping today things finally went their way. Eventually, they got a cab, jumped in, and gave the driver their destination.

The Red Hook Grain Terminal was built in Brooklyn in 1922. Twelve stories tall and composed of fifty-four circular silos, it was designed to handle two million bushels of grain at one time. But it never lived up to the lofty expectations from when it was built, and from day one fought an uphill battle. Over the years, rising labor costs and intense competition drove it out of business, and it was deactivated in 1965 due to ongoing financial difficulties. The neighborhood went downhill from there, and in the 80s and early 90s, became a infamous breeding ground for crack cocaine. Abandoned for years and now thoroughly run down, the Red Hook Grain Terminal seemed like a strange place for a meeting to Jack and Cheryl.

"Good luck," the cab driver said.

"Thanks," Cheryl said, as she and Jack got out.

They walked slowly through an open gate, towards what appeared to be the main entrance of the terminal. It was much larger in person than it had appeared on Jack's phone. It was mid-afternoon, and the sun had made its way overhead and the shadows were getting longer. As they approached the main doors, they saw a thick rusty chain and padlock wadded up on the ground. They appeared to have been very recently removed.

Jack opened the doors and a loud creak announced their arrival. The main terminal was massive, packed with rows of white columns, extremely high ceilings, and countless windows. The sun shined brightly, illuminating the ground floor as they walked slowly among the columns, looking around. Dirt and dust covered everything, and the cart rails, grain spouts, and staircases were all thoroughly rusted.

As they walked across the dusty floor, Agent Lewis stepped out from behind a column, moving slowly enough as to not startle them. She wore jeans and a white short-sleeve blouse. Her pistol was holstered on her right hip, her FBI badge shining from her belt. "I'm glad you guys made it," she said. "I've been worried about your safety since we last spoke."

"No, we're ok," Cheryl replied.

"So this is Jack," Agent Lewis said, looking at him. "It's nice to finally meet you in person."

"Likewise," he said. "I've heard a lot about you from Cheryl here."

Agent Lewis smiled slightly.

"Did you bring all the evidence you put together?," she asked.

Jack patted the bag slung over his shoulder. "Right here," he said.

"Did you come alone?," Agent Lewis asked.

"We did," Cheryl replied. "Took a cab straight from the airport."

"Yeah, I saw the cab pull up," she said.

"Did *you* come alone, Agent Lewis?," Jack asked bluntly.

"Of course," Agent Lewis said, somewhat taken aback. She placed her hands on her hips, her right hand resting on the hilt of her pistol. "Why do you ask?"

"Just curious," he replied. "Seems like a pretty strange place to meet."

"I already told you," she said. "I'm not sure who to trust anymore. I wanted to make sure we were alone and not disturbed." She looked back and forth between them. "Now, let's have a look at what you brought."

"Sure," Jack said. "But before we do, do you mind if I ask you a question, Agent Lewis?"

"What's that?," she said curtly.

"Where's your radio?"

"My radio?"

"Yeah. Cheryl tells me you always have one attached to your hip anytime you're out of the office. Where's your radio today?"

"It's in the car," she replied. "I didn't want to chance anyone overhearing our conversation."

"I bet," Jack said. "Ok, here's another one. How did Simon Gabriel know about the hacker we brought in to try and crack Dr. Holst's drive?"

"What do you mean?"

"That day in the park, when I went to meet Gabriel," he said. "When he had my daughter tied to a tree. Before he shot me twice in the chest, he said he knew about 'my pals', including my 'hacker buddy'. How would he know that?"

"How am I supposed to know? I have no idea," she said adamantly.

"No?," Jack retorted. "Only a handful of people knew about that. Most of them I trust with my life, including Cheryl. But she told you. And somehow Gabriel found out."

"Jack, Gabriel is a former Navy Seal with a long history and a lot of connections. He could have found out any number of ways." Agent Lewis managed to look offended by the question.

"I see. So you're saying there's a leak somewhere inside the FBI and I've suddenly made you aware of it? That makes me feel so much better."

Agent Lewis folded her arms with a scoff.

"It's also bullshit," Jack said.

"You're being ridiculous, Jack."

"Am I? Let's try this one... How did Gabriel's image get deleted from the FBI's facial recognition database?"

She sighed. "Again, anyone with the appropriate security clearance could have done it. As I told you, I don't know who to trust. That's just another reason why."

Jack shook his head in disbelief. "So what you're telling us, Special Agent in Charge Lewis, is that you are completely unaware of what goes on around you at the FBI and have no knowledge of the leaks and corruption that swirl abundantly under your very nose?"

Agent Lewis was about to respond when there was movement behind her. Out from behind a pillar, over right shoulder, appeared Simon Gabriel, a pistol hanging in his right hand. From behind the pillar to his left, he was joined by one of his colleagues, also gripping a pistol. They walked up and stood to either side of Agent Lewis. Gabriel looked Jack square in the eyes and said, "You're pretty smart, you know that, Jack? Smarter than they were willing to give you credit for. I told them not to underestimate you again, but they didn't listen. And now here we are."

Agent Lewis turned to Gabriel. "Why did you deviate from the plan?"

"He's on to you, obviously," he said, gesturing to Jack. "And I really didn't see the need to listen to any more of this inane back and forth. Besides, he's dead either way. Both of them. No sense playing games. Wouldn't you agree, Jack?"

Jack stood quietly still. His theory was right. He wasn't a hundred percent sure of it until Gabriel walked out from behind the column. Agent Lewis was dirty, and she had been feeding Gabriel information all along. Now here he was, holding a gun, once again poised to kill him.

"How could you?," Cheryl asked, looking at Agent Lewis with a tear in her eye. "I trusted you! Matt trusted you."

"Sorry Cheryl. I liked you, I really did. You're sweet. But there is a lot at stake here. You know that."

"What about Dresden Pharmaceuticals? You went after them. Why not AstaGen?"

"Dresden was foolish. They thought they could beat the rap, that I wouldn't dig up enough evidence against them. As the trial got closer, they got scared, and finally made me an offer. But it was insulting, so I told them to stick it. AstaGen, however, has been quite generous.," she said with a grin.

Agent Lewis paused, looking back and forth between them.

"Oh, and I have some more bad news, for both of you," she continued. "There's no help coming. I know about the other call you made to the FBI. Do you really think my superior officer wouldn't come to me with an issue directly concerning me and a case I've been working? So if you've been stalling with all of these stupid questions in the hopes that the cavalry is coming, you've been wasting your breath."

Cheryl and Jack both appeared deflated. They had no more words. It had come down to this.

Gabriel took a step towards them. "Jack, I thought I killed you once already. I underestimated you. Today, I'm afraid you won't be so lucky." He started to raise his pistol when a deafening bang rang out. It echoed around the warehouse, off the metal walls, making it virtually impossible to determine its origin. Gabriel's pal, standing to Agent Lewis's left, went flying backwards and fell hard to the ground. There was a gaping hole where his eyes used to be, blood rapidly pooling underneath and around his head.

Gabriel, his pistol only partially raised, froze and looked down at his chest. There was a red dot shining brightly, slowly moving up to his head. It was the kind of red dot projected from a laser sight on a rifle scope. The sniper, he thought to himself. He heard a sudden movement behind him, but before he could turn, Tommy and Mike, the Army Ranger he worked with at the Tower, were behind him, pistols raised.

"Don't!," Tommy shouted, telling Gabriel not to try it. "Weapons on the deck, hands up!" Gabriel let the pistol slip out of his grasp and it clattered onto the dusty concrete floor. He slowly raised his hands over his head. Tommy and Mike carefully circled around in front of Gabriel and Agent Lewis. "With your fingertips, very slowly," he said to Agent Lewis, pointing his weapon at her. She removed her pistol from the holster using only the tips of her thumb and pointer finger, and dropped it. Keeping his weapon up, Mike moved in and searched them both for additional weapons. Tommy kept his pistol trained on Gabriel. Mike found a small pistol strapped to Gabriel's ankle, and removed it. He stood back up and rejoined the others.

With a smirk, Jack said, "Looks like the cavalry came after all."

Chapter 76

Alex Volmer was a former Navy Seal and sniper who served three tours during the Iraq war. Tommy met him overseas and, as time passed, they became good friends. Alex was an elite marksman, and his skills as a sniper earned him numerous commendations for heroism and meritorious service in combat, including the Silver Star and two Bronze Stars. "He never misses," Tommy would say.

Alex sat with Tommy and Mike in the back of Tommy's SUV. They waited outside the Tower, engine running, gear loaded. As soon as they got Jack's text, they raced to the Red Hook Grain Terminal. They flew across town, encountered little traffic, and got there well ahead of Agent Lewis and her companions. They broke a window in a distant corner, far from what appeared to be the main entrance. They threw their gear in, climbed through, and moved in single line formation, careful not to disturb too much dust and dirt on the floor.

Alex found an elevated position with an excellent view of about ninety percent of the ground floor. He braved an exceptionally rusty staircase, but it held and he made it safely to his perch. Once his weapon was assembled and he was set, he radioed down to Tommy and Mike. They had taken cover behind a couple of grain silos, far from the front entrance to ensure they'd be able to cover Gabriel and Agent Lewis from behind.

When Gabriel and his pal came out of hiding and appeared before Jack and Cheryl, Tommy and Mike immediately doubled forward. They took position behind the same pillars that had just shielded Gabriel and his buddy. They counted on Alex to be quick on the trigger if anyone raised a weapon at Jack or Cheryl, and he was. After Alex put a hole in his buddy's head, Gabriel froze. He hadn't considered a sniper in a place like this. His hesitation were all Tommy and Mike needed. Gabriel and Agent Lewis had been disarmed, and were now covered by three highly trained ex-military soldiers. Alex was still perched in his elevated position, the red dot still glimmering on Gabriel's chest.

Tommy stared at Gabriel. He had been eagerly awaiting this moment. He swore to avenge the deaths of Lou and Marco, good friends who both died at the hands of Gabriel. Tommy dreamt often of putting a bullet into Gabriel's brain cavity, but that was too easy. He needed to suffer, to know the end was near. Tommy knew Gabriel was well skilled in combat, but it didn't matter. This was about honor. Gabriel had sold out. He'd betrayed the oath he swore as a Navy Seal. He'd murdered civilians, killed his brothers in arms, and sold his soul to the devil by doing AstaGen's dirty work. For Tommy, this was personal. He was willing to risk his own life to honor his lost brothers.

Mike led Agent Lewis by the arm, away from Gabriel, and pushed her face first against the wall. He zip-tied her hands behind her back and sat her down. Jack and Cheryl joined them. Tommy remained perfectly still, his pistol still trained on Gabriel's head.

"What's this?," Gabriel inquired, hands still raised over his head. "An execution?"

"Not exactly," Tommy said, arms extended, staring down the barrel of his gun. "Believe me, there's nothing more I'd rather do than put a bullet through your eye. But I'm going to do for you what you lacked the courage to do for Lou and Marco."

"And what's that?," Gabriel asked, intrigued.

"I'm going to give you a fighting chance. But know this... one way or another, you are going to die today." Tommy gave his words time to sink in. After a few seconds, he lowered his pistol, ejected the magazine, and cleared the chamber. He tossed the now empty weapon aside, removed the knife from his belt, and took off his pack. He moved quickly towards Gabriel, fists clenched. They were on each other in seconds. Tommy was six-foot-five, two-hundred and sixty pounds, and towered over the smaller man. But Gabriel was quick and well trained in combat.

With his large hands, Tommy grabbed Gabriel by the throat and started to squeeze. Gabriel reacted quickly with a sharp kick to the side of Tommy's knee. Tommy's leg buckled, his grip loosened, and Gabriel's hands chopped down on Tommy's forearms. Tommy stumbled sideways, trying to regain his balance. Gabriel didn't hesitate. He launched a barrage of rapid punches and kicks to Tommy's midsection and head. His mastery of the martial arts was rapidly becoming apparent to everyone watching.

Tommy, already bleeding from his nose and above his eye, blocked a kick headed for his ear, and landed a powerful blow to Gabriel's midsection. Gabriel doubled over and Tommy quickly grabbed him around the neck and wrapped him in a headlock. Gabriel reached both arms around Tommy's midsection, and locked his hands together. He tried to lift Tommy up and throw him backwards, but his size and weight proved to be too much. Tommy bent Gabriel farther forward, tightening his grip around his neck. Gabriel reached up with the arm closest to Tommy and put his hand on Tommy's face, pressing his thumb into his eye. As Tommy leaned away, Gabriel's hand followed, pushing Tommy's face back until he was nearly upright. Gabriel positioned his leg directly behind Tommy's and flipped him backwards, slamming him hard to the ground. Tommy's head hit the ground and it was obvious he was reeling. Gabriel pounced. He was on top of Tommy in a flash, leaned forward, and landed several sharp blows to his face. Tommy raised his arms to fight back, but his reflexes were slowed, and Gabriel was quick and skilled.

"Tommy!," Mike shouted, taking a step forward, his weapon coming up.

"Not yet," Tommy said, still battling to get off his back. Gabriel sat up quickly, grabbed at his waist, and pulled a knife from his belt buckle.

"Oh shit!," Jack exclaimed.

Gabriel made a quick slash and Tommy deflected it with his forearm. Gabriel repositioned the knife into stabbing position and thrust downward. Tommy again blocked it, but this time the blade lodged into his left arm. Tommy roared in pain, then slammed his right fist hard into Gabriel's left eye. Hit him clean and rocked Gabriel's senses. With a muffled groan, Tommy quickly pulled the knife out of his arm and lunged upwards, driving it into Gabriel's throat. It penetrated deep, only the short hilt of the knife protruding from his throat. Tommy fell back onto his elbows, knowing he'd struck the fatal blow. Gabriel, still sitting on top of Tommy, dropped both arms to his side, blood rapidly escaping from his neck. His eyes widened with the sudden knowledge that he was about to die. Tommy reached up with his uninjured arm and shoved Gabriel off of him. Gabriel fell hard onto his right side, making no effort to break the fall. He laid there in a heap, eyes open, gasping for air, gurgling through the blood that had filled his throat and lungs.

Tommy kicked Gabriel's legs off of his own, and sat up. He took a moment to catch his breath, as Gabriel got very quiet. Tommy watched as he stopped breathing and the life drained out of him. He sat for a moment as a sense of peace washed over him. He had avenged his fallen brothers. He let out a deep breath and tried to stand, but struggled to get up with an injured knee and only one good arm. Jack rushed over to help him to his feet. Tommy's arm was bleeding profusely.

Mike came over, unzipped his pack, and wrapped Tommy's arm in a hemostatic bandage to help stop the bleeding. He put in a field sling and then tended to Tommy's nose and eye.

When Tommy was patched up, Mike helped him take a seat against a pillar. Alex appeared and joined them, carrying a large sniper rifle with scope and laser sight. The three exchanged handshakes and backslaps. Mission accomplished. Tommy would be fine. He'd taken worse beatings in the field.

Jack walked over to where Agent Lewis was sitting. Cheryl stood next to him.

"What?," she said obnoxiously. "You going to kill me now too? Are you going to kill an FBI agent, Jack? Good luck. They'll hunt you to the ends of the Earth."

Jack smiled. "You know," he began, "you really shouldn't believe everything you hear."

"What is that supposed to mean?"

"About that evidence we told you about…"

"What about it?"

"There isn't any."

Agent Lewis's mouth was slightly agape. "But...," she began.

"Oh we have pictures of the Sagante' truck coming and going. And yes, Bobby and I did break into the water plant. But we didn't find anything. Do you really think AstaGen would be dumb enough to leave a paper trail? Or that some minimum wage moron working the night shift would have any clue what was going on? He had no idea what was on the truck or what they were putting in the water."

She sat there for a moment taking it all in. She'd been tricked, lured out here by phony evidence. And the meeting place *she* chose was exactly what *they* wanted. She swallowed hard and then puffed out her chest.

"This doesn't change anything," she said. "You still have nothing. No proof of anything."

"That's true," Jack said. "But you're wrong about one thing. We just got rid of our two biggest nightmares."

"You've got nothing on me. If you don't let me go, I'll have you arrested for kidnapping and assault on a federal agent."

Just as she was wrapping up her threat, Detective Mark Davies of the NYPD came from behind the nearest pillar. He was holding a digital recording device in his hand. He pressed a button and Agent Lewis heard her own voice playing back: "*Dresden was foolish. They thought they could beat the rap, that I wouldn't dig up enough evidence against them. As the trial got closer, they got scared, and finally made me an offer. But it was insulting, so I told them to stick it. AstaGen, however, has been quite generous."*

Detective Davies clicked the button and the playback stopped. "Agent Lewis, you're under arrest."

Chapter 77

They retreated to Cheryl's small midtown apartment to celebrate. They all wedged in around the kitchen table, each hoisting a cold beer. Jack, Cheryl, Tommy, Mike, and Alex had good reason to smile. Jack's phone sat out on the kitchen table, with Bobby on speakerphone, so he could join in the celebration. Cheryl had already called Matt and told him the good news.

"Umm, why aren't we doing this at the huge penthouse apartment I've heard so much about?," she asked.

"Ooh, it's really nice, Cheryl. You should really see it sometime," Bobby teased over the phone.

Jack and Tommy both chuckled. Cheryl had been wanting to see his parents' penthouse for awhile now. "I really want to keep my parents out of this. They're still traumatized from what happened in the park. After Gabriel attacked them, took Emma, and shot Marco right in front of them, they can't handle any more drama."

Cheryl nodded. It was hard to fault Jack for wanting to keep his family out of this. *They've been through enough*, she thought.

"You know," Jack said, thinking about what they'd just done, "today might be the first time since this all started that things went the way we planned."

"Really?," Tommy said. He held up his injured arm that still hung in a sling. "I wasn't exactly planning on getting stabbed in the arm."

"Oh, don't be a baby," Jack said with a laugh. He was giving Tommy a taste of his own medicine, hitting him with the same line Tommy used after Jack had been shot twice in the chest.

Everyone laughed, they couldn't help it. It was a great feeling, and they all breathed a well-earned sigh of relief. Simon Gabriel was gone. Jack, in particular, was thrilled he would no longer have to look over his shoulder for the man with the scar under his eye.

"You were incredible, Tommy. Really," Jack said with the utmost admiration.

"You really were," Cheryl agreed. The others nodded their agreement.

"It took you long enough," Mike goaded.

Tommy responded by flipping Mike off with his good hand. "He was a feisty little fucker."

Agent Lewis had been taken away by Detective Davies. The FBI was made aware of her arrest and the charges impending against her. She would no longer be feeding AstaGen information. An investigation was already underway into her bank accounts, and hopefully soon a connection would be made between her and AstaGen.

Every little bit helps, Jack had said, and if they could nail them on bribing a federal officer, that was a step in the right direction.

The laughter continued. They clinked glasses in recognition of a fine victory in their campaign against AstaGen. Two of their major players had been taken off the board, and they had good reason to celebrate. Jack felt better than he had in years.

"I hate to bring the rain to this parade," Cheryl interjected, putting her beer down, "but Agent Lewis was right. We're not any closer than we were when we started. We still have nothing. No evidence to go on, no proof of anything."

"Yet," Jack emphasized. "But what we do have is a plan."

"Yeah, about that...," Bobby chimed in over the phone.

"Yeah?," Jack said, leaning in closer.

"A couple of questions..."

"Go on," Jack said warily.

"What sense does it make to go after the drive when we still have no clue how to open it?"

Bobby asked a legitimate question, one that all of them were thinking. They exchanged glances around the table, waiting for Jack's answer. He took a sip of his beer as he considered his words. He put his glass down on the table and said, "You might be right, Bobby. But without the information on that drive, this has all been for nothing. We may not know how to access it yet, but once it's in our hands, we can take our time and figure it out. We can't afford for that drive and whatever's on it to be destroyed."

"That brings me to my next question," Bobby said. "How do we know they haven't already destroyed it?"

Jack turned to Tommy, who said, "According to Prowler, the tracking software was still active as of yesterday. If they had destroyed the drive, it would no longer be emitting a homing signal."

"They must be curious," Jack said. "They want to know what's on it."

There was a pause before Bobby said, "Did the tracking software provide a location?"

"It did," Jack said.

"I'm afraid to ask... where is it?"

"In California. At AstaGen's corporate headquarters."

"Oh, great!," Bobby said sarcastically.

"That's not even the best part," Jack said. "We need to get in, get the drive, and get out without anyone knowing we were ever there."

"And how the hell are we supposed to do that?!," Bobby said, once again verbalizing what everyone else was thinking.

"We're gonna need some help," Jack replied plainly. "Yours for starters, Bobby." They could all hear his exasperated breath coming through the phone.

Jack turned and looked at Cheryl. "And Brenda's."

Cheryl nodded. She knew this was coming. This was not a conversation she was excited to have with her sister. But she had been planning for it and was ready.

Chapter 78

U.S. Ally Security was founded in early 2002, not long after the September 11th attack on the United States. Their primary objective was to protect corporate networks from the inside against outside intrusions using data security, insider threat analysis, and advanced network protections. With thousands of clients in countries all around the world, U.S. Ally Security was one of the largest Cyber-Security companies in the world. They were routinely in the top-five on the annual Cybersecurity 500 list, and had numerous clients among the Forbes 50, including, but not limited to, AstaGen Pharmaceuticals.

Brenda was one of the assistant information security officers (AISO) at U.S. Ally Security. Her job was to assist the Chief Information Security Officer (CISO) in ensuring the information of their clients was adequately protected. She was responsible for security clearance approval, travel coordination, training process management, and processing sensitive specific data. She also assisted the CISO with the development and distribution of security visit requests to client facilities, ensuring sensitive data was maintained and secured, and company badge identification issuance and tracking.

"You're crazy," Brenda said.

"It's the only way," Cheryl responded. "Everything hinges on this, Brenda. We can't do it without you."

The two sisters sat across from each other at Brenda's kitchen table, each with their hands wrapped around a mug of hot tea. It was late. Brenda had been getting ready for bed when Cheryl knocked on the front door. Lily was already asleep. Cheryl had come straight from the airport, anxious to talk to Brenda and get the ball rolling. Everyone was counting on her. They needed Brenda on board.

"I don't know, Cheryl. I could get fired. Worse, I could get sent to prison. You don't know how many things I had to sign swearing I would never violate a client's trust."

Cheryl took a breath. This was the part she had been dreading.

"Brenda, we found out how they've been making people sick. How they made you and Lily sick."

Brenda sat up slightly in her chair, listening.

"It's the water," Cheryl said softly.

"The water? What do you mean? What water?," Brenda asked.

"The town's water. The water you drink every day. A truck visits the water station once a month. It comes late at night. They are contaminating the water with a pollutant of some kind, a carcinogen that is causing cancer in people with B-negative blood."

Brenda's jaw went slack. "What?," she said, weakly, a tear in her eye.

Cheryl nodded, a slow, sympathetic nod.

Brenda let go of the mug. She stared down at the table. "Oh my god," she whispered.

Cheryl reached over and put a hand on Brenda's arm. "They're poisoning people for profit, Brenda. You, Lily, and countless others. All to sell their drug. But we can stop them. You and me. Think about Lily. Think about all the other kids out there who are sick. Who *will* be sick. We can stop it. But I can't do it alone. I need your help."

Cheryl hated this. She was exploiting her sister's emotions, and it made her nauseous. But it didn't matter now. This was too important, and she needed Brenda's help. Without it, what they had to do next would be almost impossible.

Brenda raised her head to look at Cheryl. Her eyes were red and watery.

"How?," she asked. "How will you stop them?"

"There's information out there, Brenda. Information that will prove what they've been doing. With it, we can expose them for the monsters that they are. We will show the world what a greedy pharmaceutical company like AstaGen is willing to do, just how low they will go. Everyone will know they have been poisoning people, giving them cancer, so they can sell their drug and make more money."

Cheryl paused for a moment. As she spoke, she could see Brenda's grief slowly turning to anger. She pressed on.

"But without that information, we can't expose them, Brenda. And if we don't expose them, they'll just keep doing it. And more people will get sick, more people will die. And they will keep making money, laughing at us, all the way to the bank. They'll win."

Cheryl stood up, slowly walked around the table and sat down right next to her sister. "This is no ordinary client, Brenda. They're literally killing people. Those that can't afford EBF-14 die a quick and painful death. And the ones that don't die, the ones that are *lucky* enough to be able to take their precious drug, have to live life under a cloud of uncertainty with a diagnosis of terminal cancer looming over their head. What kind of life is that? What kind of life have you and Lily been living this past year? These people don't deserve to be protected, Brenda. They deserve to be exposed. They need to pay for what they've done."

Brenda listened intently, nodding as Cheryl spoke. When she was finished, Brenda she sat up a little taller, wiped her eyes, and said, "What do you want me to do?"

Chapter 79

With their newly requisitioned uniforms and freshly printed ID badges, the four-man U.S. Ally Security team strolled through the front doors of AstaGen headquarters.

The building was a massive, towering structure seventy-six floors high, wrapped in glass. It was surrounded by tall pine trees, green grass, and a parking lot that looked big enough to accommodate all the Black Friday shoppers in Southern California. With over 120,000 employees, many of whom worked in the building, AstaGen's corporate headquarters was like a small city. There was a cafeteria, day care, a fitness center with an Olympic sized pool, sleep pods, a hair salon, massage rooms, an on-site medical clinic, even a dry cleaner. They had anything and everything to keep their employees happy and productive.

AstaGen headquarters was also home to the most advanced research laboratories in the world. Here they developed gene-based drugs to target diseases on a molecular level. Nearly all of the company's research and development happened in this facility. Doctors and scientists worked around the clock developing new drugs and, apparently, new diseases. EBF-14 was born here. Soon, hopefully, it would be determined if Omnicarcinos was too.

The entire fortieth floor of the building was dedicated to computer servers which housed all of AstaGen's data files. Everything from employee information and financial data, to research and patents were stored in servers and storage banks that spanned the entire floor. This is where the U.S. Ally Security team would be running their information security audit today. But before they made their way to the fortieth floor, they needed to pay a visit to the security office on the ground floor.

It was standard operating procedure for the information security team to make sure the on-site security was doing their job. The four-man team swiped their card keys over the turnstile sensors, and following a quick beep, marched across the lobby making a bee-line for the security office. The lobby was a massive expanse lit by the sunlight streaming in through the windows on all sides. They walked past a reception desk, multiple fountains, TVs running different news stations, even a coffee bar. When they finally reached the security office, two knocks was all it took before the door opened.

"You're early," the security officer who opened the door said. "We weren't expecting you for another two hours."

"We like to keep you on your toes," Jack said. "It's not as much fun when you're ready and waiting for us." The audit was scheduled for ten in the morning, but Jack and his 'team' arrived just after eight. The fake mustache he wore itched his upper lip, but he tried to ignore it. They presented their IDs, then followed the guard inside the security office. Jack walked to the far end of the room, and Tommy, Bobby, and Prowler squeezed in behind him, all dressed in matching uniforms. Black polyester pants, black shoes, a white, short sleeve button down shirt with straight black tie, and black hat. No guns, or weapons of any kind were visible. Tommy did, however, have two concealed pistols and a knife tucked away.

The AstaGen security guards wore similar looking uniforms, but blue pants not black, and each of them had a pistol holstered on their hip with a nightstick on the opposite side. This level of security work required prior law enforcement, military or security experience, and some level of firearms training. Jack had absolutely no intention of finding out how good the guards were with their guns.

Since he was the only one of them who had been followed and watched, his face would be the most recognizable, and as such, Jack was the only one in disguise. He had glued on a phony mustache, wore glasses with no prescription, and a blond wig peeked out from under his new hat. Getting dressed this morning, he couldn't help but laugh at his appearance. But he hardly recognized himself, so he went with it. Plus, it matched the picture on his ID, so there was no turning back.

There were a total of three guards that manned the security office, now all seated at their consoles, watching the wall of monitors before them. They knew they were not to speak to the audit team unless spoken to directly. There were two large screens mounted centrally, surrounded by dozens of medium sized screens. Below them was a row of even smaller monitors. Mounted over the main displays were two large digital clocks, indicating east and west coast times.

The control panel where the guards were seated contained hundreds of lighted buttons, each linked to different cameras or monitors, all connected to joysticks that allowed them to pan the cameras in different directions, zoom in, and record at will.

Another smaller panel was embedded with a series of switches and buttons that enabled the officers to lock and unlock certain doors in the building, and even override security lockdown protocols in the event of an alarm.

In the center of the massive control desk sat three phone terminals, each with dozens of buttons, allowing the guards to connect to virtually anyone anywhere in the building. One of the guards was on the phone now confirming the arrival of the U.S. Ally Security Team and logging it into the computer. The system had already registered their arrival when they had swiped their access cards, but the manual entry was procedure, and ensured accurate information if a security/information audit were to take place, like today's.

Jack and his team quietly observed the guards at their consoles. Tommy held out a small foldable pad, pretending to take very thorough notes.

"Anything to report since your last audit?," Jack asked.

"No, sir," said the guard who let them into the office. "Anything that had been flagged last time has been addressed. Would you like to see the previous audit report and the changes that have been implemented?"

"Not right now," Jack said, nonchalantly. "Tell me about the server floor. Who has access to it?"

Jack and the others were eager to get to work, but it would look suspicious if the security team performing the security audit didn't ask at least a few questions. Brenda told them where to go, what to do and what to say. They needed to stick to the plan.

"Just the security team, the in house I.T. guys, and a few of the corporate higher ups. But the I.T. guys have to check in with us before they access the floor or make any modifications or repairs to anything."

"What about data theft?," Prowler asked. He leaned in between two of the guards to get a closer look at the monitors. "How do you ensure that no one that accesses that floor walks away with valuable data?" He stepped back and returned to his spot next to Jack.

The security guard on the left, closest to them, looked up at Prowler. "Once the I.T. guys check in with us, their bags and their persons are searched. No hand held devices of any kind are allowed on the fortieth floor. That includes cell phones, flash drives, digital cameras, even iPods. Nothing but the tools they need to do their work. And the search is repeated after their work is complete."

"And what about the security guards that patrol the floor?," Tommy asked.

All three guards turned in their chairs to look at Tommy oddly. With a confused look, the first guard said,

"There is no roving patrol on the fortieth floor. It's locked up tight. No one gets in or out without our say so."

Tommy screwed up and he knew it, but Jack covered quickly. "He's new, don't mind him," he said with a wave and a smile. "That's why we make him take notes," Jack said, and winked. For a moment, Jack thought they were busted, that they'd come all this way for nothing. But the guards bought Jack's story. They spun around in their chairs, returned their attention to the screens, and forgot about Tommy.

The questions were getting wearisome, but they had to make it look legit. Tommy had just raised a warning flag, they couldn't afford another. They needed to be patient.

"When was the last time anyone accessed the fortieth floor?"

"Yesterday," the same guard said. "We had an issue with a storage array and an I.T. team member repaired it. Took them about an hour. They were in and out without issue."

"Mmm hmm," Jack mumbled. He glanced at Prowler who gave him a subtle nod. "Ok," Jack said, "we're going to head up for the physical inspection and information audit. As you know, the audit team is not to be disturbed, so you need to ensure that absolutely no one attempts to access the floor while the audit is going on. Understood?"

Each of the guards nodded, practically in unison. "Yes sir," the first guard replied.

"Now," Jack went on, "I need to watch you turn off surveillance for the fortieth floor. Audio and video." Jack followed Brenda's script to the letter.

The guard in the middle brought up the cameras for the fortieth floor on the two main monitors, and about a dozen of the surrounding screens. The banks of servers and storage housings were clearly visible across the various monitors. They were lined in rows far beyond the range of the cameras. The guard then hit a few buttons and the screens all went black.

"Good," Jack said. "Now disengage any alarms connected to the server ports. I don't need to hear any sirens blaring when we plug in to run the audit."

"It's already done."

"Very good. We'll let you know when we're finished." He nodded to his team and they made their way out of the security office. They turned left and headed towards the elevators. Once inside, Jack hit the button for the fortieth floor. The doors closed, but the elevator did not move. The light around the button Jack pressed was red. Then he remembered the card. He inserted his security access card into the slot above the floor numbers. A small beep sounded, the light on the button changed from red to green, and they started to move. They knew the elevators had audio and video surveillance, so no one spoke. They were quickly whisked upwards, and when they reached the fortieth floor, the doors opened and they all stepped out.

The doors closed behind them, and the elevator headed back down.

The fortieth floor was a massive expanse of servers lined evenly in rows as far as the eye could see. In order to keep the servers from overheating, it was extremely cold. They could see their breath when they spoke. Everyone relaxed a little, knowing they could no longer be seen or heard. They gathered together and Prowler unzipped his bag. He pulled out what looked like a large portable TV, about the size of an iPad.

Back in the security office, Prowler had discretely placed a small transmitter under the desk near the central bank of monitors. The device wirelessly intercepted video signals and then transmitted those same signals to a receiver with a unique frequency. A receiver like the one Prowler held now. He turned it on, and in just a few moments, four images divided the screen, bright and clear. He started toggling through the different screens, displaying every part of the building. Everything the guards in the security office could see.

He looked up at Jack with a smile and said, "We have video."

Chapter 80

"You up for this?," Jack asked.

"Well I didn't come all this way just to freeze my ass off in here," Bobby replied. They all let out a nervous laugh.

"Ok, here's the deal," Prowler said. "They can't see or hear us in here, but once you step outside this room, you're fair game. We'll be watching the screen to make sure they don't have eyes on you, but according to Brenda, they monitor the cameras in sequence. So as long as you head out right after they look at the floor above us, you should have a good forty-five minutes before they look again. They don't spend much time on the stairwell, but they do check it. If anyone is coming your way, we'll let you know. But remember, that's about all we can do from in here."

"Got it," Jack replied.

"Earpieces," Prowler said. He handed out a small plastic case to each of them. Inside was a small earpiece, similar to the one Jack had been given by Gabriel that day in the park. They each opened their case and inserted them into an ear. Now they could communicate hands free. They could talk and hear each other, and it was small enough not to be seen by anyone looking.

"I really think I should come with you, Jack," Tommy said. "If you run into trouble, like an armed guard, I'm gonna feel pretty helpless sitting in here just watching on Prowler's stupid little screen."

"Hey man, this thing is state of the art!," Prowler objected.

"Whatever," Tommy replied flatly.

"I appreciate it, Tommy, I do," Jack said. "But we can't afford even the smallest encounter with a guard. We need to get the drive and get out of here without raising any alarms. If we attract attention, it's over. If AstaGen knows I was here, and the drive turns up missing, they will stop at nothing to get it back. They will kill me, you, and anyone else they think was involved. Then they'll go after my family. I need you and Prowler to be our eyes and ears to make sure that doesn't happen. They can't ever know I was here."

"Who's gonna know you were here with that awesome costume you got on?," Bobby teased.

"Alright," Jack said with a smirk, brushing off Bobby's remark. "Say when, Prowler."

Not being able to use the elevator meant they had to climb thirty-six flights of stairs. Bobby was not excited. He slung his bag over his shoulder. It was an official U.S. Ally Security bag, but it was loaded with his tools. Jack carried a similar bag, full of miscellaneous parts Bobby wanted with them. "Just in case," he'd said. They stood near the door that led to the stairs. The tracking software still indicated the drive was on the top floor, in a large corner office. According to the building blueprints Prowler had 'found' online, it was the office of Dr. Albrecht Müller, the founder of AstaGen. The fact that the drive was in his office meant the conspiracy went all the way to the top.

"Ok, here we go," Prowler said. "Sixty seconds. Get ready." He watched the screen intently. "Remember, forty five minutes to get up there, get in, get the drive, and get back down here. You ready?"

"As ready as I'm gonna be," Bobby quipped.

"I'm ready," Jack said.

The seconds ticked down and everyone watched nervously.

"Go!," Prowler said.

With that, they opened the door onto the stairwell and started climbing. It was a steady pace for the first ten flights, but fatigue hit quickly, and Bobby slowed down. Exercise was not one of his favorite things, and he was panting heavily. Jack, on the other hand, had barely broken a sweat. "Don't say a word," Bobby wheezed, as Jack gave him a look of derision.

"I told you to get off that stool once in awhile," Jack teased.

Bobby was conserving his breath and opted against making a wiseass remark. Instead he just flipped Jack off with both hands. Jack laughed.

Though they were moving slowly, they were ahead of the schedule Jack had mentally drawn up. Even at twenty seconds per flight, it would take just twelve minutes to get to the top. That left thirty three minutes to get the drive and get back down to the server room. As they passed the sixtieth floor, Bobby stopped.

"I need to sit down."

"Bobby, we really need to keep moving. I know you're tired, but we're on the clock here."

"Would you rather I drop dead right here?"

With a sigh and a 'gimme-a-break' eye roll, Jack put his hands on his hips, as Bobby caught his breath. He began tapping his foot as he waited impatiently

"That's not helping," Bobby said.

"Right now, neither are you. Let's go already."

"Umm, why is Bobby sitting?," came Tommy through their earpieces. "Is he waiting to have a pizza delivered?"

"Fuck off, all of you." Bobby pushed himself up and they were moving again. Several minutes later, they reached the top floor. Bobby was breathing hard, but he'd live. The door from the stairwell into the building was locked. A few clicks later, and Bobby had the lock open. "Child's play," he said. Jack always enjoyed watching Bobby at work.

"You're good to go," Prowler said. "The hallway is clear."

They stepped out of the stairwell and started making their way down the hall towards Müller's office.

"Hang on," Prowler said. "There's a receptionist desk coming up on your right. It looks empty. The computer is off and the chair is pushed in. Doesn't look like anyone has been there yet today. Keep moving."

"That's comforting," Bobby said sarcastically.

They eased past the reception desk. Prowler was right. The light was off over the desk, the chair was pushed in, and everything was straight and neat on the desk. No one had been there today. Down at the end of the hall they could see Müller's office. They approached the door, and

322

Jack turned to wave into one of the security cameras mounted over head.

Prowler saw him on his screen. "You're doing great, guys," he said.

"Oh, shit," Bobby said.

Jack turned to see why. "What is that?!," he asked.

"It's a biometric scanner locking system. It requires a positive fingerprint and retinal scan for entry. I have one on order for the shop. It hasn't come in yet."

"Well here's your chance," Tommy said. "Have at it."

"It's not that simple, sport," Bobby retorted. "This is not like picking a lock. It has an internal locking mechanism that will slam into place the second it realizes we're not Dr. What's-his-face."

"Müller," Jack said.

"Whatever!," Bobby snapped. "This wasn't on the blueprints. I have no idea how to defeat this thing." He threw up his hands in frustration.

Jack ran his hands roughly through his hair and started to pace. "We have to try something. Prowler, how we doing on time?"

"You have about twenty minutes left before they start scanning the upper floors."

"Goddammit," Jack replied. "Bobby, come on! If this was the shop, what would you do?"

"I would take the piece of shit completely apart, like I always do, to see how the internal mechanisms work. Then I would find a weakness, something I could bypass or defeat, then put it back together, and test my theory. I would do that over and over again until I beat the sucker. Not really an option here."

Jack resumed pacing. He walked back and forth for several minutes before an idea struck. "Hang on!," he said, excited. "Who makes that thing?"

"Samsung. Why?," Bobby asked.

A big smile spread across Jack's face. It took Bobby a moment before he realized where Jack was going with this. He smiled in return.

"Umm, what are you guys smiling about? The clock is ticking here," Tommy said.

"Let's just say I've been here before," Jack said, as he remembered standing outside Dr. Holst's office door. "Think it'll work?," he asked Bobby hopefully.

"No idea," Bobby said. "But it's all we've got." He reached into his bag and grabbed a couple of tools. He went to work on the device, and managed to pop the outer housing off, revealing some of the internal electronics. Jack fished around inside his bag until he found what he was looking for. His hand came out with a nine-volt battery and some loose wire.

"Just in case," he said with wink.

He set the bag down and moved over to the door, near Bobby.

"If this doesn't work, we're screwed," Bobby said.

"I'm so glad you're here," Jack said, sarcasm painted on his face.

Jack wrapped one end of each wire to a post on the battery. As he brought it close to the device, a thought occurred to him.

"Hey, Prowler?," he said.

"Yeah?"

"Is anyone inside this office? Is Dr. Müller working in there?"

"That's a good question," Bobby said with a nod.

There was a short pause.

"I don't know," Prowler replied.

Jack stood up straight, turned, and looked up at the camera overhead. "What do you mean you don't know?"

"I don't have a video feed from inside his office. Either there's no cameras in there, or it's being monitored from somewhere other than the security office."

"That's just great!," Jack said. "What if he's in there?"

Suddenly Bobby balled up a fist and rapped twice on the door.

"What the hell are you doing?!," Jack shouted in a whisper.

"Quickest way to find out," Bobby calmly replied.

Jack scurried behind the reception desk while Bobby placed the cover back on the lock. If Müller was there, he might recognize Jack, even in disguise. Hopefully, he would think Bobby was just a random security guard. His heart was pounding as they waited for what seemed a very long time. Ten seconds later, Bobby knocked again. Still no answer.

"I don't think anyone's home," he said. "Let's try this."

Jack crawled out from behind the desk and went back to the door. Bobby popped off the cover once again and Jack got the battery ready. When they had agreed on what they both believed was the processor, Jack brought the two exposed wires in close, the nine-volt battery dangling from the other end. He touched the wires to the processor. They was a small buzzing sound, followed by a ding, and then a click. He turned his head to look at Bobby, who was smiling.

"Bingo," he said.

Chapter 81

The handle turned smoothly and the door opened without resistance. They pushed it open slowly and quietly, but the office inside was empty. Bobby had been right, no one was home. It was not yet eight-thirty in the morning, so it was possible Dr. Müller's office hours started a little later. They were hoping for a lot later. Jack scooped up his bag and threw the battery and wires inside. Bobby replaced the cover of the lock, making sure it snapped into place. He picked up his bag and they stepped inside, closing the door behind them.

Morning light blazed through the windows of the massive corner office. The word 'office' didn't have the right feel for this room, Jack thought. It was more like the Presidential Suite of a luxury hotel had been merged with a conference room. There was a grand desk in the corner where the two walls made up of only windows met, accompanied by two plush chairs facing it. Several feet away was a huge mahogany conference table with at least twenty chairs circling it. There were several elaborate chandeliers hanging high over polished marble floors, a koi pond snaking its way through the office, a full bar, several couches, and multiple wall-mounted televisions. The walls were also adorned with expensive paintings, wall hangings, and shelves filled with books, small sculptures, and collectibles.

"Jesus Christ," Bobby said, awed by the magnitude of the room. He stood just inside the door, taking it all in. To their right, hanging on the wall over the bar was a painting of Dr. Albrecht Müller. "What kind of asshole hangs a picture of himself in his own office?," Bobby asked.

"The kind that's willing to poison and kill people for money," Jack replied.

Bobby slowly nodded in agreement. "Touché."

"Now let's find the drive and get the hell out of here," Jack said.

"Ok guys," came Prowler over their earpieces. "The tracking signal is coming from the northeast corner of the room. Should be in the far corner to your right. What's over there?"

"A big-ass desk," Bobby replied.

"Let's go," Jack said. They moved quickly, but carefully, across the office, looking all around as they walked.

"Hey, there's fish in there," Bobby said, pointing to the small stream winding through the office.

"Great. Come on," Jack urged.

As they approached the desk, Jack looked up at the ceiling. He didn't see any cameras anywhere. Evidently, Dr. Müller didn't want anyone seeing or hearing what took place in this office. "No cameras," he said.

"Hmmf," Bobby replied, looking up.

"Strange," Prowler said.

Jack and Bobby walked around to the front of the desk. It was the most beautiful desk either of them had ever seen. It was a rich rosewood with a glossy, polished surface that stretched wide across the top, before rounded corners dove into smooth, curved edges. Each drawer had a handle shaped like a golden leaf that pulled them open. Jack ran his fingers over one of the leaves, wondering if it was made of real gold.

The desk was immaculately clean, without a scratch, smudge or fingerprint visible. The sheen of the polished surface was so bright and clear, it allowed them to see every detail of the wood. The desk even smelled expensive. There was a long leather blotter on the surface, with a matching pen set, clock, and paper tray sitting behind it.

"Wow," Bobby said. Jack nodded in agreement.

"We're at the desk," Jack said, letting Tommy and Bobby know of their progress. He pulled out the high-backed leather chair, took a seat, and started opening drawers. The inside of the drawers were lined with brown, hand-stitched leather. The four top drawers of the desk opened with ease, but contained nothing of interest. Two of the lower drawers on Jack's left were locked, but were opened easily by Bobby. They quickly thumbed through them, but neither contained the drive.

On the right side of the desk, near the bottom, Jack pulled on a golden leaf which opened a larger, deeper drawer, about twice the size of the others. Inside the drawer, facing up, was a black safe with a ten-digit keypad and a small key lock. Bobby scratched his chin, opened his bag of tools, and got to work. The safe was open in less than sixty seconds.

There it was. Just inside the safe, on top of a stack of papers, sat a small, black portable hard drive. Jack recognized it immediately. He grabbed it out of the safe and tossed it into his bag, wondering if the security guards downstairs would insist on searching it later. Right now, that didn't matter. They'd found it, and the adrenaline made his heart race. Jack reached into his back pocket and pulled out a duplicate hard drive.

"Just in case," he said to Bobby with a wink.

He wiped it down carefully with a rag to remove any fingerprints, and put it in the exact same spot and orientation as the one he'd just removed from the safe.

Bobby closed it back up, made sure it locked, and they closed the drawer. Jack wiped down all the drawers, the surface of the desk, even the arms of the chair.

"We got it," Jack said to Tommy and Prowler, trying to contain his excitement. "How we doing on time?"

"They should start scanning the upper floors again in about twelve minutes," Prowler replied.

"Oh shit!," Bobby exclaimed.

Jack pushed the chair back under the desk and gave it one last wipe. Together, they checked to make sure nothing on the desk had been disturbed. The two looked at each other, shared a nod, and began moving quickly back to the door.

"Wait, how are we going to re-lock that thing on the door?," Jack asked urgently as they walked.

"We're not," Bobby replied simply. "They'll just have to wonder if they remembered to activate it last night, or if it might be malfunctioning. They will have no way to tell we bypassed it, so don't worry."

"Ok," Jack said. There was nothing they could do about it now anyway.

"Umm, guys," Tommy said over their earpieces. "We have a small problem."

Jack and Bobby both stopped in their tracks, just a few feet from the door.

"The secretary is sitting at her desk, right outside the door."

Chapter 82

They were stuck, and the clock was ticking. Security would begin scanning the upper floors in a matter of minutes, and they were trapped inside Dr. Müller's office. With the secretary sitting just outside, they didn't dare open the door.

"Even if we left now, they'd see us in the stairwell," Jack said. "We'll never make it back down in time."

"We have to do something," Bobby said. "We can't stay in here."

There was a pause as everyone tried to think of what to do.

"Actually," Tommy piped up, "that's exactly what you should do."

"What do you mean?," asked Jack.

"Prowler said security will begin scanning the upper floors in about five minutes. It takes them about twenty minutes to get down below the fortieth floor. So hang out in there for the next twenty-five minutes until it's clear again. In the meantime, let's work on getting the secretary out of there."

Jack and Bobby looked at each other. Since neither of them had any better ideas, they shrugged their shoulders, and Jack said, "Ok." He checked his watch. It was going to be a long twenty-five minutes.

"Should I fix us a drink?," Bobby asked, gesturing to the full bar on their right.

"I think it's a little early in the day for that, don't you?"

Bobby shrugged, not sure he completely agreed with Jack's sentiment.

They stood just inside the office, staring at the door, wondering how they were going to get rid of Müller's secretary. Jack folded his arms, and stared up at the ceiling. Above them was a beautiful chandelier, with five tiers of crystal cones connected in the shape of a ring, each ring getting smaller as they descended. Bobby, curious as to what Jack was looking at, also looked up. For a moment, they just stood there, mesmerized by the beauty of the chandelier. From behind them, inside the office, they heard what sounded like a door opening.

"Hello, Jack."

Startled, they both turned. A man was standing across the office, just outside a now open door, in front of what was clearly a bathroom. He looked to be in his early to mid-sixties, with white hair, silver glasses, and a neatly groomed goatee. He wore grey suit pants, a white long-sleeve button down shirt, a black and grey silk tie, grey suspenders, and black dress shoes. The only thing missing was his jacket. He was smiling at Jack as he dried his hands on a small beige towel. Jack did a quick scan of the office. To his immediate left, just inside the doors was a coat rack, on which hung a grey suit jacket. Neither he nor Bobby had seen it, and he wondered how they'd missed it. Dr. Müller had been here the entire time.

"I must admit, I'm extremely impressed," he said. He spoke with a German accent, one that had lessened from years of speaking English, but was still present. He turned partly around, tossed the towel into the bathroom, and started walking towards his desk. Jack and Bobby instinctively headed that way too. They were caught and had no idea what was going to happen next. Dr. Müller pulled out his chair and took a seat at his desk. "Please," he said, gesturing to the two chairs across from him. Jack and Bobby reluctantly took a seat.

Dr. Müller propped his elbows up on the desk and interlaced his fingers.

"You're in the lion's den now, huh?," he asked with a smirk.

Jack and Bobby remained silent, not sure what to say.

"By the way, that painting of me was a gift from a very old friend." He pointed across the office to his portrait that hung over the bar. "He's a very talented artist. It would have been an incredible insult not to hang it so people could enjoy his work."

Again, they said nothing. Jack peeled off the fake moustache, took off his phony glasses, and removed his hat and wig.

"That's better," Dr. Müller said with a smile. "Now, let's get down to it, shall we? Surely you must realize the depth of trouble you're in. Your two friends on the fortieth floor have already been detained, and there are armed guards standing just outside the door to this office."

He gave them both a moment for that information to sink in.

"The security office downstairs has been notified that you're all imposters and your information audit is fraudulent. And despite your previous declaration, there are, in fact, cameras all over this office. They are monitored and recorded from a smaller security office on this floor, that's not on any blueprints."

Jack and Bobby sank lower in their seats. Their situation was getting worse by the second and both of them couldn't help but wonder if they were going to survive this.

"So, we have video evidence of you breaking into this office... again, very impressive... breaking into my desk, and stealing private property."

"Property that doesn't belong to you," Jack snapped.

"Pish posh," Dr. Müller replied. "And you can prove that? Of course not. Just like every other contention you've made about my company. You've never been able to prove anything, and you still can't."

"You're a real piece of shit, you know that?," Bobby said angrily.

Dr. Müller turned calmly to Bobby. "And you are?"

"I think you know who he is, Dr. Müller. You've known what we've been up to all along, haven't you?"

Dr. Müller simply smiled at Jack. "I have my resources. Now, I believe you have something that belongs to me." He extended an arm towards Jack and held his hand out, waiting.

Jack leaned over slightly, reached down into his bag, and pulled out the hard drive. He placed it in Dr. Müller's hand.

"Thank you," he said.

"Do you mind if I ask you a couple of questions, Dr. Müller?"

"I see no harm in that now," he replied. Both Jack and Bobby knew what he meant by that.

"What's on that drive that's so important that you would kidnap and murder to get it back?," Jack asked.

"I have no idea what's on it," he admitted, looking at the drive in his hand. "Dr. Holst was remarkably effective in protecting whatever information is on it."

"Is that why you killed him? Because of whatever's on that drive?"

"Dr. Holst developed a conscience. He suddenly became uncomfortable with the agreement we'd had for years. And he was planning to reveal our secrets to a reporter. I simply could not allow that," Dr. Müller said matter of factly.

"And Jonathan Aker?"

"Ah, Dr. Aker. He felt he was being treated unfairly despite his continued and prolonged absences from work. While he was one of our most valued researchers, and, if I'm being honest, the father of EBF-14, his absence from the lab could no longer be tolerated. Initially, we had just planned to terminate his contract and let him go, but when he decided to reveal confidential information about his work here, he had to be silenced."

"His wife was sick!," Jack said.

"A lot of people are sick, Jack, but the world keeps moving forward."

"Yeah, you're making them sick!," Bobby shouted.

Dr. Müller sighed as he turned to look at Bobby. "Let me explain how science works in terms that I think even you will understand. In order for us to sell a drug, there needs to be a disease. And in order for us to treat a disease, we need to have a drug that we can sell. Dr. Aker and some of our other researchers stumbled upon an extremely effective formula for reducing, and even eliminating, tumors. It was like nothing we'd ever seen before. But it wouldn't work on the majority of cancers, only rare forms, that would occur in patients with uncommon blood types."

"Like B-negative," Jack offered.

"Precisely," Dr. Müller agreed. "So we needed to increase the number of people exposed to the disease in order to create a great demand for the drug. And we did that very effectively."

"You're killing people, you know that? And the people that don't die are sick. They're living with cancer. Adults, children... don't you care?" Jack asked the question, but he already knew the answer.

"The people that died were simply casualties of the situation, Jack. Some couldn't afford our drug, while others had dosage related deaths. We had been calibrating the dosages to find the exact number that would keep patients alive and relatively well, without curing them altogether. When the dosage slipped too low, patients would often suffer seizures, and even die. It was unfortunate, but unavoidable."

"My son was one of those people. His name was Nate. He's dead because of you."

"Don't be so naive, Jack. I'm very sorry about your son, but people die in the name of science all the time. We now have a drug that we can continue to research and develop, that other cancer patients will benefit from in the future."

"You mean *you* will benefit from. More patients means more money for you and for AstaGen."

"I'm afraid you got me there. Yes, in the end, AstaGen will make more money. That's why we're in business. To make money. Like it or not, that's how business works, Jack. The pharmaceutical business is no different. We're not in the healthcare business, we're in it to make money."

Jack and Bobby sat there, stunned at this brutal admission. Finally, Jack thought, the truth. He had been right all along.

"And now, I think we've wasted enough time, don't you?" He stood from his seat, pressed a button under his desk and looked towards the door.

"Yes," Jack said. "I do. Now!," he shouted.

The doors to the office burst open and half a dozen FBI agents wearing blue blazers swarmed into the room. Weapons raised, they moved quickly over to Dr. Müller's desk. The agents formed a semicircle around the desk, weapons trained on Dr. Müller. Jack and Bobby remained seated and very still. Another agent entered the office and casually walked over to where the others stood, hands resting comfortably behind his back.

He stood directly behind where Jack and Bobby sat, and spoke right over them. "Dr. Müller, my name is Special Agent Jeffrey Walsh. I believe you knew my subordinate, Agent Donna Lewis, who is now sitting in a federal detention center. It is with great pleasure that I say the following words to you... Dr. Albrecht Müller, you are under arrest on the charges of kidnapping, bribing a federal officer, conspiracy to commit fraud, racketeering, and murder. And I have no doubt we'll be able tack on a few more charges before you stand in front of a judge."

Jack was beaming. Bobby had no idea what was happening, but was thrilled at the sudden turn of events.

Agent Walsh went on. "You have the right to remain silent. Anything you say can and will be used against you in a court of law. You have the right to an attorney. If you cannot afford an attorney, one will be provided for you. Do you understand these rights as I've just read them to you?"

As he spoke, two other agents were patting Dr. Müller down and placing him in handcuffs.

"This is preposterous!," Dr. Müller shouted. "You have no proof of anything!"

Agent Walsh removed a small recording device from his jacket pocket. "Well, we have your confession, for starters," he replied with a smile. He pressed the play button, and Dr. Müller's voice started playing for everyone to hear. Everything he'd just told Jack and Bobby, clear as day.

"That still doesn't prove anything!," he said.

"We'll see," replied Agent Walsh. "Get him out of here."

The other agents escorted Dr. Müller from the room, leaving Jack and Bobby alone with Agent Walsh. They rose from their chairs and turned to face him.

"Are Tommy and Prowler ok?," Jack asked.

"Your friends are fine," he said. "They're down in the lobby waiting for you. Nice work, Jack. I'll be in touch." He shook Jack's hand, then Bobby's, and left the room.

Bobby looked at Jack, his jaw agape.

"How?," he asked, baffled by what just happened.

Jack held his tie and turned it around for Bobby to see. On the backside, attached by a tiny clip, was a small microphone. Jack was wired. Bobby leaned in for a closer look, then back up at Jack.

"Just in case," Jack said with a smile.

When Jack tripped over the body of Lou Embers that night at the Tower, he didn't know for sure what had happened. He'd later learn that Lou had been murdered by Simon Gabriel, his throat slashed, as Gabriel made his way up to the penthouse apartment. Laying on the floor in the darkness next to Lou's body, Jack knew he needed help. He took Lou's cellphone and texted Tommy 'Tower 911 - Jack'. He put the phone in his pocket, then headed upstairs, forgetting about it for a while.

After Agent Lewis was arrested, Jack needed to find someone at the FBI he could trust. He would need their help before this was over. He and Cheryl did some digging and ultimately came up with the name Jeffrey Walsh. He was the bureau chief in New York and Agent Lewis's boss. He also had lost a sister to breast cancer.

Jack couldn't risk using any of his own phones, but then he remembered Lou's cellphone. No one would be monitoring it, Jack thought, and he was right. He used it freely to contact Agent Walsh, and kept in touch throughout the process as he made his plans to infiltrate AstaGen. Walsh hated the idea of Jack sneaking into AstaGen and fought him every step of the way. But in the end, he believed in what Jack was doing, wanted him to be proven right, and showed up when it mattered.

Chapter 83

It had been two months since Dr. Müller had been arrested. As it turned out, he was right. Jack and the FBI had no material evidence proving any of the things Dr. Müller had been accused of, despite what he admitted on the recording. To make matters worse, a team of AstaGen lawyers did a superb job getting the recording thrown out as inadmissible in court. Jack and Bobby were on the premises illegally, the recording was made without Dr. Müller's consent or knowledge, and the FBI had no warrant or even reasonable suspicion to burst into Dr. Müller's office and subsequently arrest him. His inadvertent confession simply wasn't enough.

The judge had been disgusted by what he'd heard about AstaGen's business practices, but he was bound by the law, and there was nothing he could do. Dr. Müller was released and all charges were dropped. All but one. Agent Lewis did a rather poor job of hiding the money she'd been paid by AstaGen, and a connection had been made between the two. But, the AstaGen lawyers were able to convince the judge that the payments received by Agent Lewis were not a bribe, but a graft. Agent Lewis had used her position of influence as a Special Agent with the FBI to extort money from Dr. Müller and AstaGen. Just as she had tried to do with Dresden Pharmaceuticals.

Dr. Müller walked away scot free, and AstaGen didn't receive so much as a slap on the wrist. Jack, Matt, and

Cheryl had been at every court appearance, and were appalled by the lack of justice served. Despite everything that happened, AstaGen faced no penalties for their actions. No punishment was handed down for the deaths of Nate Turner, Jonathan Aker, or any of the other countless victims of AstaGen Pharmaceuticals.

Agent Walsh had been sympathetic to Jack and his friends, but in the end, there was nothing he could do. He'd overextended his bounds by agreeing to the operation in the first place. But Jack had guaranteed him proof, and had offered enough circumstantial evidence that Agent Walsh bought in. Agent Lewis refused to talk, even in exchange for a reduced sentence. But it was unlikely she knew anything substantial about the inner workings of AstaGen Pharmaceuticals.

Out of options and without hope of anything new happening that would turn the tide in their favor, everyone simply went home.

Tommy, Mike and Alex continued working at the Tower. They left with Jack's sincerest thanks. They were all honorable military men who had truly gone above and beyond for Jack and his family.

Prowler went back to doing whatever it was he did. He still refused to tell anyone who he actually worked for.

Bobby went back to Keeler Locks and Bolts. There was a package waiting for him when he returned. It was the biometric scanner locking system they'd encountered outside of Dr. Müller's office doors. He wanted to throw it away, but then he'd never get his refund. He returned it without ever opening it.

Jack went home to Amy and Emma. He told them it was finally over. He convinced Amy they were entirely safe, even though he didn't completely believe that himself. They were of no threat to AstaGen moving forward, but what was to stop Dr. Müller from exacting a small degree of revenge for the trouble they'd caused? The negative press and the rumors caused a sharp, though brief, stock dip. But what choice did they have? Jack ran, filled in at the shop with Bobby, and loved his wife and daughter for as long as he had them.

Cheryl and Matt resumed their jobs at the New York Journal. They were now both investigative journalists, and often collaborated on their work. They had also finally gone on that date. True to his word, Matt took her out for drinks and dinner. Again and again. Their relationship progressed quickly and there was talk of moving in together. This was it, they both knew it.

It was a typical Thursday morning at the Journal. Matt and Cheryl were at their respective desks, doing research, writing, returning calls, and otherwise pecking away at their computers. Every day it got a little easier to put the AstaGen mess behind them, but not much. They kept their focus elsewhere by keeping busy pursuing other stories.

Cheryl was bored. It was almost eleven and the caffeine from her morning coffee was wearing off. She stood, stretched, and meandered over to Matt's office. His door was open. Cheryl strolled in, plopped down into one of the chairs and said, "Wanna go downstairs and grab a coffee? Maybe even a blueberry scone?"

Matt was preoccupied with his phone, staring at it with a confused look.

"What's going on?," Cheryl asked.

"No idea," he replied. "I got this bizarre text. Total gibberish, and I have no idea who sent it."

"So delete it," she said. "Who cares?"

"I know. I just feel like I've gotten this text before," he said, still staring at the screen. "And I don't give out my personal number much. You know that."

"When was the other time?"

"I don't know. A while ago. Maybe a few months."

She leaned across the desk to look at his phone. "You think this nonsense is the same nonsense you got a few months ago?"

"Maybe. Weird, I know. But I think so, yeah."

Cheryl sat back in her chair. The hairs on the back of her neck were standing up. Something about this felt weird, important in a way she didn't understand. She tried to think back, and then suddenly it hit her.

"Wait a minute!"

"What?," Matt said curious.

"The day you were supposed to meet Dr. Holst downstairs. He didn't show up, but you told me he texted you a bunch of gibberish before he was found dead. Is that the text you're talking about?"

Matt sat up tall in his chair, suddenly excited. "It might be. But I don't have that phone anymore. I had to ditch it when I was being followed." He sat back, deflated. "I guess we'll never know, huh?"

"Maybe, maybe not. Did you try calling the number from today's text?," she asked.

"Yeah. Repeatedly. No answer."

"Hmmm," Cheryl said. "There must be something we can do."

"I'm all ears. What did you have in mind?"

"Hang on," she said with a wink, and pulled out her cellphone. "I made a friend during my stay with the FBI. His name is Lonnie, a very bright tech guy working with Agent Lewis. Nice call on that one, by the way."

"Yeah, my bad. But in my defense, how was I supposed to know she only investigated the companies that refused to pay her bribe demands?"

Cheryl dialed and Lonnie answered two rings later. Cheryl explained the situation, and then scribbled on a notepad as she listened to what he was saying.

"Great, thanks Lonnie!," Cheryl said, and hung up. "Ok. He says that smartphones and computers operate in much the same way. Data is never truly deleted until it's overwritten by another piece of information. He said there is software out there that lets you retrieve all old and deleted information from prior cell phones. He's done it before. He gave me a few options. Think we should give it a try?"

"It's worth a shot," Matt said.

It was a slow day at Keeler Locks and Bolts. Bobby was dismantling something on his workbench as Jack half-heartedly watched from his stool. He was hunched over with his elbows on his knees turning the hard drive over and over in his hand. When Agent Walsh had left Dr. Müller's office, he hadn't noticed the drive sitting on the desk. Dr. Müller had put it down as he was being handcuffed and led away. Jack scooped it up on his way out and had been fixated on it ever since.

Prowler spent weeks trying to crack the encryption with no luck. He'd even brought in a couple of fellow hackers, none of whom could peel back the multiple layers of security Dr. Holst somehow managed to install on the drive.

Jack stared at the glossy black surface as it turned over in his hand. He was working hard to tune Bobby's humming out when his cellphone buzzed in his pocket. He pulled out his phone and looked at the screen. It was Cheryl. They hadn't spoken in weeks. Not since the final motion against AstaGen fell through, and Prowler and his band of hackers had thrown in the towel.

"Hey," Jack answered. "What's up?"

He listened to her talk for several minutes. She explained about the two odd text messages Matt had received, months apart, Matt's conclusion that they were the same message, and Cheryl's recollection that Holst had sent Matt a gibberish text the day he died. She went on to tell Jack about the software they'd used to confirm that the texts were, in fact, exactly the same, but from different numbers.

"What?!," he said, sitting up. "Who sent the most recent one?"

They didn't know. They tried calling the number, but there was no answer. They'd used their resources at the paper to trace it, with no luck. They ultimately concluded it must have come from a burner phone, and had probably since been destroyed. They were all thinking the same thing, until Cheryl voiced it.

"Could it really be that simple?," Jack asked hopefully. He grabbed a pad and a pen. "Ok, give it to me, slowly."

When he was done writing, he read it back to her, twice.

"Doing it now. Hang on."

He grabbed the drive and ran into Bobby's office. Not quite sure what was happening, Bobby followed closely behind. Jack sat down at the computer and plugged in the drive. When the security screen appeared, Jack carefully typed the letters Cheryl had given him. Bobby stood over him, watching.

"Oh my god..."

Chapter 84

The article was a full page cover story for the New York Journal, and, since being published, had been picked up by the Associated Press and syndicated worldwide. Written by Cheryl Anderson and Matt Cunningham, it chronicled the entire history and timeline of Omnicarcinos and EBF-14. It dove deep into the corruption at AstaGen Pharmaceuticals, revealing how they had been intentionally causing cancer in patients so they could sell their drug. And it shared every detail of perhaps the largest conspiracy ever involving a pharmaceutical company. It went on to demonstrate that a greedy, heartless drug company would stop at nothing to make money, including bribery, kidnapping and murder. It even included numerous quotes from Dr. Albrecht Müller himself, owner and founder of AstaGen.

Dr. William Holst had jam-packed the four terabytes of storage space on his portable hard drive with an abundance of evidence. Information that proved what Jack and Cheryl believed from the start, and formed the foundation of their article. He provided digital copies of internal corporate documents, emails, test results, blood panels, research reports, patient counts, raw clinical trials data, financial projections, and files on every patient he'd seen or consulted on that was taking EBF-14.

The timeline was assembled and laid out flawlessly by Dr. Holst on his drive. The information and data was meticulously dated and arranged. As Dr. Müller had said in the midst of his impromptu confession, researchers at AstaGen had discovered a formula to not only stop tumor growth, but eradicate them altogether. It was the first real and complete cure for cancer. The tumors were destroyed, the blood tests were clear, and the patient was cancer-free. But not all cancers.

This particular formulation was only effective on Rh-negative patients with a B blood type. It was a far less common form of cancer, but the potential for this new drug was too great to ignore. They needed to test it. In order to do that, they needed more subjects. Once they understood how the drug worked, they were able to reverse engineer the type of tumor, and thus the type of cancer, they needed. Now it was only a matter of developing a carcinogen that could induce this newly devised form of cancer in B- patients. They succeeded.

The next step was finding a method of infecting as many patients as possible, without creating an epidemic or attracting the attention of any government agencies like the FDA or CDC. To play it safe, they chose small towns as their initial target. Since the carcinogen was odorless and flavorless, they chose to use water as their delivery mechanism. Unless the water was tested specifically for the chemical compound being added, no one would ever know.

Twenty percent of Americans lived in small towns. But only two percent of them have a blood type of B-negative. That equated to nearly 1.3 million potential patients who would need EBF-14. If only *half* of those people contracted Omnicarcinos, at $300,000 annually, that still meant more than $194 billion in income for AstaGen, every year. And that number would only grow. Even if half of them couldn't afford the drug, it was still nearly $100 billion annually going in AstaGen's pocket.

With the financials and logistics mapped out, dosing became the next major issue. Both adults and small children were contracting Omnicarcinos and had been prescribed EBF-14. But body weight mattered. Adults and kids needed different doses. If the dose was high enough, the entire cancer would be eradicated, and patients would actually be cured. In fact, during clinical trials, AstaGen intentionally gave nearly every test subject the exact dose of EBF-14 they needed to cure them of the cancer. This was done to assure their drug received a speedy FDA approval so they could get it out on the market quickly. And with a ninety-five percent cure rate during clinical trials, that's exactly what they received.

It was a miracle drug, and AstaGen was about to bring to market the first real cure for cancer in pill form. But curing patients was not the business AstaGen was in. They were in the business of making money. They calculated the precise dosage for every body weight that would keep the patient alive, and feeling relatively well, but still technically dying of cancer and in need of EBF-14 to stay alive.

If the dose was too low, however, the cancer would progress too rapidly and, often, patients would suffer seizures, and even die. These seizures were reported by a number of physicians around the country, and the company assured them it was an unfortunate reaction to the dosing inaccuracies. Some doctors accepted this, others were vocal in their disapproval. Like Dr. Bosh and, ultimately, Dr. Holst.

Dr. Holst had been involved from practically the beginning. This was by design. As a prominent oncologist who served as a consultant and specialist to a large network of physicians throughout the country, it only made sense that AstaGen wanted him on board. They met with him a number of times, taking him to dinner at lavish restaurants and for golf on exclusive courses, often with his wife by his side. But when he learned what they were planning, he immediately refused. He would not be part of such atrocity, and even threatened to report them to the FDA and the FBI.

But, as it turned out, Mrs. Holst had a blood type of B-negative. And the representatives of AstaGen made sure she got their special water every time they met. It wasn't long before she was diagnosed with Omnicarcinos. Dr. Holst was given a choice... get on board, or watch his wife die.

He was commanded to prescribe and recommend EBF-14 to any patient he encountered with Omnicarcinos, whether it was his patient or a consult. In return, his wife would receive her treatment for free, and he would be paid handsomely for his efforts. He went along with the arrangement for the first year, but his conscience gnawed at him. The death of Nate Turner was the breaking point. A child had died from the drug he was shilling. How many more would die? How many already had? Nate's death had affected him. He couldn't keep advancing a cause that went against everything he believed in. He'd sworn to uphold specific ethical standards and to protect his patients from harm. Instead, he was a key participant in a scheme to give them cancer.

Dr. Holst began compiling everything he had and everything he knew. Once he was on board, he was given access to everything. He had insisted on knowing every detail about the disease and the medication he would be prescribing to treat it. He documented, recorded, and kept everything. When the call came from Matt Cunningham, Dr. Holst believed it was fate. It was time to let the world know what AstaGen was doing. He had planned to turn everything over to Matt, to help him expose Dr. Müller and his company for the monsters they were. And then he intended to commit suicide. He knew he wouldn't survive once the story broke, and he couldn't bear the thought of facing his wife after what he'd done, the shame of it all.

When Dr. Holst was murdered, his wife quickly had his body cremated. This was at the urging of AstaGen, in exchange for continued treatment and a generous monthly stipend. She complied. But after his death, she wanted nothing to do with AstaGen, and was more than happy to die from her disease. Without her husband, she was lost. She didn't need their drug or their money. But before she died, she called Matt Cunningham. He had reached out to her months earlier, but she refused to speak with him. This time, she sat down with Matt and Cheryl and told them everything she knew. It was her cryptic text message to Matt that gave them access to the drive and the proof they'd long been searching for.

AstaGen was vilified in the media. Never had such an immoral, outrageous and vile act been perpetrated on the American people. Boycotts were immediately scheduled, the stock, which had been trading at over $100, plummeted into the low $20's, and the public was demanding arrests. Dr. Albrecht Müller was unavailable for comment, having fled to his homeland of Germany. But thanks to the International Extradition Treaty with the Federal Republic of Germany, signed June 1978, he would soon be returning to the United States to face all manner of charges associated with his actions surrounding Omnicarcinos and EBF-14.

The courts, however, had more than enough to go on without the presence of Dr. Albrecht Müller. All assets of AstaGen Pharmaceuticals had been frozen in anticipation of the class action lawsuits that were growing by the second. There would also most certainly be hefty punitive fines, both criminal and civil. AstaGen was also mandated to cover the costs of purifying every water supply in every town that had been contaminated with their carcinogen.

And with their final and most significant ruling, AstaGen was ordered by the courts to recalibrate the dosage of EBF-14 for every single patient across the country. In a matter of months, every patient who had been diagnosed with Omnicarcinos was completely cancer free, including Amy, Emma, Brenda, and Lily.

1 - http://www1.nyc.gov/site/ocme/index.page
2 - https://www.fbi.gov/services/cjis/fingerprints-and-other-biometrics/ngi
3 - https://www.fbi.gov/services/laboratory/biometric-analysis/dna-casework
4 - http://americanpregnancy.org/pregnancy-complications/rh-factor/

Made in the USA
Columbia, SC
21 April 2018